After the Battle

Kelley's Story

S. Stieglitz

Rantings of a
Wandering
Mind

DEDICATION

This book is dedicated to my husband, without his tireless patience and relentless support, it may never have seen the light of day.

In remembrance of Steve Russell; his encouragement was the spark that started it all.

PART I – ENDINGS/BEGINNINGS

After the Battle

Chapter One

Kelley sat, staring at his drink. The first one was still roiling in his belly. The bad taste in his mouth was only partly due to the cheap whisky. He stared at his drink as he tried to block out the acrid stench from the nearby factory. He didn't want to hear the drone of the other workers in the background as they shook off the tedium of their last shift. Right now, he didn't even want to see the pretty anchorwoman on the vid.

He was sitting in the worst of dive bars on an armpit of a moon called Balin. He had taken a job at the factory, on the dark side of the moon, twenty-three days ago. Twenty-three freakin' long days ago, to wait for something to happen.

He reviewed his situation again, as he had been doing a lot recently. Major Garrett Kelley, honorably discharged from Fleet, Division One. Honorably discharged at only thirty-three years of age. His whole life was still ahead of him. All the possibilities that life could offer a former soldier were all open.

What a load of space slag. He had been caught in an explosion two years before and that had changed everything. Everything about the explosion had been wrong. He wasn't even on a mission—he had been on base, on an elevator with a Lieutenant what's his name, when it went off. The Lieutenant had been on his right, the side that the blast had come from. For him, the end was quick—probably not painless, but at least quick.

Kelley's injuries were severe, but that wasn't the worst of it. He was barely out of surgery when they had started in with their questions. That an inquiry was opened didn't surprise him. He was mad as hell and wanted to know what happened, just like everyone else. But it didn't play out as it should have. The review had been quiet, and they hadn't asked the right questions. They weren't thorough, and the inquiry was quickly closed. It didn't take a genius to smell a rat. Even though the official inquiry was closed, the unofficial snipe hunt had only just begun, with Kelley right in the middle of it all.

Laid up in the hospital with burns and breaks, and a head injury that left him unable to speak, he must have looked like easy prey to shift suspicions. It was possible that whoever was responsible had just wanted to get the heat off of themselves for a time. Kelley had had an impeccable record up to that point; nothing they threw at him would have stood up to a sustained, proper inquiry. When he started to hear accusations of his misconduct on previous missions, he decided not to wait that long. Groundless, unsubstantiated mud-slinging. He had had enough; he was done being their patsy.

Kelley didn't know who had set the bomb, if the Lieutenant was the actual target, or what the end game was, but he was *done*. Injured, barely able to stand, he had expected someone in Fleet to have his back. The load of platitudes from higher up that came his way at first stunned, then angered him. A soldier didn't get to be Division One without intelligence and the good sense to know which way the wind was blowing. Whatever game they wanted him to be a pawn in could go on without him. He didn't wait for things to get worse, for his record to get sullied, while he fought an unknown opponent blindly. Winning was only to have his good name handed back to him, when, in the first place, it should never have been questioned; it was time to go. Screw the cork out of the bottle on that front. They could plant a big one on what was left of his six; he was shipping out.

He briefly considered that his leaving would only make things worse for himself, that they would say he left in a cloud of shame and all that, but that wasn't how he had read the signs. He quietly asked for and received a medical discharge due to injuries sustained while in active service. Officially, his name and reputation stayed clean and he received his benefits, including his pension, in full. Here one day; entirely off the space grid the next.

His time in private rehab was not worth reviewing except to say that the scuttlebutt he picked up while there told him enough that vindicated his decision to leave. There were no answers to his many questions, but that was a battle for another day.

During his rehabilitation, he kept himself as up to date as possible on Sector news and events. The Confederacy governed a large part of the known universe, and Fleet was its military. Not every planet or habitable moon was part of the Confederacy; some preferred to join the League. The Confederacy concerned itself with the health and well-being of its members and was governed by very strict moral and ethical standards. The League of Planets was a financial coalition and was very selective with its membership, though it also had a military force at its disposal. Looking at both sides with an objectivity he gained after his forced retirement, Kelley thought that neither was good or evil—though he had reason to believe the League was less than ethical in certain areas.

After his rehab, Kelley elected to focus his attention in the EC4N 6HN area of the Sector because that was where his instincts told him the action was. He was no longer with Fleet, but it was where he would have been if he was.

After the Battle

In this area, the planet Iaonus was the beautiful girl at the ball. Resource-rich and well-endowed with tradeable goods, Iaonus was being courted by the Confederacy and downright lusted after by the League. The ruling body of Iaonus had been playfully flirting with both sides for some time. They were in no rush as there was no downside to them if they took their time in choosing. Kelley didn't think they appreciated the tensions that were developing in the rest of the Sector in general, and between the Confederacy and the League, specifically.

The League was a financial partnership and each planet contributed its just share to the whole that was used by the whole in the best interests of all member planets; that was the idea anyway. And for the last three hundred years, it had been a good one, until the unanticipated happened. It really wasn't often that a sun died—though one did, leaving the Tarsus 3 system with a dead sun at its center. Fortunately, there were only three habited worlds in the Tarsus 3 system—two were Confederate and only one was League.

Both the Confederate and the League took care of the people in those worlds. It was just that the League was bankrupt when it was over.

And during all this, pretty Iaonus kept herself to herself, declining to choose between her suitors.

Kelley, antsy after his rehab with no long-term plans, had traveled around and gathered intel from various sources. From the intel, he concluded that there was a high degree of probability that Iaonus was in danger of being forcibly annexed into the League. The League's financial situation demanded an influx of funds, or at least collateral, if it were to avoid collapse. Iaonus's inclusion into the League could provide the stability the League needed at this crucial juncture.

Kelley knew that many in the Confederacy would come to similar conclusions. He also knew that they would politely warn Iaonus's leaders of its peril. While on Iaonus doing recon, he was surprised that the public news didn't even hint at the possibility of an alliance with either side. He had thought that the general populace would be buzzing with speculation.

The ruling leaders were not preparing the population for a vote or even polling them for their opinion. Drawing on experience, Kelley tapped into the more sensitive areas of governmental communications to confirm his suspicions: Iaonus was in no way preparing to join the League, nor did they give any weight to the Confederacy's warnings.

The repercussions of the League forcibly annexing Iaonus would be felt throughout the Sectors. Such a move was unprecedented, and it would not go unmarked by the other planets whether Confederate or League. Battle lines could be drawn.

The Confederacy was hardly in its infancy and this situation, while unique, was not its first trial. They were not going to sit idly and watch the League implode. Its collapse would destabilize too many worlds and bring financial ruin and chaos. It was very probable that they had reached out to the League through private channels and offered financial assistance.

Kelley's intel was limited; he no longer had access to know if the League had pridefully rejected an offer of a discreet loan or not, which was frustrating, to say the least.

If the League had refused, then, logically, they would move forward with the annexation. It was a solid play. Either Iaonus would merely accept the annexation or, at worst, the annexation would tide the League over long enough to financially stabilize, should they be pressured into releasing the planet from forced membership. The Confederacy, its hands largely tied, would do nothing to stop the annexation.

They would wait and manage the situation even if it meant financial chaos, and perhaps, even violent conflict.

Kelley's experience told him that annexation was more than just a possibility; it was a threat that had to be addressed.

He wasn't sure why the situation bothered him so much, but he wanted to be involved. He wanted back in the game. Irritated that he knew so little, Kelley ignored the fact that he was no longer in service and considered how Iaonus could be pressured into joining the League. He decided that the threat of invasion would be enough. A large show of force by the League's military would overwhelm and cower Iaonus's own military and scare them into capitulation without shots needing to be fired. For this to work, Iaonus would have to be isolated and prevented from being able to call for assistance.

Was it possible for the League to move a considerable portion of its fleet through the Sector and into position without being noticed? No, but then they didn't have to. They just needed to move a couple of smaller ships and a large number of fighters into strategic positions over heavily populated cities and key infrastructures. Still, even such a reduced amount of traffic would be noticed.

Kelley considered Iaonus's solar system. She was the second farthest from her sun with one moon called Balin. Balin orbited Iaonus but did not rotate on its axis. The outmost planet of the solar system had several moons. One of these moons' orbits, at its apogee, would be at the furthermost edge of the monitored space.

Utilizing even moderate amounts of stealth technology, and given Iaonus's lack of military sophistication, the League could use the moon, Rekonda 5, as their landing zone. Powered down and therefore undetectable, the ships would travel around the sun until the two planets and their moons were at their closest point. It would then be a short trip from Rekonda 5 to Iaonus.

Okay, that was the overwhelming force part of the op, but how do you silence an entire planet? Kelley researched how to do this as if he had been ordered to do. He discovered that while the planet itself had a sophisticated communications infrastructure, it only had a limited Sector-range communications array, which was located on Balin. To make matters worse, the backup array was also located on Balin. The primary array was on the bright side and the backup was on the dark side of Balin's moon, a couple of clicks north of his current location. Apparently, Iaonus had not yet invested in a communications satellite of sufficient size or capacity to reach out past its own solar system.

Two well-trained teams could easily take out the communications arrays. Not that they even had to destroy them; they just had to take them down long enough for the ruling government of Iaonus to capitulate to the League.

Kelley told himself it was just a theory more than once, but that did nothing to calm his instinct that he had to *do* something. Even though he wasn't entirely sure why, he took a shuttle to Balin and got himself a job in one of the factories.

So now, he was in a bar on Balin after his shift at the factory; just like the day before and the day before that. Twenty-three days, in fact. Waiting twenty-three long freakin' days for something maybe only he thought would happen. He lived out of a closet-size room and worked at a job he could have handled when he was sixteen. He never thought of himself as a snob, but this was a new low for him.

Iaonus was not the first planet to shift the dirtier manufacturing operations off to a satellite moon. Kelley's father had been a miner, and before joining the military, Kelley had had a number of manual labor jobs. He was no stranger to hard work, and he fit in well enough with the other workers, but damn, he did not want to be here much longer.

After the Battle

By his calculations, the orbits had passed their closest point days ago. It was at this time that he had sent a communication to an old Fleet buddy. Calling General Walters a buddy might have been a stretch. Colonel Walters had been in charge of several of Kelley's missions. The two knew each other, but not well enough to exchange holiday cards. At this point, General Walters was now in command of the Sector Fleet.

Even so, his communication to Walters was friendly, how-have-you-been in tone, except for the part where he mentioned his theory. He really stuck his neck out. It was entirely possible that the General thought him paranoid or worse, dismissed him, thinking he was suffering the effects of his head injury. Kelley didn't like to think of the consequences of the other possibility—what if the General did believe him and the League didn't invade? Thinking about that was what had sent Kelley into his funk.

If the League had planned on invading, it should have happened by now. Grasping at the slimmest of possibilities, he stayed because of the news reports—unusually well covered by the local media—about the meteor shower activity in the solar system.

For most of the Sector, such activity was commonplace and unremarkable. However, Iaonus did not have a long history in space past is own solar system. It still had a lot of folklore and traditions related to meteor storms. The locals did not fear the storms, rather they were heavily celebrated. Apparently, there were festivals that lasted several days. This year, the local media coverage of the celebrations was getting picked up on Sector media relays. Kelley had decided to think that the localized storms were causing delays with the League's deployment. He picked up his drink, intending to down it quickly, with more to follow, when the vid suddenly cut from the pretty anchorwoman to an on-the-scene reporter.

Kelley shouted to the bartender to turn up the volume. The bartender, who went by the nickname of Sam, grunted that it was only an over-hyped piece about a fire. No big, it was under control, and it was over at the Dever settlement, on the bright side of the moon. Kelley, tensed, looked behind the reporter. She was standing in front of the communications array, and it was on fire.

At the bar, a couple of workers' pagers started going off. They hurriedly stood and started paying their tabs. They had to go, something about an explosion a couple of clicks north. Sam turned to Kelley, but he was suddenly off his stool and gone—his drink still on the bar.

Chapter Two

Finally, Kelley had had time to make plans, plenty of time, in fact. Taking out the arrays wouldn't stop the transmissions *from* the planet, it would just stop them from getting out past the solar system. So, the issue was how to get the transmissions from the planet to Fleet. The closest Fleet could come, given Iaonus's current neutrality, was the edge of the solar system. And that was assuming they were even at the edge of the solar system; it being off their usual patrol routes.

The obvious solution would be to get to the array—only several clicks north—fight his way past the League forces, somehow fix it, reboot it, and send the cached transmissions. Being only one man without sonic tools or parts that wouldn't likely be lying about close to the array, that wasn't his Plan A.

There are several ways to get transmissions through space, mostly involving satellite relays. The bigger the satellite, the fewer the relay points needed. The Confederate worlds especially used big, moon-sized satellites and often networked them together. Redundancy was a Confederate mandate. Usually, a percentage of a planet's personal communications were relayed through these moon-sized satellites, as well.

However, from a military point of view, these satellites were considered prime targets. The Confederacy, recognizing this fact, discreetly encouraged alternatives, sometimes used by its own Fleet forces. The smaller the relay point, the more alternatives are needed; this is true. It is also true that the smaller the relay, the more portable it is. These types of relays were often used by corporations and those that could afford them for their various business or personal needs.

Kelley knew all about Fleet's alternative communication relay networks. He also knew quite a bit about the non-military communication relays.

As Kelley left the bar, he scanned the street. He saw the usual flotsam of factory workers, delivery trucks, a couple of grease trucks, and a news van already on the scene to cover the explosion. That was unusually quick!

He got on his motorcycle and started towards the array. Once out of town, Kelley went to where he had stashed his gear. He would have preferred his military-grade armor, but had decided to go with the civilian gear, in case things got public. He had also taken the time to modify his motorcycle. A few quick adjustments now and his ride ran a great deal quieter.

When he was close to the site, he stashed the bike to travel the rest of the way on foot. He got out his night vision gear and scanned the array and surrounding area. His retirement hadn't been his choice, certainly not the timing of it, but he was never a soldier who wasn't prepared. He had more than one cache of gear and supplies readied, just in case.

He spotted activity. Yes, there they were. It looked to him like a five-man team. The array itself was inoperative and the surrounding area was on fire. As Kelley circled around, he could see that the array was damaged by a power line that had come down and apparently started the fire. The team was spread out, cleaning up to get ready to move out.

Kelley decided on his approach and went closer. He got in behind one of the soldiers, and after a brief, near-silent effort, put him down. He got undercover and patiently surveyed the ground he still had to cross. Still clear. He made it to the array, singed and sooty. He climbed as quietly as he could to the data center.

He heard shouts as the soldier's absence was noticed. He got to the hub and, no longer quiet, opened it up and took the entire data rack, which was not as heavy or large as they had been in the older days. He quickly wrapped it in a protective cover he pulled from his backpack.

He ran to the opposite side of the array and dropped a line over the railing. He secured it quickly and went over the side, repelling down to the ground. He ducked as a couple of shots went his way from one of the soldiers. He was sprinting back to his bike as he heard her shouting.

He gunned it to put some distance between him and his pursuit. Up ahead, headlights briefly flashed off the side of the road. He steered towards the vehicle. As he approached, the side door of the van opened, and a man shouted to him. Kelley didn't have much time for an assessment, but he noted the man had agency credentials around his neck. He threw the data panel into the van and kept going, his pursuit following him back into town.

The soldiers from the array caught up to him in the street not far from the bar, and while they couldn't shoot him in front of so many witnesses, two of them beat on him while another went through his pack. He didn't resist as well as he could have and made it look like he was getting worse than he was. As expected, his fellow workers were coming over to help him.

When the leader saw that he didn't have the panel, he hissed at Kelley to tell him where it was. Kelley grinned, his lip bleeding, and said that it was already too late. The workers closed around them and started shouting at the soldiers. The leader, realizing he couldn't take them all out, started backing away and called off his team.

Kelley calmed the workers down and said that he'd buy them a round at the bar by way of thanks. He called out loud enough for the retreating soldiers to hear, that they should watch the news—he was sure there was something they had to see.

Not long after entering the bar, the vid abruptly cut out. Before the workers could moan, it came back on, but it was not the news. Everyone was quiet as they stared at the vid, which was blaring with Iaonus's distress call on loop. One of the workers found their voice and nervously asked what was going on, the Legion what, and why was the SOS on the general news channel?

Kelley, leaning up against the bar, had a beer in his hand. He opened it and took the time to get a couple of swallows down his throat before answering. "The explosion must have damaged the communications array. If so, the news media relays would be the next best way to get a signal out," he said.

The sound of agreement from his left caught his attention. He turned and saw someone who was new to the bar and too nicely dressed for a manufacturing settlement. Kelley stared hard at him while the man nodded at him like they knew each other.

Ignoring him, Kelley turned back and continued saying, "The news media is all over the solar system, covering the meteor storms. Given that the Sector media is picking up their feeds, that SOS is probably not only at the edge of the system, but already out past it." As if on cue, the vid switched to live coverage of the Confederate Fleet heavy cruisers entering local space, dwarfing the smaller Legion ships around Iaonus.

Chapter Three

Several days later, Kelley sat at a table in a bar eating wings and drinking beer. This bar was upscale and on a rather nice moon. He faced the bar's vids, where he had a view of the game, the door to the right, and the shapely bartender.

General Walters walked up to his table, dressed in civilian clothes. Kelley was not at all surprised by the visit. He stood out of habit, grunting a greeting as he cleared his mouth and wiped his hands. When his eyes met Walters's, he was surprised at the surge of anger in his gut.

Part of him was still mad, and even though he had no reason to take anything out on Walters, he was just plain angry. This was the first time since the explosion that he'd met face-to-face with a brass of such rank.

Kelley got himself under control and offered his hand to the General saying, "General, nice to see you." Walters shook his hand strongly and looked straight at him. Having been sized up many times, he calmly stared back, then said, "Want a beer?"

Walters snorted, grinned briefly and said, "Sure," as he sat down. Neither man said anything for a time and just watched the vids, until the waiter had taken the General's order of a stout and another basket of wings.

"So, what the hell, Kelley?" asked Walters, who apparently had decided on the direct approach. "Everyone is standing around, wound tight enough to pop their heads off about the League/Iaonus situation, and I get this message from you, *casually* laying it all out like its nothing. You didn't even use a communication channel I could reply to. Just, 'this is what is going to happen, so be ready.' What the hell?" he repeated.

Kelley shrugged nonchalantly, amusement perversely starting to surface, now that Walters was starting in on him. "I didn't have anything solid, General," he admitted. "It just seemed obvious to me. Did you want the annexation to happen?"

"No, of course not." He paused as the waiter served him his beer and wings. He took a sip and a wing and continued, "No one in the Confederacy wanted that."

"So, did I get in the way of an op then?" Kelley asked, not looking at Walters, and took a bite of his wing.

The General didn't answer right away, preferring to get a couple of his own wings down.

"Yeah, didn't think so," Kelley answered for him. "Iaonus being neutral and the Confederacy's policy on non-interference and all."

"Still wasn't right, though."

"People still would have died or suffered financial ruin, though."

"Who are you to tell *me* where to position my ships?" Walters growled.

"You were in a position to tell me to fly off or just ignore me altogether." After a pause, Kelley continued, "It was a good idea to get the Sector media to pick up on Iaonus's news feeds. Saved time."

Walters just grunted, not liking a former Major complimenting him. Kelley finished his beer and signaled to the waiter, who came over. Kelley asked for water and extra napkins.

After the Battle

"But you didn't ignore me. You averted a Sector-wide conflict by somehow being in the right place at the right time. All the glory to you with no downside. C'mon, it couldn't have been that hard to get the Sector media on Balin?" Kelley asked innocently.

Walters glared at him. "I had to promise to attend the next awards show, in uniform, with the Sector media president."

Kelley brought his fist to mouth, covering a laugh with a burp, his eyes on his empty glass. Then he asked, "So, who was the stooge in the bar on Balin? He wasn't babysitting the news team because they weren't there. Damn if he didn't stand out like an outsider."

The General looked at him, "That was Agent Edwards of the Galactic Investigative Services. Apparently, one of their best."

Kelley made a derisive face but left it alone. Both men sat for a minute, having finished their beer and wings. Finally, Walters quietly asked, "What now for you, Kelley? Do you think you can stay out of my hair?"

"I don't know. I doubt it," he answered. "I get bored easily."

"Well, I can't have that. I don't like to think of what you would get yourself into—what you would get *me* into."

Kelley kept his face neutral. "What do you have in mind?"

"I'd like to get you into GIS. It wouldn't keep you out of trouble, but at least it would keep you out of my inbox."

Kelley involuntarily sat straight up, "Well, it sounds like they could use the help," he said, trying to sound casual. "Go ahead and set it up."

PART II – MIDDLE

Chapter One

"I failed my psych eval?" Kelley asked indigently. He was sitting in the counselor's office, staring at the tablet displaying his evaluation results. He hadn't read it; he had skipped to the end for the recap. "What the..." he started to say but stopped himself from completing that sentence and ground his teeth instead.

It had been eighteen weeks since he had beer and wings with General Walters. In a remarkably quick time, he had packed up his gear and been on a shuttle to a GIS training center.

He thoroughly enjoyed training. The other agents-in-training moaned and groaned practically every day, but not Kelley. He had been out for too long; he knew he needed something like the GIS agent training to get back on his game. He put his head down and got on with it.

He listened to his instructors, even though some of them were younger than him, and generally did what he was told. He wished he could compare his current results with his Fleet records, but they said they didn't do that. He breezed through training and expected to be assigned to a field office in short order.

He hadn't expected this; to have his world stop spinning all over again.

Kelley looked down at the tablet but couldn't make himself focus enough to read the words. *Not again.*

"No, you didn't fail anything," the counselor said calmly. "That isn't the way an evaluation works. Based on the results, you have not cleared for Level III operations, that is all."

Kelley waited for Counselor Crane or Agent Crane—he wasn't sure which title the messenger of death preferred—to go on, but he didn't. Crane sat patiently in his over-stuffed desk chair and just looked at him calmly.

Crane, Doctor/Agent Frank Crane, was a bipedal humanoid from some planet or other. His appearance just said 'generic human' with no identifying colors or other physical characteristics. Not that it mattered to Kelley which flippin' planet or moon or asteroid or whatever he was from.

After they stared at each other for a while, Kelley finally said, "whatever you call it, it is still a big deal."

"Agent Kelley, I know it isn't what you expected or what you wanted. Let us talk about why you feel that it is such a big deal."

Kelley gaped back at Crane, his mouth moving but he couldn't decide where to begin to enlighten the doc. He felt like he was being asked to state the obvious.

"I've washed out of GIS; I'm done. It's over."

Crane's face actually changed expression at this, moving from calmly patient to slightly concerned. "No, Agent Kelley, that is not what the evaluation means. Again, it just means that you haven't cleared for Level III operations. Everything else is still open to you."

"'Everything?' Like what? I'm not good at...well, much."

"We should explore that. Let us start with why you were accepted into GIS. Your recommendation from General Walters stated you would make a first-class analyst..."

"Analyst?!" Kelley burst out, interrupting him. "What? Me, behind a desk?"

"Yes, you," Crane said, stressing the words. "Your analysis of the Iaonus situation was excellent. You were not the only one to be concerned about the League's intentions. However, you were capable of seeing the entire situation, including anticipating *how* the League would take action. GIS values such abilities very highly. And what is wrong with a desk job?"

"Look, I'm sorry. I didn't mean to offend you, but it's something I never saw myself doing."

"No offense taken. You misunderstood my question. I can see that your perception of yourself and your capabilities is very… focused. I am trying to get you to reflect on your assumptions and expectations."

"Why? Is all this really necessary?"

Crane smiled slightly. "That is really up to you. I will give you the bottom line. GIS wants to keep you. As an analyst. You want to be a soldier again. You were expecting to be a Level III field agent so you could be a soldier again. However, GIS doesn't need another Level III agent. It has enough of them now and I think you overestimate how often we need those we have."

Still looking directly at him, Crane continued, "Before you leave GIS, I would like you to consider several things, such as, since you can't go back to Fleet you may want to move forward. I suspect moving forward or rather, letting go, may not be easy for you right now. I recommend talking about that.

"If not that, we could talk about your limited perceptions of yourself and your capabilities. You were a highly decorated officer in the Confederate Fleet, Division One. You have many skills apart from the knowledge of weapons and how to use them.

"You know how to manage a team before, during, and after a mission. That is a lot. You know how to choose the right people, train them, gear them, and guide them to a specified objective. And from what I have read of your service record, you also stay around and make sure your people are taken care of after the mission is over. Those skills alone would be enough for GIS to be interested in you. I can walk you through how these skills translate to several GIS job opportunities."

"However, you also possess the abilities to gather intelligence *and* be able to interpret the said intelligence to predict outcomes. This is what makes you highly sought after by GIS as an analyst." Crane paused, gauging Kelley's reaction. Seeing he was listening and attentive, Crane went on.

"I am curious as to what your life plan would have been, should you have stayed in Fleet. Did you expect to die in service, or did you have other ideas? As you took the time to advance your education and earn a tertiary degree, you appear to have had some sort of back-up plan." Crane paused again, this time to give Kelley a chance to answer him. Kelley didn't respond but maintained a look of interest.

Crane was a patient man. "I think we should begin with making sure you understand what the Galactic Investigative Service does, what its mission is, and if you find it a good fit for you."

Kelley sat for a while, his head full of questions. He was surprised and a bit overwhelmed by Crane's candor.

"Geez, doc… I mean, Doctor Crane, talking about all that sounds like more than one or two sessions."

"Agent Kelley, if you choose to stay, it's going to take a hell of a lot more than just one or two sessions to sort through it all. The question is, do you have the brass to do what it takes to work it all out? And I mean, to really dig down and be honest with yourself and me?"

Kelley didn't say anything. Agent Crane decided to take Kelley's hesitation as a good sign. After all, Kelley hadn't flat out said no. He might be hesitant at self-exploration, but Crane knew he had intrigued Agent Kelley with his challenge and the possibilities GIS offered.

"You don't have to decide right now. In fact, you have another matter that may take precedence," Crane said. "Swipe over to your medical results."

Kelley swiped for several screens before asking, "What am I looking for?" Suddenly he stopped swiping and stared at the tablet. On the left side of the page was a DNA profile with his name at the bottom. On the right side of the same page was another DNA profile with the name redacted. In the center of the page, the text read: Match found.

Seeing his pale, stunned face, Doctor Crane decided not to wait to be asked and said, "No, based on the DNA comparison, you are not this child's father. The results suggest that you are a close relative though. An uncle, perhaps."

He continued, "It is standard GIS policy to run our agents through a database search. As we are an intergalactic organization, with share agreements with 90% of the known species and/or habited worlds, our database is fairly comprehensive. Your profile says you have a sister and a nephew, but this match is not either of them. Therefore, we are bringing this child to your attention. It is your choice what to do next."

Chapter Two

Kelley pulled himself together. He felt oddly relieved at being able to focus on something other than himself and his 'future.' He also pushed the implications of being an uncle to the side; he would deal with that later.

"You said child. How old? And how did he or she get into any sort of database?"

Dr. Crane answered, "She. She is fifteen and was taken into custody by the local PD of planet Tycor for possession of narcotics. She has been sitting in their cell for a week now." He stopped.

"Is that it? No information on her trial or arraignment?"

Crane swiped back and forth several times. "There isn't much here."

Kelley stood up and started moving towards the door before stopping himself. He sat back down again on the edge of the chair. "I would like to go now. Are we done?"

"We are done talking about you today, yes." Dr. Crane replied. "But, no, we are not done. I expect you will want to take some personal time, which is not a problem. However, I would like to know what you are going to do."

"I want to figure this out. I want to talk to my sister first. Then, if this girl is family, I want to see what is going on with the PD on Tycor. Why are they keeping her without moving her through their judicial system?"

"Yes, I expected as much. Would you like assistance in booking travel to Nibiru? And while you are there, would you like me to send a legal asset directly to Tycor and start looking into the girl's situation from a legal standpoint?"

"Well sure, yes. That would be great. Thank you." Kelley stood again and offered his hand to the doc.

Crane shook it and said, "Keep in touch. I'm here to help; just ask, Agent Kelley."

Kelley nodded in agreement and left. He decided to ignore Crane's implication that he needed or should want his help, even though a GIS trained lawyer had been a good idea.

As he walked down the hall, the idea of his sister getting pregnant and having a baby started crashing down on him. If it were true, why hadn't she told him? How had he not known? They had been very close, especially after their parents died. He had done everything he could to take care of her. He had become a cop on their homeworld, Blerreon 4, because the pay was good, and the job came with decent family benefits. It wasn't until he enlisted with Fleet that their relationship started to get distant. At least that was when he thought it had been.

He made his way out of the GIS building and went to his apartment located nearby. As he entered, he saw the blinking light on the communication console, indicating he had a message. It said that his flight to Nibiru was arranged. He tapped his tablet to the console and transferred the itinerary to his tablet. He hadn't expected GIS to spring for him to actually go and meet with his sister; Fleet would never have done that. As he got his gear together, he supposed that this was better. The conversation he wanted to have probably shouldn't be over a vid.

Chapter Three

All during his flight, he thought about his sister, Mel. Her name was Melvina, but she went by Mel. She never told anyone her full name. Kelley wouldn't be surprised if even her husband didn't know. He called her Melody from time to time. Kelley assumed it was some cute pet name thing and didn't say anything because Mel never objected.

Her husband, Hugo, was nice enough. Hugo Turner. Kelley had always thought he was on the bland and boring side; not that he ever gave Hugo much thought. He always just assumed it was because he had never really got to know the guy.

He remembered he was already in Fleet when Mel told him she was getting married. He had managed to get leave for the ceremony but hadn't stayed around long afterwards. Mel hadn't like being asked why she was marrying when she was only twenty-three.

They had a son, Brian. Brian wasn't born until almost two years after they got married. But wait, if this girl was fifteen, then Mel would have been eighteen when she was born. So why marry Hugo? If she was eighteen, then he would have been twenty years old. He had joined the Blerreon 4 PD when he was seventeen after convincing them to take him on early due to family hardship. He had enlisted with Fleet when he was twenty years old. Is that why Mel hadn't told him?

After the Battle

The shuttle shook lightly as it landed, rousing him from his thoughts. It wasn't until he had finished arranging for land transport that he started to wonder if he should have let Mel know he was coming.

He went to a private area and tapped in her code on his tablet. After a minute, his sister's face appeared on the screen. She smiled when she saw it was him, not a big smile, but at least she looked pleased to see him.

"Garrett! Wow, this is a surprise." Mel looked him over. "You look a *lot* better than when I saw you last. Have you *finally* come to pick up your stuff?"

"Hey, sis!" He tried to smile back, but he was confused. When was it that they last met? "I have some time off and thought you and I could get together. You know, catch up and all."

"Okay, sure." She was noncommittal. "When did you have in mind?"

"Got any time today? And what do you mean 'my stuff?' What did I leave with you?"

She looked very surprised and hesitated before answering. "Today? Sure, I guess. It must be important, so I will make time." She paused again, looking at him. He couldn't be sure, but he thought she was making his image bigger on her side, to get a better look at his eyes.

"You don't remember? Just after your 'accident' almost two years ago now."

"Mel, I'm sorry. No, I guess I don't remember. I didn't even know I wasn't remembering." He stopped talking, upset with himself. For the past two years, he had assumed she hadn't been there. He had never considered the possibility of memory issues.

She nodded and said quietly, "Sounds like we have a lot to catch up on. I'll see if I can get Brian and Hugo out of the house for a while."

"Actually, maybe you could come to me. This might take a while. I would like to talk further back than just two years."

Her face got strained and her eyes looked scared. She nodded again and said, "Send me the address." Then the screen went dark.

Chapter Four

Kelley quickly searched the local listings for a property rental. He had a bad feeling and didn't want whatever was about to go down to happen in a hotel room. He wanted privacy and didn't want nosy guests getting involved or listening through the walls.

He found a fishing cabin a good distance outside of the city from his current location but fairly convenient for Mel. It was a solid structure, not at all fancy but nicely isolated. He sent her the address and his ETA.

When he arrived, he found Mel sitting on the front steps of the cabin. She was looking out towards the water. She didn't move or turn to look his way while he pulled up and got out of the vehicle.

She seemed small, small like when she was a child. When he last saw her—when he last remembered seeing her in person—it was a holiday dinner at her and Hugo's house. She had been calm and confident and had organized and prepared everything like clockwork. No half-frozen main courses or burned side dishes for his sister. Nothing had been forgotten, she even remembered his favorite dessert. Thinking about it, that was the last time she had invited him to anything. They had kept in touch after that for a time but when she stopped answering his communications, he had taken the hint and left her alone.

Now, he walked over and sat down on the steps near her. She finally turned to look at him. She looked him over, especially his face, and then smiled. "Hey, bro, you're looking good these days."

He wasn't sure how to respond. He wanted to hug her but was unsure; she had her arms folded and was slightly hunched over. Was she scared?

"Melvina. Mom's little chieftain and Dad's favorite. How are you doing these days?"

Mel smiled, really smiled at the reference to their parents. "I wasn't his favorite. He just liked that I took the time to learn our family's history. It was very important to him that we knew our story and where we came from."

Their father had been a miner and the Kelley family had lived on Blerreon 4. As their father moved up from working in the mines to management, he would take jobs that took him off the moon, weeks at a time. Finn Kelley had always said it didn't matter where he was or where they were; they were always a family.

"I still miss them sometimes, Garrett," she said looking back out towards the water. "Do you?"

Kelley inhaled through his nose and let it out again, taken by surprise at the question. "Well, yeah, I guess." He paused. "Yes, I do miss them, when I think about it."

Turning back to him she said, "But you don't think about them, do you? You always have something else to keep your mind off them." Her grey eyes looked straight into his, intent but not hostile.

Where the hell was this going, he wondered to himself. He was uncomfortable and wanted to talk about other things; practically anything else in the galaxy, in fact, rather than talk about the parents they lost within one year of each other when they were just children. He had only been fifteen years old when their father died. A thought struck him; that was the same age as the girl currently sitting in a cell on Tycor.

He bowed his head and leaned towards her, his head almost touching her shoulder. "It hurts, Mel. It still hurts even now. And back then, I didn't want to be hurting. We were alone; I had to figure out how to care for us and not get swallowed up by it all."

She leaned against him and gripped his hand. "And you did. You did find ways to take care of us. You kept us fed, you fought to keep us together. I still don't know how you did it, but you did." She sighed. "Or rather why you did. You joined the police. What do you think Mom and Dad would have thought about that?"

He took a moment to think about her question then said, "Well, okay, I guess they both would have been an odd mix of proud and not so happy at the same time." Tara and Finn Kelley were upstanding citizens and believed in the law. They just weren't overly fond of its interfering ways.

"You know I took the job for us. It was good money and came with benefits on top of the pay, instead of out of it."

She frowned and pressed her lips together. "Yes. The pay was good. I liked being able to eat and have a decent place to live and finish school. But that is when it started."

"What started? Started what?" he asked confused. Still confused. He was trying to keep hold of his patience.

"Your adrenaline habit. You were a good cop; good at your job. You could have made detective, but no. You liked getting in on the busts and takedowns. You didn't want to do anything else if it took you away from being in the middle of the action."

She barely paused, giving him no time to respond before she went on, "Did you have any idea how much I worried about you, how often I would lie awake at night until I heard you come home?"

"No, no, I didn't, but we needed the bonus money," he said defensively.

"NO, no we didn't!" she shot back. "You just liked how it felt. You preferred the adrenaline surge over your grief."

He sat back; it was his turn to look away from her. He looked out over the water. After a time, he said, "Okay. Yes, maybe I did. Was it so wrong?"

She reached out again taking his hand. "No. Yes. No, there are many ways to grieve. And yes, because I don't think you ever actually did. I tried so hard to be proud of you. You got injured three times in three years. I got three calls, each time wondering where they were going to tell me to go—to the hospital or the morgue."

He looked down and held her hand tightly. He didn't have any words.

"I loved you, Garrett. You were my brother, my only family. I tried so hard to be strong." She sniffed and cleared her throat. "And then you had to join the freakin' Fleet."

Ah. The fog was maybe beginning to clear.

"You left," she continued. "You were gone, always on some mission or other. I couldn't decide if it was better that you weren't there to worry about, or worse because I couldn't see that you were all right and so I worried even more."

"I was so tired. Tired of being worried, tired of waiting for Fleet to tell me you had been KIA. Just so tired of waiting to live my life."

Mel stopped talking. Garrett, caught by surprise, didn't say anything; he just nodded for her to go on.

After a moment, she continued. "I had my own way of dealing with their dying and your leaving. I married Hugo because he gave me what I wanted the most. Freedom. I didn't marry him because I loved him; I married him because I didn't. He is nice enough, but what is wonderful is not caring."

After the Battle

Mel looked defiant and seemed to be waiting for him to challenge her choices. It may have been a while, but she hadn't changed that much over the years; she still had a knack for being evasive. It was the same as when she was a kid. She would get their parents wound up about something to distract them from what she didn't really want to talk about.

"Mel, if you think I'm shocked; I'm not. If you think I'm going to tell you that you were wrong for marrying a man who gave you a nice house, treats you well, and paid for your doctorate..." answering her surprised look he said, "Yes, I did know that you earned your Ph.D. in Psychology, Dr. Turner. I kept up with you even when I thought you didn't want me around. Maybe I had my head up my six about, well, maybe about a lot of things but, we can talk about me later.

"You just skipped five years. Want to tell me what you were doing? Or who you were doing it with?"

Mel shook her head. "No, I can't."

Garrett said, "Of course you can. I'm your brother and I can't think of anything you could tell me that I wouldn't understand. Here, let me start. Apparently, GIS does galactic background checks on its agents, including DNA sweeps. They found a match but... Mel, what's wrong?"

He stopped because the color drained from her face and her body jerked liked she had been punched.

"Stop, Garrett. Stop talking. Stop talking. I can't talk about it. I CAN'T TALK ABOUT IT!" She would have screamed if she could get her breath.

"'It', what it? Mel? Mel!"

Mel was choking; her face now a bright red. She swiveled around so that he could see the right side of her neck, still unable to breathe.

He put his hand on her neck and felt the pulse of something like an electrical charge going through her. He stood up, pulling her to her feet with him, and then suddenly hit her hard in the jaw, hard enough to drop her back down on the steps, unconscious.

He felt her neck again. Now that she was unconscious, he no longer felt the electrical surge and she seemed to be breathing normally. He picked her up and carried her into the shack. He still didn't know if he was going to stay with GIS, but he was grateful for their training program. He looked for scars on the left side of her neck and didn't see any. As suspected, there were very faint scars on the right side of her neck, just below her skull; faint with age and easily missed if you weren't looking for them. There were more scars at the base of her skull, high enough for her hair to hide them. He turned her over and hitched up her shirt to see her back. He had to pull her pants down, just a little, to see the base of her spine, where he wasn't surprised to find more fine, faint scars.

"What are you doing?" Mel asked thickly, slurring slightly.

"Mel, listen to me. Don't say anything. Look at the lake, think of puppies or something. Don't talk. Just relax and breathe. I don't want you to say anything. Do you understand?"

Mel started to turn back over and groaned as she moved her head. She stopped suddenly as she remembered what had just happened. Garrett held his breath, hoping she wasn't going to be choked again.

"The lake is very pretty," she lied. At the moment, she couldn't even see the lake. "We can talk about the lake, if you'd like. Not puppies; Hugo doesn't like dogs."

Garrett got up and went to the kitchen side of what was basically a large one-room shack. He came back with a glass of water and some ice wrapped in a towel.

"I don't suppose there is anything to drink around here?" she asked, holding the ice to her jaw.

Garrett smiled slightly. That was the Mel he remembered. He got back up and looked around. As he searched, she got herself comfortable on the bed, propping up pillows and pulling the blanket around her.

He found a bottle of something the previous people had left or forgotten and poured them each a drink. He knocked his back.

"Okay. Do not say anything. Just listen. I'm going to tell you about my GIS training."

She raised her eyebrows at this and said, "When did you join GIS?"

"For freakin' sake, would you stop talking! School your mind to just *listen*. Yes, I joined GIS. It's a long story that I would actually like to tell you, but not now. Part of the training was about the current threats to the galaxy and what to look for. For example, I learned about 'collars.'"

"In the past, people who didn't want their secrets known, and assuming they didn't kill them outright, they would get other people to sign Non-Disclosure Agreements or pay them lots of credits to not tell anyone these secrets. Or maybe they would cut the person's tongue out if they felt like a middle of the road option. Of course, all these things are often not very effective. So, people came up with implants."

He stopped to see how Mel was doing. She was listening intently. Still breathing; in fact, she was breathing a little fast. She nodded for him to go on.

"They are known as collars even though they aren't. These implants are connected to the brain and nervous system. They are coded with what the person is never supposed to talk about and if the person tries in any way to communicate this taboo topic, the implants punish the person. The punishments vary from shocks to paralyzing certain muscles, such as those muscles associated with breathing. A fascinating tech in the way it can detect a person's thoughts.

"Highly effective, too. Wonderful devices in many ways, if you don't start counting the number of fatalities. In fact, doctors despise these things. The tech is very difficult to detect and, of course, the person is forbidden from disclosing that they are collared. There have been instances where doctors have killed their patients because their treatment interacted negatively with the implanted tech. This causes a dilemma for the docs—do they waste precious time scanning for tech and have the patient die from the delay in treatment, or treat without confirming the absence of tech but kill the patient because the tech and the treatment conflicted?"

"These collars are outlawed on many worlds but that doesn't stop people from using them. As I said, they are highly effective and once implanted, virtually impossible to remove."

"GIS trained me on what to look for and what to do if I suspect someone has an implant. For example, do not provoke the subject and certainly don't ask them to talk about what they are forbidden to talk about. I'm sorry, Mel. So sorry. I must have slept through that day's class."

She reached out, took his hand, and squeezed it hard but didn't look at him. "The lake is a pretty blue and you can see waterfowl on the far edge."

He waited until she finished her drink and had settled back against the pillow, eyes closed.

"Is your family expecting you back soon?" he asked.

Mel shook her head slowly. "Nah." As she moved to put her glass on the table, he caught her eye, his hand on the bottle. She shook her head again and continued, "I said I would be gone for a couple of days. They are used to me going away once in a while. Now that Brian is older, I can leave him for a little while if I need to. I figured if you were reaching out, it might take a while."

"Do they know you are meeting me?" he asked.

"No, Hugo thinks you are a bad influence on Brian, and Brian would have wanted to come with me."

Garrett didn't know his nephew even liked him, let alone that he had any sort of influence over him. He thought Brian was about six when he last saw him.

"Mel, can we talk about the last two years?" he asked tentatively.

"Sure. If you make us dinner." She looked up at him from the bed, with a look on her face and the ice pack on her jaw.

"I didn't bring anything, and I don't want to fish right now." He wanted to say that he only hit her because he had to, but he couldn't. Plus, he was sure she knew why; she was just busting him anyway.

"In my trunk," Mel said, taking her vehicle fob out of her pocket and handing it to him.

He dutifully got up and went outside, casually picking up his tablet on the way out. He established a connection to the main communication grid—being a GIS agent did have some nice benefits—and tapped out a quick message to Agent Crane.

He said he was with Mel, who wasn't talking due to being collared, and asked Crane to advise the legal brief sent to Tycor to take every precaution. He then brought in the bags of food. Real food, fresh and uncooked.

Back in the shack, Mel said, "If you don't remember how to cook, I can walk you through it."

"I got it," Garrett answered as he started rummaging around.

"I remember lots of things, like how to cook. I remember the explosion. I remember details like what the guy next to me looked like before he was blown apart. I remember waking up in the hospital and being questioned by a bunch of idiots."

He started banging the pots and pans as he got more agitated.

"I remember getting fed up and getting out of there and going to rehab."

After a pause, Mel asked, "That's it? You don't seem to remember me."

He stopped chopping and stared at her. "You? No, I don't remember you at all."

Mel got up from the bed and went to sit at the table. "Okay, here is what *I* remember. As your emergency contact, I got a call from Fleet saying you had been injured and they asked me to come right away. They never gave details; they just said that it was an explosion. They just asked me to come right away as if you could be dead any minute."

He resumed cooking but listened intently to the new information.

"So, I get there, and I find you in a coma. Half of your face was missing. Well, half of *you* was missing." She paused and looked at the glass on the table.

"They tried to get me to sign some release forms. That really ticked me off. Here I was, your sister, right off the shuttle, just getting a look at the mess that was you, and they had the nerve to start in on me."

This time she reached for the bottle and poured herself another.

"I gave them hell. Straight up. I let them have a piece of *my* mind." After a pause, she said, "Actually it felt kind of good. I had just gotten the call I was dreading my entire life. It was kind of a relief to let it all out. Idiots walked straight into my cross hairs," she grumped.

Garrett smiled to himself. He hadn't realized how much he missed someone caring about him.

She took a deep breath, "So, I got a hold of your doctors and made them tell me everything, medically speaking, about your condition. I made them replace your jaw and start the tissue regeneration process, despite their advice that I should wait and see. You were in a coma for three weeks space station time."

"When you woke up, they forced me to leave. They said it was a matter of security; classified and all that space slag. I guess they were afraid of what you might say."

She looked at his face. "They didn't tell you anything about me?"

"No," he said simply, but she could tell he was angry. He came and sat down at the table, dinner simmering on the stove.

"Well, I stayed close and made them give me updates. When I heard they were starting to process your discharge, I started to research rehabilitation centers. I got a referral from one of my colleagues and sent them your medical file. They agreed to take you."

"Wait. Stop. That was you?" He was clearly trying to remember. After a minute, he stopped trying. "It's no good."

"Yeah, you were pretty drugged up. But I was happy to arrange for your transport out of there."

He stood up and went to check on their dinner.

"The last thing I did was to make them get me into your place to pack up your belongings. I still have your stuff in storage."

At that, he put his hands on the counter, back to her, head and shoulders down.

She waited a moment and then got up and went over to him. She hugged him for a long time.

When he turned to her, his eyes were red and wet. "I had no idea. It was months into my rehab before I even thought about my place. When I checked into it, they had assigned it to someone else. I assumed they had thrown out my stuff. I had no idea it was you. I don't know how to thank you or pay you back."

"Garrett! Stop talking nonsense! We're family. We take care of each other. You took care of me. I took care of you. It's how a family works. Remember, it doesn't matter where we are, we are always a family."

The pan on the stove started to sputter and pop. They both reached out at the same time to grab for the pan. They looked at each other and Mel smiled at him. He pulled the pan off the heating element and tried to smile back at her; he managed to nod. She squeezed his arm and went to the cabinet to look for plates.

After eating and clearing up, they went outside and walked around the lake. Garrett told Mel the redacted version of Iaonus and how that got him an interview with GIS. He stopped there and asked her to talk about herself.

And she did. It was for the first time in a long time they really just talked. They fell right back into their way of talking like they used to. On previous visits, she had always been reserved around Hugo and Brian. Here with him, she could talk freely about her life as it was now. He couldn't decide if it was ironic or surreal that she seemed to be talking so openly when he knew she was collared. Whichever it was, at least she seemed content with her life. He felt good about that.

Chapter Five

The next morning, Garrett woke up and stretched. He got out of bed and quietly shuffled over to start making coffee. Mel was still asleep on the couch. She had insisted he take the bed as he was too tall to fit on the couch. He hadn't protested that much, and looking at her now, she seemed to fit well enough where she was; he didn't feel guilty.

He looked at his tablet and saw he had a message from Crane. He decided to contact the doc and went outside even though it was chilly; he didn't want to risk Mel overhearing something she shouldn't.

Crane's face appeared on the screen. He looked like he had been sleeping. Kelley hadn't even tried to calculate the time difference. "Morning, Doctor."

"Evening, Agent Kelley," Crane answered evenly. "Your last communication was somewhat terse. How is your sister?"

"It was close, but she made it through the collar being revealed. The damn thing didn't give her any warnings that I could see. It went straight into punishment mode."

"I see. I have already advised Agent Sofia Deleon to proceed with all due caution. She will arrive on Tycor later today."

Kelley thanked him and tried to sign off, but Doctor Crane kept him on the call. He finally gave Crane a brief recap.

When he went back inside, Mel was sitting at the table drinking coffee. It looked like she had showered. Her jaw was bruised and a little swollen. He didn't mention it.

"Morning. You should probably wait to shower, I might have used all the hot water," she told him.

He grunted, got himself a cup of coffee, and sat down at the table rubbing the chill from his arms. Mel got up and pulled a blanket off the bed and put it around him, briefly hugging him, before turning to start making breakfast.

He looked at her. She was different this morning. She was small and scared yesterday but today she was calm and confident.

Which he supposed made sense. She was afraid of him finding out about her daughter and probably terrified of him finding out about the collar. No wonder she pushed him away; between his missions and her secret, it must have been hell for her. It's not like they could talk about his work, and there was always the danger of him bringing up the past, which could have killed her. Today was very much a brand-new day. He knew about his niece and the collar, and knew he could never bring them up again.

"So, do I have any nieces you need to tell me about?" she asked, as if causally.

He turned around so fast, he spilled his coffee, "Mel, stop! What the... What are you doing?"

"Whatever are you referring to, Garrett?"

He continued to gape at her while she finished making breakfast and sat down at the table. "Here. Maybe you would like something to read while we eat." She tapped her tablet to his. He accepted the file she had pushed to him and opened it.

It appeared to be an academic paper from several years back. He read the premise and checked the author. The author was Dr. M. Turner and she was arguing how it was possible to lie while never saying anything that was untrue.

He thought for a time and then he got it. She could obfuscate. She couldn't say anything directly that would trigger the collar, but if she was vague enough, the collar wouldn't be able to differentiate and establish a cause to set off a punishment.

Of course, this depended on the other party knowing what was being implied, and knowing her well enough to follow her logic. Like him.

He looked over at her and mouthed a silent ahhhh. She grinned wickedly. Okay. She couldn't talk about her daughter, but no reason why she couldn't talk about her niece. Her niece being his daughter. *What?*

"What's next for you, Garrett? Are you going to stay with GIS and settle down?" Mel asked, starting in on him again.

He set his empty coffee mug down hard on the table and glared at her. It had barely been a day. They went from being estranged to back to being family, close enough to share secrets in a single planetary rotation—that wasn't enough apparently.

She glared right back at him and handed him a napkin to wipe up the spilled coffee. She then picked up his mug, filled it, and set it down with an equally loud thump. She settled herself in her chair, crossed her arms and legs, and gave him a look that told him she wasn't going to let it go.

He tried waiting her out and just stared at her, but it was like when they were kids. When she made up her mind, a grenade couldn't blow her out. He groaned and gave up.

"Mel. I don't know. Look at me; I'm a mess." He gestured at his un-showered, coffee-stained person. "I barely have a job, both you and the Agency shrink think I have 'issues' to talk about. I can't wait to add your list to his. This, this is not what I expected. Hell, even what I thought was, wasn't. *And*, and GIS only wants me as an analyst."

"Well, I agree you are a bit of a mess, but I don't see why your shorts are in a bunch." Mel was perfectly calm, though less belligerent.

"Let's think this through. Let's *assume* you planned on living to retirement from Fleet; what would you have done then?" He gave a half-shrug but didn't say anything. She made a face but didn't call him on it. She sighed.

"No, life isn't like a well-planned mission that you execute to perfection. Life out here, outside of the military, is uncertain and unpredictable, and I can see how you would be disorientated."

Kelley thought that 'angry' would be a better choice than 'disorientated' and she was way oversimplifying his situation, but he didn't want to interrupt, nor did he feel like arguing with her.

She went on, "Instead of chasing after what you can't have, maybe you should look and see what you do have. You have a job, a great job, in fact. Good pay, solid benefits. And it even plays to your strengths."

"I'm a soldier, not an analyst," he objected.

"You were a soldier, but you were and still are a very intelligent man with an analytical mind. Have you explored what it means to be a GIS intelligence officer?"

That was a nice touch, he thought, linking a GIS analyst to a military intelligence officer.

"And what about family? I thought family was important to you," she said pointedly.

Ouch. He didn't like that poke. He got up, agitated. So, if he didn't adopt this girl he'd never met, he was rejecting family? Rejecting Mel's daughter? Rejecting the values their parents had taught them? The simple yes bounced around his brain like a ricochet. He felt like he'd been hit but he couldn't see where.

After the Battle

Mel came over to him and hugged him. "You can do this. Look how far you got, all on your own. Now you don't have to do it alone anymore. You have all of GIS's resources to help you sort things out. And you have me."

He hugged her back for a long time. He looked down at her, took a deep breath, and nodded.

Mel's face lit up. He couldn't recall seeing her that happy in a long time, certainly not since their parents died.

She said, "Just focus on family and it will be all right; it will all work out."

Chapter Six

Kelley was tired. He leaned back against his seat on the transport to Tycor. He had expected to bolt from the fishing shack soon after he agreed to adopt Mel's daughter as his own. However, Mel had thought otherwise. She insisted on arranging for his belongings to be shipped to his current residence near the GIS training center. He was reluctant to agree. He had gotten used to the idea that his stuff was gone, and it wasn't like his current place had any room for it. His apartment was hardly bigger than the students' quarters.

To make it more uncomfortable, Mel had babbled on happily about her new-found niece. Kelley had been on edge the entire time, but evidentially Mel was pretty good at obfuscating.

When he checked in with Doctor Crane, he surprised himself by wanting to talk to the doc. After a general update, they discussed the collar in more detail and Mel, in general.

Dr. Crane's perspective was informative and helpful. He agreed to research the collar to see if it would help figure out who had implanted it.

He felt Mel's study of psychology was suggestive, as was her current choice of counseling pro bono at several health centers on Nibiru, even though Dr. Turner was highly respected in her field and had published several well-received papers.

Crane also suggested that perhaps Mel had always wanted the girl to be found, why else would she allow herself to be collared instead of simply aborting it? While Kelley didn't disagree with the premise, he thought the doctor's reasoning was flawed. Kelley believed that Mel had had more choices than just a collar or abortion. Kelley refused to discuss this aspect further saying that they would never know, and speculating wouldn't help deal with the situation now.

Crane was also supportive of Mel's opinion when she had said that he had always been more than a foot soldier. An elite foot soldier, he had wanted to correct the doc.

He was grateful that the doc hadn't pressed him too hard about Mel's suggestion that he had been running away his entire adult life. Although Crane did take advantage of Kelley's state of mind by getting him to agree to reoccurring, periodic check-ins.

After all that, he was finally able to get transport to Tycor. So, here he was, the initial shock of the revelations of the past couple of days wearing off, as was the initial panic of becoming a father.

Well, the initial panic was wearing off. He was still dealing with the bitter irony. He had been *so* very careful all his life when it came to his liaisons with females. Now after all that, he had agreed to be a father to a kid that had suddenly popped up out of nowhere. And he hadn't even met her yet. The beer had helped take some of the edge off, but he asked the attendant for coffee instead of another one. He still had to review the report from the legal brief already on Tycor.

Agent Sofia Deleon had made discreet inquiries about the girl and the charges against her. She also worked with a local brief to get context around the other parties.

In short, there had been a raid and a general sweep of a club whose owners were suspected of dealing narcotics to its clientele. Narcotics had been found on several people, including Duine Arbith. He paused; it was the first time she had been named. He wondered if the name meant what he thought it did. And if Mel had known that was going to be the girl's name, and if she agreed?

Pushing the name aside, he focused on the report. According to Miss Arbith's statement, she saw the owners dispose of something just as the police were storming in. They, of course, denied it and said it was the girl that had been the one. The report did not say anything had been found in the club, but there also didn't seem to be anything in the report about a search of the club either.

There was no evidence of drugs in the girl's system and there was no evidence to support she had been buying them, yet the girl had not been released. Agent Deleon's source had suggested that the owners were well-connected and as the girl was not, they were trying to shift the blame to her.

Kelley suspected that by keeping her locked up they hoped she would eventually take a deal. However, if this was the case, it meant the local PD was in some way collusive. As former PD himself, he wanted to believe there was another explanation. He put away his tablet and settled back into his seat to catch some downtime. His last thought before dropping off was that Agent Deleon had gotten a fair amount of intel in a very short period of time.

Chapter Seven

When he landed on Tycor, Kelley immediately went to the Police Precinct. After establishing his credentials, he was shown into the observation side of an interrogation room. Inside there was only one person, a woman, dressed very well, watching the interview in progress. "Agent Kelley?" she asked, barely taking her eyes away from the interview.

"Agent Rogers?" he asked, deliberately using the wrong name.

"Deleon," she corrected him tersely, though not visibly upset.

"What is the latest?"

"They are losing patience. I think they are going to get rough with her soon. I didn't want to leave her; I think it's only my interest that is keeping them in check."

Kelley joined her at the window and focused on the interview in progress. Tycor was one of the many worlds where humans cohabited with the locals. The interview was being conducted by a native of Tycor wearing a police uniform—the same uniform Kelley had seen the officers who were directing traffic on his ride from the Port wearing. He looked at Deleon quizzically. She answered him with, "No, he isn't a detective, just big. Looks like they are trying the intimidation approach. Want me to stop it?"

He just shook his head. He turned back and got his first good look at the girl. Mel's daughter. His niece. He involuntarily took a step forward and put his hand out towards the glass. She looked so much like Mel when she was fifteen; same general build, same hair and eye coloring. This girl had a long, thick mane of rough unkempt hair though. Their mother would never have allowed Mel to look that wild. She was hunched, her arms folded, looking tired but resolute.

She just sat without speaking and listened to her interrogator drone on and on about what she *thought* she saw. He gave a detailed, grisly description of what would happen to her if she went to prison. He finished by asking her if she understood.

Her answer surprised Kelley. She said, "Yes, you want me to lie." She was quite defiant. The youngster had guts.

The cop, caught off guard, was momentarily speechless before he started to yell at her in his native tongue. The girl's poise left her as he pushed his angry face in close to her. She was scared, making Kelley feel the need to intervene.

He turned to Deleon and demanded, "Make it stop."

She nodded and left the room. A moment later she appeared in the interview room and identified herself as GIS Agent Sofia Deleon, a lawyer, and claimed the defendant to be her client. The cop tried to intimidate her, but she held her ground and started listing the many violations of the girl's rights under the Confederate guidelines.

The officer rudely interrupted her saying that Tycor's laws were paramount. Agent Deleon calmly contradicted him and explained that while each planet of the Confederacy had their own local government and laws, they also agreed to abide by a baseline or framework of the Confederate guidelines.

This made the officer nervous. Seeing he was out of his depth, Agent Deleon advised him to go and get the lead agent on the case. Her tone was strong and commanding; she might have well as said get out.

The officer was barely out of the room before Kelley was in through the other door. The girl was looking at Agent Deleon in awe. When she saw him, she looked scared again, taking him for someone who was going to attack her too.

He stopped, made himself relax, and took a breath. "I'm not here to hurt you. We," he said gesturing to Deleon, "are here to help."

"Why? What is going on that involves GIS?"

"It's a long story actually. Right now, we don't have much time before the locals come back. I would like you to tell us what happened at the club. Were you buying or selling drugs?"

"Neither. I was in the kitchen of the club, cleaning dishes for food. The cops burst in and, all of a sudden, this woman was in my face, shoving something in my pocket, telling me to take it, and that she will take care of me later."

"The police arrested me and when I told them what happened, they took me to a cell and just left me. I could hear them arguing about something. One of them tried to take my statement once, but I haven't seen him since. They ask me to change my story at least twice a day. They tell me just own up to the charge and make it easy on myself."

"Then today, they bring me here and that huge officer comes in and starts threatening me. Then she comes in and drives him off and now *you* come in. You are the first person to actually listen to me since I got here." Her voice was tired and shaky.

"How long have you been on Tycor?"

"Not long. I've been here mostly," she said, indicating the Precinct.

"How did you get to Tycor and from where?" asked Deleon.

She looked wary at the question. "Does it matter?"

Kelley answered, "To the case, probably not. To me, yes." He looked over at his colleague and said, "This is going to take a while to sort out. Interviews, identifications, formal statements. Does she have to stay here? Can't we get her a bail hearing or something?"

"We can try and take her into our custody, but we don't really have a cause. She is a witness, but we aren't even sure as to what."

"What do you need? How about I know where they hid the rest of stuff?" the girl piped up, suddenly more animated.

Kelley and Deleon looked at each other. Deleon said, "It's thin but I can make it work, for a short time; longer if your intel is actually good."

The girl looked defiant again and refolded her arms. Agent Deleon smiled briefly and said, "Okay." To Kelley, "Stay here." She left the room.

Kelley and the girl just sat for a minute, staring at each other. Finally, Kelley broke the silence by introducing himself. "Garrett Kelley. And you are Duine Arbith?"

The girl shrugged. "I guess so."

"You guess? You don't know your own name?"

"I grew up in an orphanage on Pagnol. I am not sure of anything." Kelley didn't contradict her, but she was hardly grown up in his opinion. However, she somehow managed to get herself a good distance across the galaxy, he had to give her that.

"How did you get from Pagnol to Tycor?"

"A cruise liner came in. They did every so often. I managed to sneak aboard and just got off when it berthed at Tycor."

Kelley tried to give her his best imitation of his father's look, when Finn knew his son wasn't being completely truthful.

"You just walked on board a space liner and no one saw you over the course of the trip?"

She shifted nervously. "Okay, no. I managed to stay hidden long enough to get into orbit. One of the crew found me and I begged him not to turn me in. He wasn't sure at first, but when he talked to his mate, she convinced him that it was the least they could do for me."

"I stayed in their quarters and they brought me food. They almost turned me in when Spectrum sent a message saying I had gone missing. The ship didn't think I was there, but they had to comply with the request to do a search. The two were terrified at the thought of me being found with them. I ran and hid. They didn't find me, and when the shipped docked, I put on one of the crew uniforms and walked off."

"Once here, I took to waiting at the back of the restaurant, I mean the club. I would wait until they came out with the trash and got what I could before they threw it out. One of the managers saw me and told me he would give me food if I worked in the kitchen. Seemed like a fair enough deal to me."

Kelley doubted the manager's intentions when he looked the young woman over again. "How long were you in the kitchen?"

She shrugged again. "Not long at all. He said he was going to let me use the shower at his place after the shift was over. The police came before that, and then this nightmare started."

"Kid, as bad as it's been inside, you got lucky. It was better than being out there with that perv."

"So *you* say," she said defensively. "Who are you anyway? Why do you care? What is this long story?"

Before he could answer, Agent Deleon came back with several police officers behind her. Kelley stood and moved in front of the girl.

Agent Deleon said, "The Tycor PD have agreed to release Ms. Duine Arbith into our custody pending the outcome of our investigation." Kelley noted that none of the cops looked at all happy, in fact, he wasn't sure they agreed at all.

He moved to block them as Deleon ushered the girl out and kept close on their six as they exited. Agent Deleon had the lead and a good hold of the girl's hand. When they got into a local transport she said, "This is going to be interesting."

Chapter Eight

Over the next several days, Deleon interviewed Duine extensively. She found the officer who Duine said wanted to take her statement; he had been transferred to another district. He gave them a wealth of information, apparently not liking his unexpected transfer. He told them that the club owners were known drug traffickers and several in the PD were on their payroll. Duine positively identified the wife as the one who put the drugs into her pocket.

Deleon brought the weight of GIS down on Tycor and initiated a full investigation. After a large quantity of drugs was found just where Duine said they would be, Tycor's ruling body decided that it was better to cooperate rather than oppose GIS.

The investigation and indictment of one of Tycor's leading families created a media storm. In contrast, the thorough review of Tycor's PD was quiet and discreet.

The legal proceedings took time to work out, during which Kelley was anything but idle. He got himself assigned to the case and assisted Agent Deleon, where needed. He also began looking into Spectrum Orphanage and he dutifully remembered to keep his check-ins with Crane.

When he told Crane that he wanted to look closer into Spectrum Orphanage, Crane first wanted to know why. After he explained his reasoning, Crane arranged for Kelley to liaison with local GIS agents in the Pagnol system.

He also spent a lot of time with Duine. He was impressed at how solid she was throughout it all. Deleon arranged for several rooms at a local hotel where they lived and worked during the investigation. When not working on the case, Duine talked with Kelley about growing up at the orphanage on planet Pagnol.

He was glad to hear that she had been decently treated, and her living conditions were well within the Confederate standards. At first, he supposed it was because it was a private orphanage. As they talked though, he started to get suspicious. It was at this time that he started a discreet inquiry with the help of the GIS agents local to Pagnol's system.

Spectrum Orphanage was exclusive. They did not disclose how the children they cared for came to be there. It was suggested that the rich and connected disposed of the products of their illicit liaisons at Spectrum. They, of course, never confirmed this. When audited, they always passed. The living quarters were clean and well-maintained, tailored to the specific needs of each particular bipedal humanoid. The children never had any complaints when interviewed and seemed happy enough. Spectrum's records were always in order, though often discreetly redacted. There were never any grounds to open a formal inquiry.

From the start, Kelley felt conflicted. He was very aware that he just met the girl, but at the same time, he felt a connection to her. He certainly felt protective of her. This made him want to pull back and be aloof. He didn't want to scare her or seem overbearing. Yet, he wanted to know everything about her. Kelley was grateful for Crane's guidance on how to deal with it all.

He arranged for a GIS medical doctor to come to Tycor and examine Duine. The doctor was shocked that she had *none* of the immunization antibodies in her system. It was extremely rare that a space-faring colony of any size or allegiance did not adhere to the basic immunization protocols.

The doctor immediately threw a quarantine ring around her. Fortunately, for everyone, he was able to confirm Duine was not carrying anything infectious. He was similarly shocked she hadn't caught anything over the last couple of months since leaving Pagnol. Eventually, he discovered that she had a sophisticated prophylactic chip implant.

The doctor disagreed with Kelley's decision to remove the implant and started immunization treatments, but he yielded as Kelley was her provisional guardian. Kelley pressed him as to why the orphanage would go to the trouble and expense of chip implants, arguing that surely immunizations were cheaper. The doctor agreed; in fact, they were free to accredited facilities such as orphanages. When asked to speculate why implants from a medical viewpoint, the doctor was hesitant, and finally said that perhaps they wanted the children to be kept pure, antibody free. When asked the benefits of this, the doctor initially refused to answer, and only after being pressed did he say that in some cases, organ donations were rejected because of antibody conflicts between host and donor, especially between different or mixed-race species.

Kelley requested the implant be studied as closely as possible and any findings to be reported back to him. The doctor agreed though he maintained his objections at its removal. It was a medical boon; the girl would be immune to countless diseases and parasitics, but Kelley was adamant.

Working with the local agents, he learned that not only was there a planetary alert on Pagnol for Duine Arbith's safe return to the orphanage, that same alert was also being broadcast system-wide.

It was clear Spectrum wanted her back. They managed to get a mandatory search on all vessels leaving the planet. That took considerable influence of the Pagnol government. It had gone into effect the day after the girl said she left. What was strange was for all their insistence for her return, they only included her picture, general physical description, and fingerprint information in the alert, but there was no mitochondrial profile. They apparently did not want her DNA made public in any way.

From his perspective, Kelley thought this was a mistake. If he had been looking for her, he would have taken the risk. Appearances could be altered in countless ways, with or without technology. Even fingerprints weren't reliable with limb replacements being prevalent and even fashionable.

Between Mel being collared and Spectrum refusing to disclose the girl's DNA profile, it was clear that the father did *not* want to be identified.

If it wasn't for the lack of antibodies, Kelley would have focused on figuring out how to get custody of his niece straightaway. At least that is what he tried to tell himself. He was still very unsure if he wanted full-time custody of the girl. She was a great kid; surely the father would see that and want to keep her, if only they met.

He decided he was going to wait until the situation on Tycor was resolved before asking Duine more pointed questions about her time at Spectrum. Kelley felt that she was dealing with enough with the investigation, however, Duine didn't want to wait that long.

Chapter Nine

One night, after Agent Deleon had gone to bed, Duine came over and sat down at the table where he was working. She didn't say anything, she just watched him work until he stopped and asked, "What?"

"Who are you? I mean, really. Everyone else is very clear about who they are and what they are doing. But not you. You help Agent Sofia out on the case, but the doc listened to you about the implant. You are constantly working on something or talking on the vid but it's not about Agent Sofia's case. Is it about me? Why would you still be here if it wasn't about me?" She sat back against the chair, arms crossed.

He saved the file he was working on and closed the device. He also sat back in his chair. "You have a lot going on right now, kid. Maybe we should wait on this."

"And that is another thing," she said. "You never call me Duine. Why is that? Isn't that my name?"

He surprised her by shaking his head and saying, "I don't think so, but I don't know what it was meant to be. Tell me, you have been called Duine Arbith your entire life, why do you think that isn't your name?"

She shrugged and mumbled an 'I don't know.' Duine didn't trust him and he could tell she was getting frustrated at being kept in the dark.

He looked at her for a minute and his resolve wavered. It had been several Tycor weeks since she was released from jail. She seemed close with Deleon, but not him. Thinking about what she said, he decided she had a point. Okay, into the breach.

"Here it is. I'm Agent Garrett Kelley, a relatively new agent with GIS. I haven't even been assigned to my first post. This is my first assignment. Before that, I was in Fleet Special Forces. And before that, I was on Blerreon 4 with my sister." He paused, the girl was listening, but showed no reaction at the mention of Blerreon 4.

He continued, "Part of GIS hiring protocols is a full background check which is pretty thorough. They even check for DNA matches." At that, she tensed and started breathing faster.

He shook his head slowly, "No, I'm not your father. It looks like I'm just your uncle."

He was about to continue, but she interrupted with, "JUST?! Just my uncle? And you wait until now to tell me?" She was up and out of her chair. "Well, go on, *UNCLE!*" she demanded.

"Kid, calm down. I will if you sit down." She glared at him, still pacing. "Please."

Still glaring, she sat down with a thump, jaw tight.

He took a breath and let it out again. "Please listen."

"Why? Because it's complicated?" she interrupted with a tone.

"No, it's actually pretty simple. Saying that you are her daughter could kill your mother." He was stern and looked her straight in the eye. "No lie, kid," he said more softly.

She listened while he explained about the collar. He gave her time to process while he got them both something to drink.

"You can't admit that I'm family. So, what happens now? Do I go back to the orphanage?" She held her mug tightly with both hands.

"No. Not if I have a say in it," he answered firmly. *What am I saying?* he asked himself. His response had been automatic, straight from his gut. She looked at him, unsure but hopeful.

"I have to figure all this out. We don't know who your father is or what his rights are. So far, it looks like you were legally placed in Spectrum's care and they currently have a system-wide alert out for your return. Your mother can't exert her rights on your behalf, and as you say, I can't either without compromising her life. Right now, Tycor also has a claim on you, though Agent Deleon is doing a very good job of getting that sorted out."

The girl said nothing, so he continued, "You have gone from being confined in an orphanage, to space liner crew quarters, then to a jail cell, and now to a hotel room. You've been charged with a felony, jailed, harassed by the cops, had surgery to remove an implant, and are currently undergoing immunizations that normally are administered over the course of several years."

"That is a lot to process. I was just trying to keep it all as simple as possible."

"Yeah, I get that, but finding out about you and my mother is what I want. I've always wanted to know if I had a family. I can handle *that*," she said with emphasis.

He smiled and reached out to rub her arm gently. She had guts, he liked that.

"*Now*, will you tell me why you doubt your own name?" he said with his own emphasis, gently mocking her tone.

She took a sip of her drink before saying, "My adoption record lists my name in quotes; like a fake name or pseudonym. My birth date is incomplete as well. It lists a year, but not a full date or from what system; so I can't calculate and translate it into Confederate dates."

"And how did you get to see your adoption record? Did you break in somewhere?"

"No." She was defensive. "I got a job in the office and the admin left her password where I could find it and I got curious. That's all. I didn't break anything." She continued before he could comment. "Tell me why you doubt my name is Duine Arbith."

Pronouncing slowly, he said, "Duine ar bith is no one's name. It means 'no one' in a very, very old language. I think Mel called you that for a reason. I just don't know why." The girl looked sad and tired.

"We will sort it out." He rubbed her arm again. "Do you know how many GIS agents are working on this? You have an entire legal team here on Tycor and another medical team in another system that is analyzing the implant and researching the collar. The doc here is making sure you are healthy. And I am working with the GIS agents nearest to Pagnol to learn more about Spectrum."

She smiled shyly. "Okay, it sounds like a lot when you say it that way." She leaned towards him and put her hand on his. He turned his hand upwards and gently squeezed her hand.

"Go to bed now. We have a lot to talk about in the morning."

Chapter Ten

The next morning, she was up early, almost bouncing in her eagerness to get started. "So, what do I call you now? Uncle?"

Deleon, at the table with Kelley, looked up, startled at the question.

"Agent Kelley for now, kid. Someone has gone to a great deal of trouble to keep you out of the system. Let's keep a low profile until we know more," he answered.

"Who is going to hear? The hotel bot that brings the food?"

"I don't anticipate being here for much longer. I just need to talk it through with Agent Deleon first. But yes, you need to be careful even in front of a bot. It's actually very easy to get a listening device onto a bot. Now, please scoot."

She looked at Deleon, who nodded, then she said, "Bye Agent Sofia," and went to her room.

Kelley and Deleon discussed the state of the case. Deleon agreed to seek permission to depose Duine in lieu of her testifying at the trial due to extenuating circumstances. He asked if her record could also be expunged. She was never formally charged, but he didn't like her time in jail as part of her record. Deleon agreed and further suggested that her testimony should be sealed. It would be as if she had never been on Tycor.

This led to talking about jurisdiction and custody of the girl. Deleon reminded him that he already had provisional custody. The doctor also confirmed GIS's initial report—the girl was a mitochondrial match to him. They ended their discussion with Deleon agreeing to finish the case on Tycor and for Kelley to take Duine with him when he left for the Pagnol system.

After Deleon left, he reviewed the medical report that listed the probably model of the collar, as well as a short list of manufacturers. He decided to make a discreet request and see if he could get a list of customers from fifteen or sixteen years ago. It was a shot in the dark, but these days with different species living two to three times longer than humans, records were kept for a long time.

He hadn't told Duine that the medical team's report included the results of their analysis of the chip implant. In short, it was a nasty piece of tech. It was brilliant in its ability to protect its host from disease but, what worried him, was the team couldn't be sure what else it did. There was enough coding to make them think there were additional functions, but they couldn't determine what. In addition, they could not find evidence of any safety protocols. The Confederate mandated that all medical tech, especially implants, had safety protocols that would protect the host from any sort of harm; Duine's implant did not.

The lack of protocols plus the undeciphered part of the implant made him wonder if it was capable of killing her. Spectrum clearly wanted her back, but at the same time, they were not doing absolutely everything they could to get her back; as if they had a contingency plan.

If the implant could kill her, there was no way to determine if it would automatically switch or Spectrum had to trigger it. Either way, Kelley was glad it was out.

Finally, he checked in with and updated Crane on his activities as it related to Spectrum. Crane listened but seemed more interested about he having told Duine that he was her uncle.

"Does that mean you are going to keep custody of her?" he asked.

"I'm getting used to the idea," he admitted cautiously. "But there is still a lot I have to figure out." He was not ready to commit and say anything for certain.

Crane, however, replied as if he had agreed. "Yes, and currently part of the detail on the Tycor litigation, but you should find a permanent assignment."

"I've been looking."

Crane caught the dejected tone of the reply and asked him where he had been looking. Kelley ran down the list; it didn't take long.

Crane was thoughtful for a moment, then said, "Normally, I would refer an agent to our Interspecies Relations area for guidance on permanent placements. In your case, I think it would be beneficial if you and I went through your curriculum vitae and GIS's current list of open assignments. For now, can you tell me what your immediate plans are?"

"I want to continue looking into Spectrum. I think there is something there. As you know, I've been talking with the agents in the Pagnol system and they have been suspicious of Spectrum for a while, but have never had grounds to do anything more than tag along on the occasional audit. And the audits never turned up anything. However, this time we have Duine. I would like to take her with me and see what she can tell us about her time with Spectrum."

He paused. Crane nodded, his face impassive and his tone decidedly neutral, and said, "It is worth investigating. As you say, we have access to intel we have never had before. Though you should keep in mind that it might be difficult for her."

Now Kelley nodded, though he wondered if he heard a difference in Crane's voice when he switched from talking about his lead to Duine. "Yes. I know. Ideally, I would like to find about her father at the same time. Something. Anything. Enough at least to know what I am getting into. I mean, can she go out or does she have to stay in hiding for the rest of her life?"

"I understand. Stay put on Tycor until I can get the Spectrum investigation approved, though I don't think it will be a problem."

Kelley agreed, not sure how a psychiatrist could get investigations approved, but he didn't question the doc. Things were moving in the direction he wanted them to.

Chapter Eleven

Several days and a grueling deposition later, Crane contacted him. As expected, the Spectrum investigation was approved. What Kelley didn't expect was the amount of virtual paperwork that came along with it.

"What is all this?" he asked Crane.

"Standard jacket for a new investigation. As lead, you need to keep good records."

Kelley tried not to gape at Crane, so he took a deep breath and tried to look thoughtful instead. "Lead? Does GIS often give new agents point on such politically sensitive investigations?"

"No. Very few new agents have your background. In Fleet, you planned and led many operations. It is doubtful that you will be infiltrating Spectrum, but your experience with the intelligence-gathering aspect should serve you well. Also, new agents have little understanding of politics. You, however, are both aware and sufficiently motivated to avoid an incident."

"In addition, you found the lead and provided the necessary foundation to open an investigation. You have already reached out to the local agents and gained their cooperation. You have a relationship with the source and a vested interest to protect her at the same time." Crane finished by asking, "Should anyone else be lead on this?"

Kelley hesitated before answering, wondering what Crane wasn't telling him. He decided to play along and assured the doc that he was both capable and willing to lead the investigation. "No, you are right, this won't be my first time leading a team to gather intel. Yes, I do want to make sure Duine isn't subjected to unnecessary unpleasantness. I'm in."

He liked that he could take the investigation where he thought best. He also liked being in charge again. It felt good.

"Excellent. Make sure Agent Deleon signs off on you leaving her detail and her witness leaving the planet before departing for Spectrum," Crane reminded him.

"Yes, sir," Kelley said automatically. Crane smiled briefly and ended the call.

Later that day, Duine came into the shared space that served as their war room. She looked at Kelley and Deleon, seated next to each other at the table, and said, "Oops. I can come back later."

Kelley looked up, surprised, "Come on in, kid. We're not working on anything sensitive; no reason you can't come in. I should probably give you an update since you are here."

Duine looked at the table, with the two wine glasses and the half-empty bottle, and then at Deleon, who had no expression. Kelley pulled out a chair next to him. Duine gave a half shrug and sat down saying, "What's up?"

"Well, as you may be aware, your involvement in the case here on Tycor is winding down. With Agent Deleon's permission, we are going to leave. As lead, she will stay and finish what needs to be done here."

Duine looked quizzical at his phrasing, so Deleon said, "The public trial of the drug ring is only one aspect that needs to be concluded. In addition to that, there is the PD collusion with them and your treatment during your time in their custody. The rulers of Tycor are cooperating with the

Confederacy and have agreed to a GIS review of their law enforcement network."

Duine was surprised, "Their entire network? Over me?"

"Yes, because of the size and extent of the drug ring and how many of their own laws had to be bent or broken to keep you unprocessed in jail for so long," Kelley answered.

Deleon nodded agreement and added, "They violated their own laws and the Confederate guidelines regarding citizen rights."

"And when there is one, there may be more. The situation requires a thorough review," Kelley finished quietly.

After a moment, he went on, "So, if you have seen enough of the hotel here, I would like you to come with me on another case. What do you say?"

Duine peered at him doubtfully. She had been sequestered during the current investigation; her movements restricted to the hotel and its grounds. Seeing he was serious, she perked up and said, smiling, "Come with you? Sure!" Then her smile just as quickly faded, "On a case? What case?"

"I have been given permission to look into Spectrum. I was hoping you and I could talk."

"And after that case is over, then what?" she asked warily.

He looked her straight in the eye, "I don't know. It depends on what we can find about your paternity. We know essentially nothing, which could mean we find a lot of good things or some very bad things. I can't say until we know more."

She looked back at him and swiveled her chair around while she thought about it. "But you are looking into it?" she asked.

"Yes. I have a whole team to help me and everything. Do you want in or not?" he said, his tone slightly challenging.

She smiled again, "Yes! I want in!"

Chapter Twelve

Leaving Tycor took more time than Kelley thought it would. He was used to travel, and like most military personnel, he was able to be ready at a moment's notice. He had not thought about gearing up a fifteen-year-old female civilian. That she came to Tycor with barely more than the clothes on her back should have made packing easy.

As she had been living in the hotel for several weeks, he assumed she had acquired anything necessary during that time. He was mistaken.

He had to take her shopping, which was very awkward for them both. He was looking for her to tell him what she needed, and she was looking at him to tell her what she could buy. At the end of a very long day, he decided to take her to a nicer restaurant for dinner, as a treat for them both. Duine looked like she enjoyed her meal and behaved very well.

She had a natural sense of discretion about what should and should not be discussed in public. Which was fortunate, as she had plenty of things she wanted to talk or ask about. He found her chatter almost as tiring as shopping, though at the same time, he enjoyed her curiosity and intelligent questions. He scrupulously limited himself to only two beers.

He was somewhat distressed about one thing but had no idea what to do about it. Duine was a young woman and he would have thought she would be wearing a supporting garment of some type. She wasn't. He felt like a complete pervert for noticing and could not bring himself to ask her about it. It was possible she didn't feel comfortable purchasing such garments with him around.

He couldn't give her a GIS credit stick and let her wander around unsupervised. For one thing, there was the issue of her safety. It had been established protocol that she was only allowed to leave the hotel with an escort. He felt the danger was minimal, but there was still an alert out for her. He ultimately decided to leave the issue of her wardrobe for now; she seemed happy enough.

They made it back to the hotel where she left him for her room, to see if her purchases had been delivered by drone. He sat down heavily and put his head back, trying to think if there was anything decent to drink in the suite. Deleon looked up from whatever it was she was working on and said, "You look like you have had a long day."

He just grunted agreement. He was tired and somewhat irritated with her. He knew it wasn't her job to gear up the girl. She was the lead on an important investigation and at the moment, his boss. She probably didn't have time for shopping trips.

Just because she was a female like Duine didn't make the girl her responsibility in any way. He knew that, but it didn't matter, he was still annoyed with her.

Deleon came over and sat down next to him. Her hair was around her face, not pulled back like it usually was and her blouse was not tucked in. She tried to engage him in conversation, but eventually gave up. He was civil but curt, and his answers were short.

She got up and went back to the table, pulling her hair back as she sat down. Together, they finalized the details of his and Duine's departure, and then he left for his room.

The next morning when it was time to leave, things got awkward again. Kelley was used to leaving after an assignment, which often came with brief, but intense relationships.

Duine clearly found it difficult. She had been with the team for many weeks and they had taken care of her. She felt close to them and didn't know what to say. They, of course, had been professional during the assignment, and while they were kind now, Duine was figuring out that she was closer to them than they were to her.

Kelley stepped in and helped her where he could, smoothing things over, though Duine got quieter as they made their rounds.

Finally, it was time to say goodbye to Agent Deleon. She was professional and offered the usual gratitude for his assistance. He replied in kind and thanked her for everything she had done with respect to Duine.

Duine, looking from Kelley to Deleon and back again, had a strange expression on her face. She looked expectant and confused at the same time. Kelley took it to mean that she wasn't sure how to say goodbye. She was most familiar with Deleon who she liked to call Agent Sofia.

Duine thanked her for everything and asked, "Will I see you again?"

"I don't know, maybe," Deleon replied, then she surprised Kelley by giving Duine a warm hug. Duine hugged her for a moment before stepping back, quickly wiping her eyes. She seemed unable to speak as Kelley gently ushered her out of the hotel and into the transport.

Duine was quiet on the way to the terminal and as they navigated their way to the gate. She pulled herself together when she realized they were boarding a private ship.

Kelley grinned at her. "Not bad, is it? It should be better than crew quarters on a space liner."

Chapter Thirteen

Kelley and Duine boarded the ship and were met by the flight crew, none of whom were human. They greeted Kelley in a formal and respectful manner. He returned the greeting and stopped to get their names and positions onboard the ship. The crew were mostly female and, as expected, all GIS agents.

Duine said little during the exchange but was polite when introduced. The crew gave her a brief verbal layout of the ship, including areas that were considered off-limits to civilians. She agreed to abide by the restrictions and thanked them.

The pilot informed Kelley that the ship was in order and ready for departure. Kelley complimented their readiness and ordered them to initiate the departure procedures.

"We need to get strapped in for take-off. I'll introduce you to the rest of the team after we are en route," he told Duine, guiding her through the ship.

The short corridor led to a large common area where three agents were sitting, two males and one female. One of the males was human, the other two agents were not. They nodded at Kelley and one was about to speak when the pilot announced their imminent take off.

They all busied themselves getting ready for departure. One agent swiveled and locked his seat into take-off position and pressed a button to reveal the safety harness. The other two got off the couch and started to take the remaining chairs, but Kelley stopped them. He curtly but civilly told them to use the other seating. He sat Duine in the chair next to the window and helped her strap in before taking the seat next to her.

One of the displaced agents immediately went to the rear wall and tapping quickly, brought out another seat. It looked much less comfortable and had a view of the back of the chairs in front of it. The other agent was looking around and seemed unsure.

Kelley taking note of this, waited a moment, expecting one of the other agents to assist. None of them spoke or moved. Kelley gave the female agent seated against the wall a hard look and said, "Show him."

She didn't verbally respond to his order but she did reach around to tap the buttons to bring out the seat next to her. The agent sat and started fumbling for his harness. By this time, the ship had finished taxing into launch position and was starting its thruster sequence.

Kelley glared at the female agent again. She nodded calmly back at him and helped the agent strap in, just before the ship fired its thrusters and began its ascent up through Tycor's atmosphere and into space. Once clear of the atmosphere, the ship switched to its engines, which could be felt vibrating through the ship.

Duine looking out the window, was excited and happy.

The pilot announced their successful launch from Tycor and their estimated time to the edge of Tycor's solar system.

Duine looked at Kelley questioningly. Answering her look, he explained, "Navigating through a planetary system isn't a straight line. The pilot must steer around the gravitational pulls of the other planets, and at the same time, has to keep clear of other traffic. Once out of the system, she will be able to set course and pick up speed. After that, you won't feel the engines so much."

"Should I keep strapped in until we are out?" she asked.

"It will be a while until we are clear, so no, you don't have to. Just keep in mind there will be a jolt when she kicks it up to full speed. It will be enough to knock you off your feet if you aren't prepared."

"You probably didn't feel anything like that on the liner because its purpose is to maximize the comfort of its passengers. This ship is much smaller and was designed with different priorities."

With that, he unbuckled his harness and retracted the straps. The seat now looked like a comfortable chair in the common area. He noted the non-human agents doing the same. The human male was apprehensive but retracted his straps when he saw Duine doing hers.

While Kelley waited for them to get settled and comfortable, Duine played with the buttons around her seat. She brought up the ship's video system. She looked out the window and back at the vid, comparing it to what she was seeing out the window. He decided to let her be for now.

"Right." He looked around, addressing the other agents, saying, "As you know, I am Agent Kelley, lead on this investigation into Spectrum Orphanage, headquartered on Pagnol. I have read your bios, but I would like you to introduce yourselves to Miss Arbith." He looked to his left, at the male non-human.

"Agent Servelun Dakki. I have been a lawyer with GIS for several of your decades." He paused before asking Duine, "Do you need me to explain?"

Kelley didn't care for his tone or the question, but he knew Dakki was deliberately baiting her. He stayed silent, wanting to see how she would react.

She stared at Dakki for a moment, looked over at Kelley, then down at her lap. She inhaled deeply and sat a bit straighter in the seat. Then, calmly looking at him, she replied, "No, thank you for asking. I will let you know if I have trouble keeping up." She had a bit of a tone, but given her age and experience, she was wonderfully poised.

"Oh, good. It's so hard for me to gauge you humans," Dakki said innocently.

Kelley and Duine both ignored his comment and as one turned to the female agent now sitting on the couch.

"Agent Chi Ting," she said. Her voice was soft, but they had no trouble hearing her words. "I have been involved in the last two audits of Spectrum." She paused briefly before saying, "Where we found nothing at all."

Duine looked about to argue. Kelley put his right hand on her arm and gave it a brief squeeze as he swiveled his chair left to say, "Agent Alban, come join us over here."

Agent Alban had been silently struggling with getting the seat to retract into the wall. He looked up and cleared his throat.

"Here, let me," Duine said, getting up and going over to him. She fixed the strap that was twisted and pushed the retract button. Now that the belt was lying flat, the seat slid back into the wall.

She looked up at Alban with a little smile, but he gave her a hard look, his jaw tight. He brushed past her and went to sit on the couch at the far end away from Ting. Duine looked worriedly at Kelley who gave her a quick wink, his face otherwise expressionless. He gave a quick jerk with his head.

Duine started to go back to her seat but, changing her mind, went over to the food unit and ordered herself a hot tea. Then, she returned to her seat and looked expectantly at Agent Alban.

After the Battle

Kelley schooled his face, so his amusement would not show. Alban was not so disciplined and was clearly irritated with Duine.

"Agent Marshall Alban. I am your technical consultant," he said looking at Kelley. Kelley knew Alban had been with GIS for several years, though never assigned to a permanent post. He bounced from assignment to assignment as a junior agent.

"Thank you," Kelly said perfunctorily. Addressing the team, he continued, "Spectrum Orphanage is a privately-owned business. This is somewhat unusual, as most orphanages are either run by the government of the moon or a planet where they are located or are Confederate subsidized. Orphanages generally don't turn a profit, yet, Spectrum has been in business for many years—that is Sigbar lifecycles, as you would say Dakki."

Dakki curtly nodded in acknowledgment of Kelley's reference to his culture's timekeeping but said nothing.

Kelley continued, "As you stated, Agent Ting, there have been audits in the past—a financial audit and a thorough review of the facilities with a focus on the health and welfare of the children. There were no findings in either case. Agent Ting, would you like to add anything about the audits?"

"Too clean," she purred succinctly. "Their finances were in perfect order. And Spectrum's staff could not have been more accommodating, overly-friendly in fact. And they liked to give us more than we asked for. Often irrelevant material that we then had to sift through at the expense of focusing on what we came to look at."

"You didn't like being treated well?" Alban interrupted.

"I do not like being directed by the subjects of my audit. And, as I was about to say, a substantial amount of their income comes from donations. Many donations come from those who are so high up in the various planetary social castes that we are unable to verify any details."

Ting continued without being prompted by Kelley, "As for the facilities review, again everything was perfect. The facilities were well-maintained and hygienic. Every species of child currently in their care was accommodated as per their specific needs. We interviewed several children and there were no complaints. We went so far as to pull records of children who had grown and left Spectrum and contacted them. Whatever their current circumstances, none had any complaints about their time at Spectrum."

"Well they wouldn't, would they? They couldn't after signing a non-disclosure agreement," Duine said.

Ting inhaled quickly in surprise, "What non-disclosure agreement? There was nothing in the children's files indicating any legal agreements."

All the agents focused on Duine. She shifted nervously in her seat and took a sip of her tea. Kelley said gently, "It's okay. Nothing you say will get you into any trouble." He turned to Dakki for confirmation.

"Within certain parameters, mostly dealing with how we publish or act on her information, yes, that is true," he said.

"Lifers are different than the Temporaries. Lifers like me don't get job training."

Alban started to interrupt again at Duine's cryptic statement, but Kelley stopped him and indicated to Duine to continue. Ting and Dakki were alert and curious but had enough sense to be patient and let her speak.

"Even though I didn't need to, I started helping out in the main building when I was twelve. I had studies, but then I would spend several hours a day helping a junior administrative assistant with whatever she wanted me to do. At first, it was just easy stuff, like tiding up a conference room and lots of beverage and snack runs, but I got trained on more as I got older." She stopped and looked at the agents for their reactions.

"You mentioned to me previously that one of the admins left her password where it could be found," Kelly prompted.

Duine nodded. "After I got that, I was able to browse around their networks. I was eventually trained on how to use the translation protocols as part of my data entry duties. It took me a while, but I figured out the file system. Each Temporary had two files, one on one network and another file on another network."

"Two servers," Ting murmured.

"Yes, I guess so. Anyway, the one file had simple stuff, like birth date if known, inoculation history, health issues, education record, stuff like that. The other file was more of a psychological profile and it always had a non-disclosure agreement. The agreement was always the same, essentially say nothing negative about Spectrum. Each agreement had an Appendix that was tailored to the individual. What each got was different; money, job reference, interview with a big firm, but they all got something, and they all signed the agreement to say nothing."

Dakki and Ting exchanged looks. Dakki said something about 'three years.' Ting was almost twitching at the questions she was holding in. They looked at Kelley.

"Do you agree we should move forward with the investigation?" he asked them. Dakki and Ting assured him they did. Their manner was more animated and perhaps even eager. Alban just nodded.

"This ship will take several weeks to get to Pagnol." Kelley tapped his tablet and the vid changed from external view to displaying their ETA in several time formats. "Most of our time will be spent listening to you, Duine. GIS has never had information from inside Spectrum before. We will be interested in everything you can tell us. Are you still in, kid?"

"Will it be like giving a deposition?" she asked.

He shook his head, firmly saying, "No. Not at all. There will be a lot of questions, though. It will be a lot for you, but we are all on the same side this time."

"I'll be okay. I've got a lot I want to say." Duine looked determined, even defiant.

"Okay. We have a lot of work to do. I'll show you your berth, then we can get started."

Kelley led the way aftwards, Duine following. They entered the shared sleeping area where there were eight berths, three of which looked claimed, all on the floor level. Their gear had been brought on board and was in the center of the room. Duine went over picked up her bag and looked around.

"I guess I'll just pick one," she said, a little uncertain.

"That's right. It will be okay. These bunks have privacy guards. I'll show you. Grab a bunk and lie down."

She chose the upper bunk on the left side of the room, away from the others. There were only two on the left side, an upper and a lower. On the back wall, directly opposite from the door were the other six bunks, three high, side-by-side.

Kelley looked at the gear on the bunk under Duine's, and seeing that it was Alden's, tossed it over to another bunk.

He laid down and leaned out, looking up. Duine on her bunk, looked down at him, but seemed concerned. He grinned. "Don't worry about it; I'm in charge, he's not."

"Is he going to be like that the entire trip?" she asked.

"You mean, the comments and attitude?"

She nodded, saying, "I mean all of them."

He shrugged. "Maybe. At least until they get used to me. It's nothing I'm not used to. From their point of view, I'm fresh out the training center and somehow running my own op—I mean investigation. I can handle their skepticism. Now, as to the berth's controls."

They went over the various options of the berth's touch screen. As Kelley said, the berths had privacy shields that isolated the occupant. He showed her how to tune out any external noises and to mask unpleasant odors, if necessary. He explained that some species, while tolerant towards each other, found it difficult to cohabitate. The various biochemistries sometimes did not combine well in close quarters.

Once she was comfortable with the controls and had stowed her gear, he asked her if she had any questions.

"Did I offend Agent Alden?"

Kelley hesitated before answering. He was thinking that the ship was not a very private place. "I don't think so, after all, he is a fully-trained GIS agent and you are just a kid. And a valuable asset for this investigation. I'm sure you two will get along fine."

She peeked back down at him, so he asked, "What?"

"Your voice is different," she said cryptically, then rolled back, out of view.

He grinned to himself. The possibility that the other agents were listening to their conversation may be low, given that they were in the sleeping quarters, but they were investigators and likely curious. He didn't mind Duine's comment. He *had* been speaking to the team. He was pleased that she caught that.

"One last thing, let's test communications while the privacy shields are on."

She didn't answer but he heard her cover slide softly closing.

He tapped his touch screen for a moment, calling her berth on a secure channel. She answered with, "Can we do visual, too?"

"Just tap the button on the lower left." A moment later his screen displayed her face and his in an inset.

"So, this is how we can talk in private?" she asked.

"Yes. Generally, I don't want to keep secrets from the team. I need them, and I want their cooperation. As I told you before we left, they know everything about you except that you have known relatives. Your relatives are on a need-to-know basis and they don't need to know."

He was glad they had switched the vid on because she only nodded.

"We should be getting back. I just wanted to check to see if you were ready. It's going to be tedious for you. They will ask a lot of questions, sometimes the same ones over and over. And it's going to get personal." He paused seeing her face get worried.

"How personal? Why?"

"For the most part, they will just be trying to understand. And a good investigator does not assume, they ask and then they look for verification on what they are told. It's nothing you should get upset or offended by. Remember, you may not know what you know or why something may be relevant."

"Do I have to answer them? Can I just tell you?"

Something in his chest tightened. "I'd rather you could bring yourself to tell the team. They wouldn't have been assigned to this investigation if we couldn't trust them."

"Even Agent A?"

He could guess at what she was calling Alden by shortening his name. He said sternly, "Agent Alden may have the manners of a school boy, but he is a member of my team. And you will not be helping yourself or anyone else by holding grudges and keeping the tit-for-tat going. I suggest you let it go."

Surprised, she said, "Yes, sir. I will try."

"Good. I appreciate it. One school kid is enough for me to handle. Let's get back to the others. You will want to see the ship jump to full speed."

Chapter Fourteen

Back in the common area, Duine saw the seat she had earlier was empty, so she sat there, even though Alden was next to her where Kelley had been previously. She smiled tentatively at Dakki and Ting as she went by them.

Kelley noted that they both made pleasant gestures of acknowledgement back to her. They were seated on the couch having just eaten. Each had covered beverages in their hand.

Kelley, still on his feet, took Duine's tea container and deposited it into the recycler. Alden didn't say anything and seemed mildly defiant. He had an open beverage container in his hand. Judging by the type of container, it was probably something hot.

Kelley got himself a drink and asked if Duine wanted anything. Knowing she would turn towards him to answer, he reached up and grabbed the support bar and gave it a slight tug, drawing attention to his action, and nodded at her. She nodded back and braced herself.

Just a few moments later the ship jumped to full speed. Duine let out a squeal of delight and Alden a howl of pain. Kelley carefully turned around and saw Duine looking excitedly out the window. Alden was shaking his hand in pain, his container on the floor, the contents all over his hand, shirt, and lap.

A short time later, the ship reached full acceleration and the pressure eased.

Alden got up angrily and headed towards the sleeping area. Kelley followed him.

In the sleeping area, Alden made it up to his former bunk before noticing it was no longer his. Turning around he saw Kelley, leaning casually against the wall, quietly watching him.

"You moved my stuff!" he told Kelley angrily. Kelley gave him a simple, calm yes and continued watching him.

"I have seniority over you!"

Kelley took his time before replying with, "Doesn't matter. I am your team leader."

Alden just stared angrily at him, too frustrated to speak.

"Alden, are we going to have a problem? Tell me now if you want out."

Alden still glaring, just shook his head.

Kelley knew from Alden's bio that he was in his late twenties and GIS was his first job out-of-school. To have so many years of service and still be considered a junior agent had to be frustrating. Kelley wondered if there was more going on with Alden for him to be behaving so badly.

Alden wasn't moving, so he said, "Go ahead, get cleaned up and get your geared stowed."

"And then you will give me some speech about getting myself together or will you go straight to threatening to reassign me?" Alden said as he reached up to root through his belongings, now on the upper bunk.

"No. I'm not the maternal type and I don't threaten those under me. I am wondering what is going on with you. Did you mix up your space sickness meds?" he asked.

Alden turned quickly around to see if Kelley was being sarcastic. Kelley was still leaning casually against the wall. "No," he said, shaking his head, "And I wasn't recently notified of a death of a relative." His tone was less angry; he turned back and started taking off his shirt.

Kelley went over and sat on his bunk, not wanting to watch Alden get changed.

"It sounds like others have tried to help you before. What were they? Complete idiots or wildly off the mark?"

The question made Alden pause for a moment. "I wouldn't say they were idiots. I just don't think they understood."

"Okay. I'll skip ahead and assume that all doesn't work because you don't need help. I'll even skip the pep talk. I'm sure you know what you want and where you want to be."

Alden, now in a clean coverall, was about to put his soiled clothes into the recycler, so Kelley said, "Wait," and pointed to the garment chute.

Alden, silently cursing, shoved his clothes into the appropriate chute.

Kelley tried hard to read Alden. Nervous? Angry? Anxious? He didn't get a thanks, but he didn't get a defensive 'I don't need your help' either.

"Have you been given the 'we all make mistakes, just shake it off' speech?"

"Yes. And I have been on a lot of different ships, I know how they work."

Kelley wished Alden would give him something to work with. Marshall Alden had skills that should make him an asset to any team. Well-educated, highly intelligent, strong technical skills, and an analytical mind; he had the makings of a good agent, and after nine years, he should have had a good amount of experience. Why hadn't he been assigned to a permanent post?

Strangely enough, there was nothing in his bio that suggested poor interpersonal skills. None of his previous assignments had anything negative to say about him, but no one wanted him either.

"Walk me through the last couple of minutes, Alden."

Alden stopped trying to put on his shoes while standing and said, "What? Walk you through what?"

"Alden, sit. Just stop. Go back and tell me what you were thinking, you zipped up your coverall and bent over to pick up your clothes...," Kelley trailed off, wanting Alden to pick up the narrative.

"I zipped up the coverall I was going to wear tomorrow and wondered if the laundry bot would get the stain out of my shirt, and I was so relieved about not having to sit through another useless lecture, and I wanted to ask you what it would take to also skip the 'can't you just try and work as a team' speech, and if I could get Duine to talk to me about the second server, and both panels looked alike, I just chose the wrong one."

Kelley looked at the wall. The two panels did not look similar, visually speaking. They were labeled with the common verbiage and symbols the majority of species understood.

"Now you are going to tell me I need to learn how to focus."

"No. Your thought process is your own. Whatever works for you," Kelley said. Alden was happily taken aback. "What I want to know is if you have any cranial tech implants?"

"Yes. I have an ocular implant. Information about my ocular implant should be on file. If it isn't, I can explain," Alden answered, a little quickly.

Kelley decided to gamble on a hunch. "So, yes, you have a cranial implant, in addition, to the ocular implant on file." He stated it as a fact, not a question.

Alden looking both scared and a little impressed, blurted out, "You caught that?"

"The perfect truth? The yes answering my question while at the same time misdirecting me to the known ocular implant, along with the most helpful offer to discuss that implant? You mean, that?"

Alden nodded still scared. Kelley continued, "I don't care so much about how Medical missed the tech, but more about why you are keeping it a secret? Even the best tech needs maintenance, and then there are all the drugs that are needed for the body to maintain the neural interface and to prevent rejection. That is a lot to manage. Why aren't you letting the GIS docs help you?"

"I am doing just fine without them." Alden was defensive.

"Alden, you can barely see in the visual spectrum! You are *not* fine. You need help. You couldn't see the strap was twisted on the auxiliary chair. You missed that Dakki and Ting were getting ready for the jump and you couldn't read the service panels."

"I can, too," Alden protested. "It's just hard to focus, I get headaches."

"Headaches that make you irritable and difficult to get along with. And by not being able to see properly, you make mistakes that make you look foolish and inept to your colleagues, and belies your competency. This is your definition of 'fine'?" Kelley demanded.

"I don't want them to take the implants out and I don't want to be transferred out of investigations. You don't understand, they help me in my job; how I can see and process data in milliseconds!"

"And your processing time is worth more to you than good working relationships with your colleagues? More important than finding a permanent post?" Kelley asked him.

"Yes! Well, sometimes. Yes, I would like both. I don't want to have to choose." Alden was almost pleading.

"I understand that. But you can't hide from it any longer. You. Need. Help. You don't know the damage that could be happening with improperly calibrated tech along with uneven neural conductivity."

Alden stared at him. "How do you know all this? Do you have implanted tech?"

"Implants yes, technical no. I spent a lot of time in a facility with patients with implanted tech. I heard a lot from the doctors while I was there. And I got along with the patients, they talked with me a lot, too."

Alden looked down. "So, I guess that means I am off this team. After one day. A new record."

Kelley was inclined to agree. He had seen a lot of soldiers dealing with implants and replacements over the years. It was complicated even when managed properly. Even so, as Alden's supervisor, he felt obligated to discuss options, so he said, "Maybe. Maybe not. Depends on where you got your tech."

Alden looked shocked, "What? No! All completely legal and above board. Except maybe the part where I didn't mention the additional capabilities to GIS Medical."

"The doctors and meds, too? All legal and certified?"

"Yes," Alden assured him. "Though it is difficult to get the scans and blood work processed being away so much on various assignments."

"Exactly my point. Now let's go." Kelley got up and headed for the medical suite, Alden trailing resignedly behind him.

Chapter Fifteen

The GIS ship, though small, was extremely capable. It was designed for the needs of a GIS team and was agile enough to be piloted by a small crew. It was not meant to carry cargo or to be a transport vessel. The ship comprised of a bridge, crew and agent quarters, common area, medical suite, and engineering, including the engines. The ship was networked with other GIS ships and facilities. This particular GIS ship rivaled, if not exceled, the military in tech and galactic access.

The medical suite was neither physically populated or entirely automated. GIS partnered with a wide range of doctors and medical facilities throughout known space. These doctors could virtually see the patient on board the ship by way of a comprehensive, continuous MRI scan of the patient that would be replicated in 3D images to the doctor's location in real-time. Doctors, by controlling and manipulating bots on the ship, could perform almost any physical task, including surgery.

Lab work was more difficult, though not impossible. If it could be seen under a microscope, a doctor could see it. The medical suite bots, with assistance from an agent, could perform a limited range of lab tests, as long they were not overly complex in nature.

Kelley asked Dakki and Ting to initiate building a rapport with Duine while he focused on being the medical liaison in the med suite for Alden.

In a mercifully short period of time, it was established that the tech in Alden's head was, in fact, improperly calibrated with his neural network and optical nerves. The doctors also believed that the medications Alden was taking were insufficient, if not completely wrong.

Alden was devastated. Kelley didn't care. He was tired. It was well into the sleep period and it had been a long day for him. He didn't have it in him to deal with Alden's whining. He ordered him to get some rack time. Period. No discussion.

The others were berthed when they entered the sleeping area. Kelley laid down and put up his privacy shield. He worked a while longer from the screens in his berth before finally getting some sleep.

He woke about the same time as the others, except for Alden who was still in bed, screen closed. They looked refreshed, while he felt groggy. It was a relief when they managed to get themselves bathed and clothed without any issues.

They ate in the common area, now laid out as a war room. He briefly related Alden's situation and directed them to assist where they could while he remained onboard. Dakki and Ting agreed without any comment. Kelley ate quickly; he wanted something in his stomach before dealing with his agent.

Alden entered the room looking defiant and ready to argue. Kelley greeted him pleasantly and suggested he get something to eat so they could get started.

Alden made his way to the food dispenser and started tapping. After waiting a moment and seeing that he was having trouble, Dakki used the remote to change the display on the food dispenser. The selections were now bigger and easier to see.

"You told them?!" Alden asked, upset.

"Yes. They have a right to know something that impacts this investigation and even possibly their safety." Alden looked about to argue, so Kelley said sternly, "Sit, eat, and listen."

Alden took his food and sat down. He didn't acknowledge when Ting silently moved another chair out of his way.

"We are still en route to Pagnol, but we are going to drop you off at a med facility in the WS1 1XR sector. There, you will get your tech properly calibrated and get your meds straight. I have also recommended you for rehab. Be quiet." He had to stop Alden from interrupting at the mention of rehab.

"Yes, rehab. Call it training if it makes you feel any better, but you weren't born with those parts in your head, so you need the training to know how to use them like they were."

He stopped to take a sip from his mug and to give Alden a chance to think.

Instead, Alden immediately protested that this meant he was off the team, his tone peevish. Kelley wanted to throw his coffee at him.

"Would you prefer that I recommend you for suspension? You neglected to disclose tech that could endanger yourself, not to mention be a potential security liability. You should be reprimanded. Instead, I am offering you the help and training you need." Kelley's voice was hard and uncompromising.

Alden wisely said nothing, but glowered, eyes down. Kelley, now trying to sound relaxed, explained that it did not mean he was off the team, not entirely. Leveling his meds would take time, but it was possible that he could work virtually as a data analyst on the investigation, provided he was cleared to do so by his doctors. He reminded Alden that should he complete his rehab, his value as an agent would most likely increase. He felt like adding and as a bonus you'll stop putting your clothes into the food recycler.

After a long silence, Alden reluctantly agreed. Kelley, used to the military, was surprised he thought he had a choice.

Chapter Sixteen

Now that everything was understood, Kelley briskly directed Dakki and Ting to let Alden ask his questions first. They didn't argue as they knew they wouldn't have to put up with him for much longer. Alden began by putting a plan of Spectrum's buildings and grounds on the main screen. After scanning the image, Duine asked if he had the most recent version.

Alden immediately took offense at her apparent insinuation of incompetence. "Well, I should think so. I thoroughly reviewed both sets of audit files, so yes, I have the most recent version."

Kelley raised his hand to stop Alden. Looking at Duine he said, "Why do you ask? What do or don't you see?"

"You only have half of the complex." Gesturing at the screen, she said, "That grassy area there is where the Lifers live. That area has...," she paused to count silently, "six buildings surrounding a large courtyard."

Duine's revelation surprised the agents, especially Ting who looked stunned. Kelley let Dakki and Alden argue how this couldn't be possible, while he just listened and kept an eye on Ting. Spectrum could have supplied false building plans, but the routine scans of the orphanage from orbit had confirmed them.

Alden gave them an exhaustive explanation of the multifaceted way sensors detect or 'see', and how they could be fooled. Apparently, it was easy enough to do, especially if the party doing the scanning isn't looking very hard.

Dakki argued there was the site audit. Surely, a complex as large as Duine suggested could not have gone unnoticed?

At that, all three agents and Duine looked at Ting. She cleared her throat and opened her mouth but didn't say anything. She looked at Dakki and said, "We could have missed it." She seemed unable to meet Kelley's eyes, so she continued speaking to Dakki. "We took the scans at face-value. We focused our efforts on what we believed was Spectrum Orphanage. I can tell you, we were *very* thorough with our review of those facilities."

"But you never did a perimeter walk of the complex or surrounding area," Kelley stated matter-of-factly. Ting nodded confirmation.

"Right. Mistakes were made but, let's not dwell on it." Ting stared at Kelly, surprised by his brisk tone. "I am not going to criticize a past investigation. I would much rather focus and make sure we get it right this time. Can I count on you, Agent Ting?"

"Yes, Agent Kelley. I promise you I will do everything I can to assist in this investigation," Ting answered him, her eyes defiantly meeting his.

I'm sure you will, Kelley thought to himself. While he didn't condone her past mistake, he liked that she was determined to rectify it.

Fortunately for Kelley and the team, there were no further revelations during their trip to the med facility in the WS1 1XR sector. Unfortunately, Alden was no easier to work with.

When it came time for him to disembark, Kelley had to escort him. Alden kept telling him what he would be doing to help while he was at the medical facility. He said he would write a program that would essentially reprogram the ships' sensors to deal with the most likely shields or barriers Spectrum was using to cloak itself. Kelley agreed, thanking him, but warned him not to do too much. He closed the door as soon as Alden was clear.

Chapter Seventeen

Kelley used the time during take-off and acceleration to full speed to clear his mind and focus. Once underway, the team unstrapped themselves. Dakki used the remote to bring up Spectrum on the vid and Ting got herself a hot beverage. Duine stood up out of her seat, stretched, and made herself comfortable on the couch. Everyone seemed to be reacting positively to the relaxed atmosphere of the cabin.

"What now?" Duine asked everyone.

"For now, more talk. Keep talking and as we go along, we'll ask questions here and there. We'll go back and elaborate if we need to," Kelley answered. Seeing her hesitate he said, "Tell us about Pagnol. Was it nice there?"

And so it began. The three agents kept Duine talking the entire trip to Pagnol. The went through everything from the climate on Pagnol to the color of her room.

The team worked very well together. Kelley instituted a set sleep time for Duine, and after she went to bed, they would compare notes and discuss any points of interest.

The agents were careful not to react to anything Duine said with anything other than polite interest. This became difficult for Kelley as his initial suspicions found solid ground.

Ting eventually asked Duine what she meant about Lifers and Temporaries. She explained that Temporaries never knew about Lifers, but all Lifers knew about the Temps. The Temps left. When the Temps reached legal age for their species, they were gone. As far as Duine knew, Lifers never left Spectrum until they died.

They, the Lifers, had different rules than the Temps. For example, interactions between the Temps were strictly monitored and sexual interaction was forbidden. Lifers, however, were encouraged to interact with each other. It was not uncommon for staff at Spectrum to make suggestions as to who someone should choose as a partner.

Not surprisingly, pregnancies happened. Sometimes one or both parents raised the infant, other times the child was sent to a 'facility more capable of caring for it.' In such cases, neither parent was ever told anything other than the child was doing well.

Dakki asked Duine about her implant. She said she didn't remember getting it, shrugging as if it was nothing important. Due to the lack of scarring, the doctor who removed it had postulated that it must have been put in when she was very young. Dakki pressed her, but Duine insisted that sickness among the Lifers was very rare. She looked at Kelley when she said that they did seem to be accident-prone. Dakki scoffed at her, asking how could that be in such a safe, carefully monitored environment?

Kelley kept steady eye contact until she went on. A Lifer would be completely fine one day and be missing an eye or a limb the next. Sometimes the accidents were fatal, but the other Lifers were never told any details.

Dakki and Ting were so taken aback at what was finally sinking in that Kelley changed the subject. He asked Duine how she had gotten a job at the Spectrum's offices. She was cagy and only said that she had wanted to find out anything she could about her parents. Something in the way she answered reminded Kelley of Mel when she was being less than truthful, but he left it for the time being. He let her continue with what she was ready to tell them.

Lifers never left the orphanage, but they were not expected to work; if anything, they were encouraged to play. For those that did want to work at something, mastering a trade was encouraged or studying one of the fine arts.

Duine, however, wheedled a Spectrum staffer into letting her help out in the administration offices. The staffer, Juxa, a junior assistant herself, was tasked with menial duties. It wasn't difficult for Duine to persuade Juxa to pass the tasks along to her. Eventually, Juxa had trained Duine so well that Juxa started leaving early to steal away and spend time with another Lifer. From her perspective, Duine must have seemed like the perfect cover for her illicit tryst.

That evening, after Duine had gone to bed, the team discussed the possibility that Spectrum was engaging in illegal limb or organ harvesting. Ting admitted it was *possible* but would not commit to taking a stand. Dakki did not voice his opinion but agreed to ask for a search warrant. They both wanted more from Duine. Seeing the rapport he had with her, they expected Kelley to get her to open up.

Chapter Eighteen

The next night, after they had eaten, Kelley told the team they were taking the evening off. He brought up the menu of games on the wall-monitor and asked who wanted to play? Dakki and Ting declined. Duine with an 'I'm not surprised' eye-roll, accepted eagerly. The two played for hours, even past her bedtime, which Kelley 'forgot' to remember. When he felt it was time, he asked her, "What really made you want to get into Spectrum's offices?"

Duine didn't answer right away and continued playing until the round was over. Setting the controller down carefully, she looked at him without speaking. Dakki and Ting, alert to the change in atmosphere, stayed silent and tried to appear nonchalant.

Duine finally answered, "I wanted to find out what happened to my friend." Her tone was flat, and she was breathing just a little harder, eyes down.

Kelley took a chance and said, "Was this friend one of the Lifers that went missing?"

She only nodded. Her eyes were starting to get red, as she tried to hold back the tears.

"Come here, kid. It's okay. C'mon. It will be better if you talk about it," he said quietly, holding his hand out to her.

Duine got up and flopped down on the couch next to him. She didn't take his hand, but leaned back against him, tears starting to roll down her face. He shifted a little and put his arm around her. "Tell me about her. What was her name?"

"Tanya. She was only a little older than me, we thought, but she was born on Pagnol. She always wondered why she wasn't raised by one of her parents, as I told you sometimes happened."

"We did everything together. She was my best friend. We shared everything. Then one day she was gone. Just gone." Duine was crying and starting to sniff.

Dakki surreptitiously put several tissues into Kelley's hand. He gave them to her as he continued to hold her. After a minute, he asked, "And you decided to find her?"

She nodded again, but now looked angry. "I wish I hadn't."

Not if you are anything like your mother, he thought. "What did you find?"

"It took me a while. I mean, a long while. I had to get into the offices and then into the computer files and *then* I had to figure out the files." She wasn't crying anymore. She was still leaning against him, facing away, but had a hold of the arm he had around her.

"I finally figured out where the Lifer files were. We each have one. My file didn't have much that I could see. Most of it was restricted above Juxa's security level. My file was different from the others too in that it had a label 'Noli me tangere' whatever that means."

"And Tanya's file? What did her file have in it?" he prompted gently.

She gripped his arm tighter and gave a half shrug. "Mostly the same as the rest of us. Except she had a date of 'termination', with a note "Heart donation successful. Client very pleased."

Kelley closed his eyes, jaw clenched, pulling Duine tight against him. She hugged his arm for a long time before pushing it away. She turned to him saying, "And now we are going back, right?" It was more a statement than a question and her eyes flashed as she dared him to say otherwise.

Dakki and Ting made comforting remarks about how safe she was and that she wouldn't have to set even one foot on the planet, but Kelley understood what she was saying.

Looking straight back at her he said, "Yes, we are. You are going back for them and all of GIS is coming with you."

Chapter Nineteen

The next day, after breakfast, Kelley sat Duine down again. "Are you okay to tell me the rest of your story?"

She didn't hesitate this time, "Lifers aren't stupid. They figure out what is going on. It's just as soon as someone starts asking questions or talking with each other too secretly, Spectrum puts an end to it. Tanya and I didn't cause trouble, so they weren't watching us. After she was gone, I started listening to what the other Lifers were saying, but I didn't join them. I made sure not to do or say anything that would get me noticed."

"When I started watching, I realized Spectrum has two sets of staff. There are people who take care of us, who are nice and friendly and only have access to the facilities. The others, the office staff, are not nice and won't even talk to us. Juxa was the exception. I think she was someone's niece or something. I'm sure she wasn't supposed to talk to me, but she was new, and I convinced her to trust me."

"What finally made you decide to leave?" Kelley asked.

"I got my, I mean, I got older." She blushed. "There was this one staff person who started talking to me about how cute this boy called Elvin was. She mentioned how nice he was and that I should go talk to him. She droned on and on. I mean, at first, I just ignored her, but she wouldn't stop.

After the Battle

Eventually, I figured it out. They wanted me to make a Tanya."

"I think if I could have started a fire big enough, I would have burned Spectrum to the ground." Looking at her face and seeing her eyes, Kelley believed her.

Abruptly shifting moods, she continued, "Since I couldn't, I stole Juxa's badge, left the grounds, and found a way to hide in the supplies being loaded onto the liner." Duine stopped speaking and just shrugged, like there was nothing more to say.

Dakki nodded at Duine, in respect for her bravery. Ting also seemed appreciative, but suggested she go lie down. Duine flatly told her, "I'm not tired."

"They want to talk and strategize how this new information fits into our current line of inquiry. No, you can't stay," he said, in answer to her pleading eyes. "Now scoot!"

When they were sure Duine was in the sleeping quarters, the agents began to discuss how to corroborate Duine's information. They were interrupted by the ship telling them there was an incoming transmission from the head of the GIS legal division, Chief Belletor and a senior diplomatic liaison, Consul Opiter.

After the initial greeting, the agents did not get a chance to speak. The diplomat did the talking. They were reminded that the Confederate does not enact laws but rather has a framework or a base set of guidelines that the member entities agree to comply with. It is actually a misnomer to say the Confederate law, although many do. The proper term is really Confederate Guidelines.

In addition, while Pagnol itself is part of the Confederacy, Spectrum is a privately-owned company. It does not receive any Confederate or Pagnol monies and as such is not strictly bound by the Confederate Guidelines.

The agents were asked to keep in mind that Spectrum was funded by the endowments of individuals of rank, position, and power from many different planets and species. And some of these species would not agree that any crimes were being committed.

While the Confederacy does believe in the rights of the individual, those rights first need to be established and proved to have been violated. The diversity of the population would make this a multi-jurisdictional matter of some delicacy.

Spectrum has been in existence for several hundred years and has multiple sites. The children placed in its care were *given* to them at the request of a parent or guardian. It was his understanding that all children receive full disclosures of the terms of their residence at Spectrum once they reach the age of consent for their particular species.

With all due respect, their source was a minor. She was not yet old enough to have received full disclosure, so naturally she assumed the contrary. Even their source said that no one associated with Spectrum forced the children to breed.

Consul Opiter finished his lecture while he understood that the agents had what they felt to be grounds for an investigation; surely now, they were open to withdrawing their request for a warrant.

Kelley was surprised; not by the amount of information the Consul had on their investigation, but how freely he had admitted to Spectrum's actions. He glanced at Dakki and Ting to gauge their reactions. Dakki was cowed and Ting overwhelmed. Apparently, neither had ever stood up to the brass before. No back up there. However, he noted that during the exposition, the GIS Legal brief had not joined in with the Consul, in fact, he was decidedly neutral.

After taking a moment to gather his thoughts Kelley said, "Thank you for taking the time to speak with us, Consul Opiter. However, we have grounds to continue our investigation." He paused, looking briefly at the Chief, "Even more so since we asked for the warrant."

He continued briskly, "From what you say, Spectrum should be able to answer all our questions and provide us with the necessary documentation to prove full disclosures were made and agreed to by the children without duress or fear of reprisal."

"I do appreciate the advice to remember who we are dealing with and how well-connected they are. We will be moving forward with the warrant, but it will have to be amended to include the special provisions associated with such a large, undoubtedly sophisticated institution. In addition, I will have to ask that you, Senior Consul, refrain from discussing or even mentioning our intentions to anyone. I believe you are aware of the Confederate Guidelines in such matters, yes?"

Chief Belletor's face was still neutral, but his eyes glinted briefly. Dakki and Ting were frozen, while Consul Opiter was furious.

Chief Belletor said, his voice even, "Yes, I agree. The Consul and I will discuss the details of his discretion, and then I will contact you to go over the special provisions of the warrant." He abruptly ended the transmission.

The other two agents gaped at Kelley for a long time. He couldn't decide if they were impressed or if they thought he was insane.

"He asked if I was open to withdrawing the warrant. I was not," he said simply.

"You defied a Senior Consul!" Dakki said. "I thought being ex-military you would have learned to obey orders!" Ting said at the same time.

Kelley shrugged and answered, "I disagree with both of you. The Senior Consul cannot order GIS to do anything; only advise. I simply declined his recommendation. Had Chief

Belletor ordered me to stand down, that would have been different. He did not. In fact, he backed me up. And he agreed to the gag order on the Consul."

"Maybe so, but your career may well be over before its begun," Dakki said.

Kelley irritated by his comment, said, "My career? I should be concerned with my career when children are being kept and bred for spare parts? You care more about the number of wins in your case file than people's lives? You don't want to look into Spectrum just because a Senior Consul *suggested* we shouldn't?" Aware his tone was harsh, he forced himself to take a breath.

Dakki said, "It's not that simple. I am taking the long view. It's better if I can stay and do my job instead of not being around at all."

"If I understand you, you are saying it is better to pick and choose which people you are going to help because, in the long run, you will help more of them, on balance, so to speak?" Kelley asked.

Dakki nodded like Kelley had made some sort of breakthrough.

Kelley took another deep breath and let it out slowly. He did not care for Dakki's way of thinking nor did he like Ting's silence. He wanted to offer them the chance to get off the team, but he knew he needed them. They were up to speed on the case and new agents at this point would only mean delays.

"I see your point. Humans have a phrase, 'better to live as a coward than a dead hero.' I think that is what you are saying."

He saw Ting jerk slightly as his words sunk in. "I am not asking you to throw away your careers. And I know this is somewhat of a risk, however, neither of you is lead on this investigation. I am. I will be the one who goes down if things go wrong. Right now, I have the Chief backing me and I will proceed as such until I am notified otherwise."

After the Battle

Dakki was slowly tapping his hand as he considered the situation. Ting sat straighter in her chair, looking disdainful at his pledge of protection.

"What is your greatest concern, Ting?" he asked her.

"This isn't going to be a win even if we prove the allegations are true. The Consul is right on several points. It is doubtful that all of the children will be granted individual rights as Confederate citizens. And there will be species, at least factions thereof, that will consider Spectrum's activities as legal, even necessary," she said.

"Necessary? As how?"

"There are governments that are ruled by oligarchies or aristocracies. Those who rule in such political environments must always appear strong. Any hint of weakness due to illness or deformity could destabilize their position or even cast doubt over the entire ruling government. What these children provide are linchpins in maintaining order on more than one world in the Confederacy."

Kelley stared at her for a moment then said, "You truly believe that we should stand down because a small percentage of the Confederate worlds think they need to maintain power by enslaving members of their own species for the purpose of spare parts?"

Dakki and Ting looked at each other for a moment. They turned back to Kelley about to speak, when Duine spoke first.

"I have a better question. You have information that this one-stop multi-species chop shop and breeding boutique exists *and* have received confirmation of this information from a Senior Consul. How can you *not* investigate without bringing the integrity of GIS itself into question, as well as your own value as agents and representatives of your species?"

Duine, who evidently had left the sleeping quarters, stood in the doorway of the war room staring at Dakki and Ting with contempt.

Stung by her words, Dakki angrily stood, his manner threatening. Ting sputtered incoherently with her anger. Kelley was overwhelmed by waves of emotions. The first being a strong sense of pride in Duine for speaking as she did, and then a second wave of protectiveness for her against the two agents. He also got to his feet and started to move in front of her.

"Excellent question, Miss Ar Bith," said Chief Belletor from the vid. There was no visual, just audio. The agents had no idea how long he had been listening to their conversation.

Even over the vid, Kelley liked what he heard. Chief Belletor's voice was relaxed, calm, and commanding.

"Chief Belletor, sir. There seems to be a glitch on our side, we don't have visual, but we can hear you loud and clear," he said.

The Chief replied, "How about now?"

The vid flicked on to display not only Chief Belletor but also Inspector Director Atris Ryante, the head of GIS.

Kelley snapped to attention, with an automatic "Ma'am."

Dakki immediately went from officious to obsequious. Ting stopped sputtering and closed her mouth.

"At ease, Agent Kelley, take a seat," Director Ryante said. She was equally calm and poised as Chief Belletor. She appraised the assembled then settled her gaze on Duine. Duine looked nervously at Kelley.

"Inspector Director Ryante is the head of the Galactic Investigative Services," he told her quietly, as he seated himself.

Duine turned back to Director Ryante and nervously said, "Hello, ma'am."

After the Battle

Director Ryante gave Duine an obvious once over and said, "You appear to feel strongly about continuing the investigation. I wonder why. You appear to be in fine health and are not missing anything."

Duine straightened her back at the Inspector's tone. "It's not about me. And I don't believe," she hesitated to shift her words around, "I mean, I don't see how it makes sense to have us separated if there were no secrets and everything was done by consent. And why were the adult Lifers kept under lock and key so they *couldn't* leave?"

"Tanya was not old enough to give consent. And even if she was the only one, you have to investigate, don't you?"

Director Ryante smiled slightly with a brief nod, saying, "Yes, you are correct. We should be discussing the case right now."

Neither of them said anything for a minute until Duine realized the Director was waiting on her. She said, "Do you want me to go back to the sleeping area?"

The Director nodded. "And stay there this time until Agent Kelley says otherwise."

"Okay. I mean, yes, ma'am," she answered the Director obediently. She boldly gave Chief Belletor a curt nod as she left the room.

Chapter Twenty

The Inspector Director and Chief Belletor briefed Kelley and his team on how the search warrant was going to be executed. It took some time as it was going to be a complex endeavor.

Spectrum had twenty-three sites across several different galaxies. The warrant was going to be served simultaneously at every location. Kelley quickly realized that their briefing was being broadcast to as many different teams. There was now a team of agents for each site comprised of a technical asset, a lawyer, and a diplomatic attaché. Kelley noted that Alden had rejoined his team, albeit remotely. It turned out that Alden was a man of his word; he had found a way to alter their sensors to make them harder to fool.

In addition, each site had a Fleet-manned ground team that included representatives from the local police jurisdictions, and several social workers.

Kelley was suitably impressed. It had taken time and resources to put all of this together. The orders had to have come from the Director herself, not only to make it happen, but to make it happen so quickly.

GIS must have started putting all this together as soon he and his team had started their preliminary investigation. This indicated to Kelley that others in GIS also had suspicions about Spectrum and Duine had given them the opportunity they had been looking for.

The Director finished the briefing saying the GIS team leads were considered the point of contact for each site and were responsible for coordinating and directing the ground team.

The planning over the next several days was intense. It was unlikely that Pagnol would be the only location where the actual Spectrum building layout would not match the plans on record.

Kelley didn't like being told that he would go in only after the site had been secured. In Fleet, he was used to leading the charge. Now at GIS, leading an investigation was different.

The landing plan included safely securing the children by Fleet and local PD where they would then be overseen by the social workers. Securing the known side of Spectrum, the Temporary side, was simple enough to arrange. Finding, entering, and securing the Lifer side required more planning. The Fleet officer took the lead on these discussions and said she was confident they could do it.

Assuming the landing went as planned, the GIS team would follow and begin their search. Kelley focused on prepping his people.

Alden's attitude was vastly improved, and he was proving himself to be very useful. In addition to everything else, he provided an excellent plan for accessing and securing Spectrum's system files. He was confident that he could locate and access the second server. Ting reengaged after getting over her fear of the brass and also provided useful input.

Dakki complied but was more obstructive than cooperative. Kelley found his negativity annoying. It was one thing to point out potential pitfalls with the intent of avoiding them, it was another to complain without offering any solutions.

Yet, somehow, they got it done. It was Go time.

Chapter Twenty-One

The actual execution went remarkably smoothly. There were glitches at several of the satellite sites, but the operation at the Spectrum headquarters on Pagnol was flawless.

After the initial search and seizure had begun, the Senior Consul tried to start a political storm. From what Kelley was able to piece together, Chief Belletor's version of a gag order was to keep the Consul waiting in his office. Kelley had no idea how long the Consul had been kept a virtual prisoner, but it proved effective in keeping the Consul from alerting Spectrum prior to their arrival.

The Fleet officer made good on her promise to locate and secure the Lifer site. Alden also came through and found the second server, which was a boon to the overall investigation. When the site and data files were secured, they started the interviews with the staff and the children.

It only took a brief inspection of the children Duine had dubbed as "Lifers" to obtain sufficient evidence that the children were in danger of life and limb. Moderately-sized space stations were called in to evacuate the children from all the Spectrum sites.

A week into the interviews and data analysis, Chief Belletor contacted Kelley for a private meeting. Chief Belletor complimented him and expressed his appreciation of his work on the Spectrum investigation; he even commended his leadership. He then told Kelley he was to step down as lead.

Kelley was not at all surprised. He knew this extremely delicate political situation was going to take a *very* long time to sort out.

He wondered why a new agent like him had even been allowed to lead an investigation this complex at all. While he hoped it was more than that he was expendable, he was perfectly fine letting a more experienced agent navigate the legal, diplomatic, and political morass. He was used to a quick in and out; stepping aside at this point suited him well enough. He dutifully expressed his pleasure to serve and his gratitude at their trust in him.

Now that the order was given and the pleasantries exchanged, the Chief relaxed and looked expectant.

Kelley was not relaxed; he knew what he should say at this point, but he was still unsure. Now that he was released from the investigation, he was free to focus on Duine's situation.

Duine hadn't been left alone on the ship, he had been ordered to move her to the space station with the other children. She was one of the many children caught in a very difficult situation. The prosecutorial aspect of the case was somewhat evident. They had the files and the children to prove a case against Spectrum on charges of murder and illegal organ and limb harvesting.

Some of the children, mostly the Temporaries, would simply be taken to other orphanages. It was anything but simple when the calls for individual children started coming in from various governments, factions, ruling families, or the simply rich and powerful, all laying claim to various children as their property.

With no records of a planet of origin, no parents, and usually multi-species DNC profiles, it was virtually impossible to establish the rights of each child and to prove or disprove the claims of ownership and/or jurisdiction.

Kelley was at a loss as to where this left Duine. She had one DNA proven parent who was literally unable to speak for her.

He decided to ask the Chief, the head of the legal branch, for his advice regarding his personal interest in the case.

The Chief was more than willing to help Kelley. He immediately pulled up and showed him Duine's Spectrum case file. It did not contain the name of her father or his family but it did have the name of the private law firm who had placed her at Spectrum on his and on their behalf.

They discussed possible options given the fact that Duine had not been harmed in any way. She had been placed on the Lifer side, like she was a candidate for harvesting, but she had been specifically classified to be left alone. This suggested that while her paternal family wanted to keep her existence a secret, they didn't consider her a parts resource.

It would be difficult to bring any charges against the father that would stick. It would be easy for the opposing side to argue that she had been reasonably well taken care of, including being educated. Spectrum could deny any wrongdoing regarding potential breeding; they could blame the individual staff person and even then, there was no way to say the suggestions were at the request of the family.

Kelley agreed that there was no cause to pursue charges against the father or his family. Belletor asked him what he wanted for Duine.

Kelley was still as uncertain as he had been when Mel first suggested he take her as his own daughter. If he didn't raise a claim for her now, he would probably never get another chance. If the family wanted to keep things quiet, they could prove *their* claim and then move her to another private facility where he couldn't find her.

If this happened, Mel would never forgive him, he was sure of that. He had been in communication with her on and off but was unable to tell her anything of substance between being on assignment and generally not knowing the pitfalls of the girl's paternity. Essentially, Mel still thought he was going to adopt her.

He just wasn't certain that he wanted to go down the path of fatherhood. He felt the same as he had when he was in Dr. Crane's office after being told that GIS only wanted him as an analyst. Fatherhood and a desk job seemed to be entwined fates and equally daunting.

The last several months had been interesting, he admitted to himself. He had liked working on the Tycor and Spectrum investigations. And he did like Duine. What the hell, it couldn't be that bad, could it?

Pushing through his trepidation, he asked, "What if we made the assumption that her paternal family simply wants nothing more than to forget she even exists? That they want nothing to do with her." Belletor nodded agreement and gestured for him to continue.

"We could make a proposal via the law firm to the family saying that if they agree to forfeit all claim to the girl now and forever, of her and any progeny she may have, GIS agrees to place her with a family as their daughter, with all the necessary documentation establishing her paternity with that family in such a way as to be virtually impossible to prove otherwise, now or in the future."

Chief Belletor regarded him for some time. "We could do that," he said slowly. "Would you agree to take responsibility for the placement of the child?"

Kelley nodded. He had to clear his throat before he could say, "Yes. Yes, I will be responsible."

After the Battle

It took longer for the GIS legal team to draft the proposal than it did for the family to sign it. Duine was free and was legally released into his custody.

Kelley did not have a permanent post or even a temporary assignment, but this did not bother him as much as being the guardian of a fifteen-year-old girl.

Chapter Twenty-Two

Kelley quickly finished the formalities of his transfer off the team, collected his gear, and got himself taken over to the space station. As he navigated his way to the girl, he was aware of how much the layout of the station resembled penitentiary cells.

Once at her assigned space, he took a moment to view her from the monitor. Curled up tightly on the bed, she didn't look so good. Even after all she had been through, being kept on the station seemed to scare her more than anything else. He opened the door. When she saw him, she immediately jumped up and came towards him, but stopped suddenly.

"You going somewhere?" she asked, eyeing the bag over his shoulder.

"Yes," he answered, "You are too."

He was going to say more but she slammed herself into him, hugging him tightly. He hugged her back almost like he missed her, then stepped back. "Gear up. Time to go." He tried to sound brisk, but he wasn't sure it came out that way.

Kelley looked around the room as she gathered her belongings. He made sure that the contents of her room at Spectrum were transferred to her here, though he wasn't sure that it had been done; she had so little to pack. "Is this all you have?" he asked her.

She nodded saying, "Most of my room was Spectrum's property. The furniture and fixtures, my clothes apparently. I had some stuff on my tablet, but they kept the tablet."

"Is there anything you want back? I'm sure I can work something out with them."

"No, these are enough," she said as she finished packing. All that she possessed anywhere fit in one large bag. He went to pick it up but she slung it over her shoulder with a little grunt. For some reason, it felt strange to him that she had so little by way of material possessions.

"You said you had some data files, were they only on the tablet?" he wanted to know.

"No, they didn't allow us to store anything privately."

He tapped a quick message to Alden and then they left the room.

As they walked down the hall, she abruptly asked, "Is it over? I mean, are we leaving for good?"

"Well, for us, yes it's over. The investigation is just getting started, in terms of sorting everything out, but we are done." He began to smile to reassure her that it was okay, but then a thought struck him. "Is there anyone you want to say goodbye to? I'm sorry, but the way things are, it will not be possible to keep in touch with anyone."

"I don't know. Are others leaving, too?"

He shook his head. "They are only in the early stages. It's going to take a while to sort things out."

"So you keep saying." She looked at him. "They are going to be here a while then. Months?"

"Maybe longer," he admitted.

She stopped walking. "I need to check on Gada."

He tapped on his tablet for a minute, and then said, "This way."

They navigated the station in silence for a time, then she suddenly asked, "What about Juxa? Is she in custody?"

He hesitated before answering, "No. She's not in custody. She is here actually."

She stopped again, looking up at him. "Here? Is she okay?"

"Yes, let's keep moving." He started walking again until he heard her bag hit the floor. He turned back to see her standing stubbornly still, arms folded.

He sighed, looked at the ceiling for a long moment, and then said, "She is here in the med wing. She was found in a locked room on one of the lower levels at Spectrum."

"Is she okay?" Duine asked again.

Juxa had been beaten, was half-starved, and had apparently been in that room since Duine went missing, but he only said, "Eventually, yes. She is being taken care of, and as I said, she isn't facing any charges."

"I'd like to see her," Duine said quietly.

"Not a good idea. She is probably upset and angry and will very likely take it out on you."

"Do you think it's selfish of me to want to tell her that I am sorry?" she asked him.

"No, not selfish; naïve yes. She is probably going to blame you for what happened to her and I don't want to put you through that. You took an opportunity. You did what you had to do to get away. Period. It's not your fault what they did to her and I don't want you to think that it was." He was getting defensive and sounded gruff.

"I still want to see her," Duine said still quietly, but stubbornly.

Kelley felt completely at a loss and a failure as a parent before he even got started. He felt things were out of control and that he was doing a lousy job of protecting the girl.

He gave up, frustrated, but managed to calmly say, "Just try and remember, it isn't your fault."

He took her up to the med wing, where, as he predicted, Juxa went off at seeing Duine. Juxa was in bed, still very thin, and her bruises were prominent. Weak as she was, she managed to hurl a great deal of abuse at Duine, even shouting, "Look at what you did to me!"

Duine had been quiet since entering the room, just standing hunched in on herself until that last bit.

"*You* don't know what they were doing to us!" Duine said loudly, almost shouting back at Juxa. She was angrier than Kelley had ever seen her. He started tapping on his tablet.

"Did what?" Juxa sneered. "You had everything handed to you and you didn't have to work for any of it. And still, you had to run away from it, you..."

Kelley interrupted by pushing his tablet into her hand. She looked down at the image then up at Kelly, confused. He just nodded at her, gesturing for her to swipe through the images.

GIS had compiled images of the 'donors' from the various Spectrum sites. They were gruesome. Some were of the donors showing their various scars from organ removals, such as kidney or liver. Other donors had parts missing, such as hands, legs, or eyes. Some were pictures of cadavers.

Spectrum gave some of the limb removal donors rudimentary prosthetics, but not when it came to eyes. Apparently, the neural interfaces of optical prosthetics were too costly or complex for something that was essentially just a walking donation bank. They had just sewed the orbital cavities closed.

"What are you saying? Why are you showing me these pictures?" Juxa asked.

"These pictures represent at least part of the allegations against your former employer, Spectrum. I cannot comment further on an open investigation," Kelley replied.

"I am truly sorry for what they did to you because of me," Duine said to Juxa. Juxa didn't say anything; she turned away, crying.

122

Kelley took his tablet back and ushered Duine silently from the room.

Out in the corridor, Duine put her back against the wall and tried to get a hold of herself after the brief but unsettling meeting with Juxa. Eventually, she wiped her eyes and asked, "Are you going to get into trouble for showing her the pictures?"

Putting his arm around her shoulders gently, he gave her a brief, reassuring hug. "Maybe, but I doubt it. Either way, don't worry about me. I look at it at this way, now, she may be willing to talk to GIS about her uncle and what she knows about Spectrum."

"Let's get something to eat before checking on Gada," he suggested.

"No. I'm fine," she protested. She continued in response to the look on his face, "I just want to get this over with."

He could understand and relate to that, so he again took to navigating the warren of cells and brought her to Gada's room. Someone from the station staff was just leaving her room.

The doctor seeing Kelley, shook her head saying, "She isn't well enough to be interviewed or receive visitors."

"Is she actually ill or just not talking to you?" Duine asked.

The female, non-human, literally looked down on Duine without saying anything, then turned to Kelley without answering.

Ignoring the doctor, Kelley turned to Duine, "What makes you ask?"

"Because she is probably terrified that she is here to be harvested," Duine answered.

The non-human protested that they had been very clear with the children as to where they were and that they were safe.

Duine shook her head. "Are you a doctor?"

"Yes, I am Dr. Frandeen," she answered officiously.

"And that is all that Gada heard. She is introverted; always has been. I mean, really introverted. Like in her own world. I doubt she heard much of anything anyone has told her since being brought here. It was scary enough for me; I knew more of what was going on than anyone and it was still pretty overwhelming all the same."

"I don't think any of you understand what it was like to have lived at Spectrum. It looked like a paradise, but a paradise where very bad things happened at random, for no reason."

"She is scared, and she doesn't trust you. You do understand that, don't you?" Duine was vehemently in earnest.

Dr. Frandeen's face told Kelley that she hadn't appreciated Gada's point of view or the possibility of her mental limitations. "What do you suggest?" she asked Duine.

"Let me go in and talk to her with you. Not you," indicating Kelley. "Too many people will overwhelm and scare her."

"I don't have to go in," Kelley said, agreeing to the restriction.

The doctor nodded and gestured for Duine to enter the room. As they entered, Kelley walked over and tapped on the monitor, so he could observe.

Duine walked into the room quietly. Frandeen, following her lead, did the same. Gada didn't react or acknowledge either of them. She was sitting on the floor with a blank expression on her face. Duine looked around the room and asked the doctor, "Where are her instruments?"

"The contents of her room were brought to her, I'm sure," the doctor answered.

"Oh right. Spectrum probably kept them." Duine was briefly annoyed; then she went over and sat down next to

Gada. "Gada, do you remember me? I know we didn't talk much, but I know you."

Gada glanced at Duine then looked away quickly. "Yes, I remember you. You didn't talk much after Tanya went away. Then you went away," she said, glancing back at Duine.

"I ran away. They didn't take me like they did Tanya. I ran away and told people what was happening to us. They listened, Gada. These people here aren't like the ones on Pagnol. They are here to help us."

Gada seemed to understand what Duine was saying, but she was still uncertain. "Are you sure?" Gada whispered, looking doubtfully at Dr. Frandeen.

"Dr. Frandeen is not one of them. She really does just want to help you. It's okay to talk to her," Duine assured Gada. Getting to her feet, she held out her hand. Gada took it and let Duine pull her up. Together they sat on the bed, facing Dr. Frandeen. Duine looked at the doctor and sort of shrugged, as if to say, 'your turn.'

Dr. Frandeen asked Gada basic questions. Reassured by Duine's presence, Gada answered. It helped that Dr. Frandeen was more mindful of the girl's limitations and conducted her assessment accordingly.

After Dr. Frandeen was finished, she and Duine left the room. Kelley was glad to note that Gada didn't appear upset that Duine was leaving, but he did think she seemed forlorn or somehow empty. It was unsettling.

Dr. Frandeen thanked Duine for her assistance, and then turned to leave. Duine stopped her saying, "Wait. Please. I know from what I was told that they are going to be taken care of while they are here. I know things will eventually get sorted out and that they will be given reading material and games and things will be arranged like classes and such."

Dr. Frandeen nodded briskly. "Yes, certainly. The children will be decently provided for until permanent placements can be found. Is that all?"

"And musical instruments? Will Gada be allowed to play her music?" Duine persisted, concerned.

The doctor was doubtful. "Perhaps. It is possible that eventually basic musical instruments will be provided."

"Dr. Frandeen, can we please do something now for Gada? Music is everything to her. It won't matter where you put her or what happens to her if she can play music. It's more than just something that makes her happy; it's who she is," Duine said, struggling to explain.

Frandeen, who hadn't changed her doubtful, dour expression, repeated, "She will be provided for."

Duine turned pleading eyes to Kelley. "Could you do something, please?"

It was evident that Duine felt strongly about getting Gada an instrument. Though he didn't agree, he turned to the doc and asked, "Would you mind if I looked into getting the child an instrument to pass the time with, while she is here?"

"I have no objections, Agent Kelley." She nodded curtly and strode away down the corridor.

Kelley checked the time and frowned. Sighing in exasperation, he looked at Duine.

"I'm sorry. Are we missing our transport?" she asked.

"We will if we stop to look for an instrument."

"I'm sorry but it's important. It's the only thing I have to do before I leave, I promise. I won't ask for anything else. I'll do anything you say after that," she said, pleading with him.

He reviewed the situation with himself. She was leaving her entire life behind with nothing more than one bag over her shoulder. She was leaving everything and everyone she had known so far in her life, with no expectation of ever seeing any of it again, and all she wanted to do was give a girl she barely knew a musical instrument.

He didn't understand it. He wasn't sure if it was a girl thing or what, but it was clearly something she felt she had to do. He considered that, perhaps, it wasn't such a lot to ask of him, given what he was asking of her.

He sighed with resignation. "Okay. We'll look for an instrument, if that is what you want." Her face lit up. "But I'm eating first!"

Chapter Twenty-Three

During lunch, he asked Duine what instruments Gada played at Spectrum. He queried what was available, but there were no musical instruments of any kind currently on board. The station had been commandeered quickly. The objective was to ensure the safety of the children, not their comfort.

Getting one from Spectrum was out of the question. He didn't think he could even arrange to go back down to the planet at this point. The planet, Pagnol, did have other cities and industries apart from Spectrum, but he couldn't get down to them.

It was impossible for anything to be delivered via drone to an orbiting space station that hadn't been there two weeks ago. Drones were used for surface deliveries, not extraplanetary ones. He doggedly researched the station itself, specifically what kind of replication capabilities it had available.

It turned out that the station that had been commandeered was outfitted with sophisticated replication technology. He briefly wondered what the station's purpose was but decided not to dwell on it. On their way to the commissary, he noted that Duine was getting tired with all the walking while carrying her bag. He offered to take it from her, but she refused. She was determined to carry it herself.

The officer-in-charge was helpful and even sympathetic to their request, but even so, said it couldn't be done. An instrument was deemed non-essential and too costly to be generated otherwise.

Kelley looked at Duine, who was exhausted and dejected. She looked at the screen image of the panflute like she was going to cry.

He told Duine to go sit down and wait for him. She did as she was told; sitting down heavily, slumping in the chair.

He talked quietly with the quartermaster and asked the cost of generating the instrument. It was more than he expected. He hadn't spent that much on anything in a long time. Even so, he asked if he could pay for the pipes out of personal funds, half hoping the answer would be no.

The quartermaster agreed and even said he would begin the process immediately. The QM was expecting a glut of requests soon, as they geared up to provide for the children, but the list hadn't been given to him yet.

Kelley dug around in his bag for his personal device and tapped it to the quartermaster's screen. The QM completed the transaction and told him the pipes would be ready in a couple of hours. Kelley said they would wait. He sat down next to Duine, leaned his head back and closed his eyes, as if wanting to sleep. He just didn't want to talk right now.

A while later, he felt Duine lean up against him. Opening his eyes, he saw that she was asleep and had fallen over against him. He put his arm around her and shifted a little in his seat to get more comfortable. He wasn't mad any more, but he was still concerned about his future. About their future.

Chapter Twenty-Four

Kelley woke up suddenly. He was still seated in the commissary, Duine next to him. He wasn't sure if he woke her up or she woke him, but they were both awake and moving to stretch their stiff muscles.

Looking around for the QM, he saw him in his office, the door open. He called out an amiable, "How's it going?"

The QM looked up and waved him in. Kelley walked back to the office, Duine trailing behind.

The QM had the pipes in his hand, examining them. Duine breathed and awed, "They're beautiful." The QM smiled and nodded, saying "Yes. Yes, they are. I haven't generated wood before. It was tricky, but they came out rather well."

Kelley didn't play an instrument of any sort, but even he agreed they were something. The wooden pipes had a beautiful sheen and were joined together with what looked like finely-braided leather.

There was a case for the pipes on the QM's desk, which was just as nice. It had a place for a small selection of tools and bottles, presumably for the cleaning and maintenance of the pipes.

Seeing Kelley's alarmed look, the QM shook his head, "Don't worry. It was all included." He carefully put the pipes in the case and closed the lid. He went to hand it to Kelley, but Duine stepped forward and took it from him.

130

"Thank you so very much," Duine told him. "They are perfect and so beautiful. She will love them."

She turned and started to leave, only stopping when she saw Kelley wasn't following quickly enough.

Kelley shook the QM's hand, thanking him. As he left, he picked up his bag and Duine's.

They navigated back to Gada's room in silence. When they got there, Kelley opened the door but stayed near the entrance. Gada was there, sitting on the floor as before, looking at nothing in particular.

Duine walked straight in and sat down next to Gada. She set the case down carefully and opened it. Gada instantly lit up when she saw the pipes. It was like flipping a switch from off to supernova.

Taking out the pipes, she looked them over and started blowing into them. The sounds weren't melodious. They varied in tone and pitch as Gada blew into the pipes, tilting them occasionally, and changing how she set her jaw. It took Kelley a while to realize she was putting the pipes through their paces, so to speak, and finding its range of sounds. Once satisfied with their range, she warmed up by taking the pipes through a series of scales.

Gada transitioned from scales into playing a song seamlessly, amazing Kelley. He was amazed at her talent and at what he was hearing. The music was beautiful. Gada played without stopping for some time; apparently just shifting from song to song without a break in between.

Duine reached out and touched Gada's arm, getting her attention. Gada stopped playing and asked Duine, "You don't want them back, do you?"

"No, they are yours. They were made specially for you. I just wanted to ask if you knew how to use the vid here. It's different than what we had before. Let me show you."

After the Battle

Duine pulled Gada, half unwillingly, to the desk with a computer terminal and demonstrated how to use it. She searched for song scores as an example of how to navigate and do searches. Gada was thrilled to find her favorite songs and at the number of new results. Kelley found it interesting that Spectrum had been selective in what it had allowed the children to find.

Glancing out the open door, he saw Dr. Frandeen coming towards him. She was displeased to see him looking in one of the girls without supervision, and was about to speak, but he stopped her and nodded at the girls.

She watched them for a few moments before telling him quietly, "This is the most that girl has interacted with anyone or anything since she came here. And I've never seen her so animated."

Apparently satisfied with her tutorial, Gada abruptly stated, "I want to play some more now."

Duine stood up, saying "Of course, but before you do, I just want to let you know that I am leaving again. I'm not being taken or anything. I'll be fine, just as you will be fine here. Okay?"

"Okay." That was all she said, but she hugged the pipes to her chest, her eyes meeting Duine's. Duine smiled and gave Gada's arm a gentle squeeze with her hand. Kelley, Duine, and Frandeen quietly left the room, closing the door.

"I gave her the pipes; is that okay? You won't try and take them from her, will you?" she asked Dr. Frandeen nervously.

"No, we won't take them from her," the doctor reassured her. "They appear to be the bridge we were looking for to connect with her."

"The pipes will be listed as her personal property? They will follow her wherever she goes, right?" Duine pressed.

The doctor didn't answer. Instead, she tapped the monitor and called up Gada's record. Duine watched as she entered the pipes into the record and also the case at her prompting. Dr. Frandeen saved the entry and asked, "Are you satisfied?"

Duine didn't answer right away. She stood listening to Gada play through the door. It really was so very beautiful.

Then she told both the doctor and Kelley, "Yes. She'll be okay. I'm ready to leave."

Finally, thought Kelley.

Chapter Twenty-Five

Kelley didn't know what to do with the girl, so he decided to go back to where he had started—the GIS facility where he had been trained and had a small apartment.

The trip back was unexpectedly frustrating. They took commercial transport as there was no need for investigative privacy. As Duine was no longer being looked for, they didn't have to worry about her security.

The transport was smaller and less luxurious than a liner, but it had a fair number of passengers and decent facilities. The transport even had an amenity that could be programed to set a sleep schedule that would gradually acclimate them to the local time of their destination.

This time, there was no case to work on and for the most part, no one else other than each other. Their quarters were fine; clean and comfortable, but small. He gave her as much privacy as he could, but he wished she would grant him the same courtesy.

She was always around him, dogging his every step. She wanted to do everything he did. He couldn't go for workouts without her wanting to tag along. If he boxed, she wanted to learn how. If he went for a run, she wanted to, too.

Kelley thought that if they did some of the onboard activities together that would earn him enough family time 'credit' to buy himself some alone time. Duine didn't see things the same way.

He ended up teaching her to box and some basic hand-to-hand. It was all he could think of. He wasn't ready to have any deep, meaningful talks with her just yet. Teaching was not new to him, whereas simple, non-specific oversight of a young civilian was. She got to be pretty good. It was a long trip and she had plenty of time to practice. It was frustrating for him, though, because it was never enough for her.

Things between them got decidedly strained when he insisted on a little personal time with one of the female crew.

He was not used to pouting and had no idea how to handle it. He also didn't particularly care for being questioned about his activities.

He asked Dr. Crane for advice but didn't think he got any. All Dr. Crane would say is that they were both going through a transition and their behavior was perfectly normal. He even went so far to say that Kelley was handling all very well.

Crane was less in the background now that Kelley was in between assignments. He guided Kelley through the process of translating his skills and life experience into GIS qualifications. Crane was now suggesting open positions for him to interview for. Kelley, his hands full with the girl, agreed to whatever interviews were suggested. Duine understood about the interviews, at least, and didn't give him a hard time there.

One morning, close to the end of the trip, he came back to their quarters in the early hours ship time. He was quiet, so as to not wake her because the young girl needed her rest, of course. She was already up but looked tired and moody. He didn't say anything, but his shoulders dropped in resignation.

"Hey there! Have you eaten?" he asked her as brightly as he could manage.

She shook her head, not answering him.

He made his way to the catering unit and started getting them both something to eat.

"Who was it this time?" she asked with more than a bit of tone.

"Why do you want to know? Does it matter?"

She gaped at him. "Does it matter to you?"

He gave an involuntary shrug, then tensed, waiting for her reaction.

"Don't you care about them?" she wanted to know.

He didn't understand her insistence. His downtime had nothing to do with her.

"Why does it bother you so much?" he asked.

"Do you not care about me the same way you don't care about them?" she continued answering his questions with a question.

He almost choked on his breakfast. He saw absolutely *no* parallel between those women and her.

"Where did that come from?! You are nothing like them. Of course, I care about you." He set his bowl down and grabbed a napkin to wipe his face.

"Do you? You haven't told me anything since we left Pagnol's system. What is going to happen to me? Am I going to stay with you or not? Apparently, my father's family doesn't want me. My mother can't talk to me without dying. And you don't want me around either." Duine looked at him, her face worried and eyes scared.

Kelley just stared back at her as he tried to get himself together enough to answer.

Finally, he said, "Come on. Let's sit down and talk." He moved to the couch and she plopped herself down on the opposite end, eyes down, arms folded.

"Yes, I do care about you, kid. And you are right, I haven't been talking much this trip. I'm sorry." He paused. She didn't move or say anything, so he went on, "I know it has been

136

hard on you. It actually has been difficult for me, too, you know."

She turned towards him with a skeptical look. "Why?"

"Because I never thought I would *ever* be in a situation like this and I have no idea what I am doing or what to do next."

"Seriously? The way you carry on with those women?"

Kelley was back to being annoyed. He was being honest, and it seemed to him that they were on the verge of a moment, and she went right back to where she didn't need to go. He had not answered to anyone about his conduct in a very long time.

He gave her a stern look and just waited.

She dropped her eyes. "I'm sorry. It's just, how hard can it be? Am I that difficult to get along with?"

Sure are moody as hell, he thought, but answered instead, "No. Of course, not. Being a, a father, is just not something I ever thought I would be. And all that it means."

"Like what? What does it mean?" she asked, genuinely interested.

"Job. House. School." He left the list there, not sure himself.

"You have a job," she answered naively. "I can help find us a house. And you don't have to worry about going to school," she finished with a teasing grin.

He tried to smile. "It's not that simple."

"Sure it isn't. <u>*But*</u>, what I am saying is you don't have to do it all by yourself. Let me help."

She was so damned earnest; he wanted to believe her.

"Why would you want to hang around an ex-soldier like me when you could have a real family, with parents who know what they are doing, maybe with brothers or sisters?" he asked her.

Her face got pouty for a moment until she realized he was being sincere. "Because you are family," she answered, like it was obvious. "I would rather be with you, however messed up or flawed as you think you are, than with anyone else." She paused. "Back at the orphanage, after Tanya died, I was too scared to leave; to face the unknown alone. I only left because I was too mad to stay."

"Then you found me and told me who I was and where I came from, and it was like everything changed. I mean, I didn't really like most of it, but I *knew*, for sure. And there was you. Since you came along, I don't feel alone."

Kelley swallowed, his throat tight. He was glad when she went on.

"It wasn't easy, especially the deposition but the only time I really got scared was when I was on the station and I didn't know where you were or if I was ever going to see you again."

He inhaled through his nose and let it out quickly, his mouth opening to say something comforting, when she abruptly changed moods on him. "But now you're stuck with me. You just try to get rid of me." She crossed her arms and legs defiantly, jaw set, eyes fixed on his. So very much like Mel.

He laughed; it just burst out of him. "You are a Kelley all right. Decide on a course and stick to it. I can see it's no use trying to tell you otherwise. And I know what you mean about family. Your grandfather used to say, 'it doesn't matter where you are, we are always family'."

He saw a light go on in her eyes as he spoke. A light coming up from somewhere deep down. He thought he understood; having family is like a cosmic compass, because of them you always know where you are, and which way is home.

He lost that feeling when he lost his parents. It wasn't that Mel hadn't been enough; he was just so scared of losing her too that he pushed her away. He let her and that spark out of his life. He let Fleet and the next mission fill the void. After

138

the explosion and cutting ties with Fleet, he hadn't turned to Mel because he thought she had abandoned him. Before leaving for Tycor he found out that he had been wrong.

And here he was, still scared. Too scared to accept that he could have a relationship with his sister again. He didn't want to adopt the girl because he was scared that if he got a family and that feeling back, he might lose them all over again. *Damn it; I'm done being scared*, he thought.

He reached out and pulled her in for a hug, holding on tightly. When he let her go, they were both teary and she reached for a tissue.

She bounced up, asking, "What do we do now?" She was fired up, ready for anything.

"Now? I go for a shower." She glared at him, exasperated and disappointed at the anti-climax. He grinned. "Don't worry. That isn't all; I've got it planned."

Chapter Twenty-Six

Kelley, energized by his shower, not because he made a life-altering choice or anything, initiated a session with Dr. Crane to let him know of his decision. Crane was more than pleased at his progress and even called it a 'breakthrough.' He told Kelley that he would start the process of disassociating Duine Ar Bith from the girl in the next room immediately. Essentially Duine Ar Bith would have to end. Or more accurately, records would show Duine Ar Bith as being transferred to another orphanage and never being heard from again.

Part of the disassociation would involve untangling her from anyone she had met since leaving Pagnol, save him, of course. Fortunately, they had kept things locked down tightly; it wasn't going to be that difficult. Kelley was more concerned about getting her set up with a new history, so to speak. That was going to take some thought.

He sent a message to Mel telling her he was sorry he hadn't been in touch lately; he had a lot going on. He just found out that a past relationship of his had produced a daughter and he was dealing with that. He would explain when he saw her next.

Mel replied that she would be happy to welcome her new-found niece into the family and that she had sent his stuff from storage to his apartment.

Okay. That was curious. When she previously said that she had saved his things for him, he had been both touched and grateful. He hadn't thought too much about his stuff since. He was getting the idea that he should now though.

Going through his communications, he was surprised to find several job offers. Not just temporary assignments but actual permanent posts. The interviews hadn't been a waste of time. He was as fired up as the girl was earlier and it felt good.

Leaving his room, he went back to the common area. The girl, he had no idea what to call her, was there looking like she just had a shower.

"I cleaned up breakfast and went for a run. I just got myself cleaned up," she told him.

"Great. Is it time for lunch already? Anyway, can you sit down, please? There are some things I want to start talking to you about."

Smiling brightly, she said, "Sure!" and sat down at the table with eager anticipation.

The door to their quarters chimed. He gestured for her to answer it, while he started getting them something to eat.

She got back up with just a little eye roll and came back with a package. "What's this? I guess it's for you."

"No, it's for you. Open it." He watched her open it.

"It's a tablet! Like yours. It's for me; its mine?" she was incredulous. "Thank you!!"

"Well, not entirely like mine. That's the latest version," he said, pleased that she liked it. "Let's get it set up."

It didn't take long to do that. She wasn't a novice to tech, it was just that the tablet was the first one that was *hers*. He tapped his tablet to hers, saying, "Here. I got Alden to give me your data from Spectrum."

She tapped and swiped for a time before stopping, her eyes reddening like she was going to cry. He leaned over to see her screen. It was a picture of two girls, one of whom was Duine. The other, presumably, had been Tanya.

He reached over and gave her hand a brief squeeze before saying, "Okay. First lesson. Let's talk about your past versus your new past." She looked at him confused.

He explained how her real past was going to have to be integrated into her "real" past. For example, she could keep the picture, but it wasn't her "Duine" and a friend. She got the idea. He knew this was going to take a while to sort out and to get used to; the sooner they got started the better.

Later that day, while they were taking a break, he went through his prospective jobs in more detail. He also listed out where they were, planet versus moon or station and their amenities such as the size of the cities, the local neighborhoods, and the quality of their school systems.

"Ooh. That one looks good. Take that one." The girl, having just come back from the facilities, was looking over his shoulder at his tablet.

"This one? Let's see, one of GIS's bigger sites. The planet is very nice with a mixture of rural and urban development. The schools are *very* good in the area where the job is. I don't know though; the job at this location is above me. I made it through the first round of interviews but I don't actually have an offer yet. I need to take a couple of tests and arrange for an in-person meeting. I was thinking about it as a pass."

"Above you? How?" she asked.

"It's for the lead of the analysis team," he answered.

"You mean like the team on Tycor? Sounds like a lot of travel."

"No, they were an investigative team, in that there was already a case to investigate. This job is to find the cases to send other teams out to investigate. The job is more analysis and would have minimal travel."

"Oh. Then it is ideal for you," she said confidently.

He was pleased at her confidence in him but didn't share it. He was still used to being out in the middle of the action, not in the back, or in his opinion, on the sidelines. She kept at him until he promised to arrange for the tests and interview. He rationalized that the pay was too good to not even try for it.

Chapter Twenty-Seven

The transport landed in the middle of the night local time. They were both tired but fortunately neither had much to carry. Kelley supposed it was good that it was so late; the fewer people they saw the better. They hadn't decided on a name for her yet. She swore to him she hadn't really liked 'Duine.' He was dubious, but he had told her that he thought it meant 'no one.'

When they got to his apartment, he used the keypad and his thumbprint to unlock the door. Opening the door, he saw a wall of boxes that kept him from going in. Swearing to himself, he pushed his way carefully inside. He was in no mood to have a box fall on his head. The girl followed in his wake.

"What's all this?" she asked.

"Your... Aunt. Your Aunt Mel sent around a bunch of my stuff that she had stored for me. I didn't know she managed to have it stowed *inside* my apartment." Kelley grumbled the last part, still trying to get around.

"Why did she have this much of your stuff?"

He looked at her. Apparently, she had passed from exhausted into over-tired and wired.

"Let's just find you somewhere to sleep and talk about it in the morning, okay?" he suggested.

144

"Okay." She agreed but started poking around the boxes instead of moving them out of the way.

He used a bunch of the boxes as a bed platform for the temporary mattress. Then, he ended up being the one to sleep on it because he didn't have any spare blankets or pillows, so he gave her the bed.

She woke him early the next morning. She was dressed and going through the boxes again.

"You know it's rude to open what isn't yours, right?" he asked her.

"I'm sorry. I was just curious. It's a lot of stuff."

He started to tell her his apartment wasn't that big but stopped as his back twinged as he sat up. He groaned and tried to stretch out the ache.

"You should take a hot shower," she told him.

He got slowly to his feet saying, "You sound like your grandmother. You would have called her Grandma Tara." She smiled and nodded.

When he finished dressing after his shower, he went out into the main room, hoping to find some coffee waiting for him. Instead, the place was even more in chaos; she was actively rooting through the boxes again and taking things out. It had been a while, but he swore there was stuff here that hadn't been his. What had Mel given him?

"Hey! What are you doing?" he was stern but didn't shout.

"I want to know more. I want to know more about my dad's side of the family," she replied, not at all contrite.

He noted the reference to himself and it still felt odd. He was getting used to the idea of having a daughter, but he had a way to go.

Looking around, he saw his entire life scattered everywhere about the small apartment. He saw his Fleet dress uniform. A medal from a high school competition was hanging from a light fixture. A cap with a GIS logo on it was sitting on the counter. The shirt that belonged to his father was over the back of a chair. There was more; a lot more.

A wave of emotion unexpectedly crashed into him, slamming him hard. He started breathing through his mouth to try and loosen his throat that was suddenly tight.

"Are you okay?" she asked, concerned. "I can get you some water, I couldn't find any coffee."

The couch and chairs were piled with stuff; with nowhere to sit he slid down until he was sitting on the floor, back against a wall. She handed him the water and sat down next to him.

He decided to skip pretending he was okay. "It's all here," he said gesturing around the room with his arm. "Each time something bad happened to me, I cut myself loose from it and just went on to something else. Like it never happened. Done. Over. I just moved on and got to the next chapter of my life." He cleared his throat. "It just feels like it's all here; waiting for me." *Like walking into a freakin' ambush*, he thought to himself.

He tilted his head back against the wall, eyes closed, tears down his face. He didn't know where they came from or why. She didn't say anything, she just nestled close to him, holding his arm tightly.

Eventually he pulled himself together, after the unexpected connection with his past, and wiped his eyes with his free hand. She was still curled up close to him, holding his arm. He looked down at her until she tentatively looked up. He gave her a half-smile and told her, "It's okay. I'm all right."

"I'm sorry I went through your stuff," she said very quietly.

"Don't be. If it wasn't for you, I probably would have just thrown it all out without looking at any of it. And really, I probably wouldn't have ever known Mel had kept any of it if I hadn't gone to talk to her about you."

He thought for a minute before going on. "I understand your wanting to know about your family, your history. And I will tell you. I promise I will tell you everything I can. It's just going to take me a little time to get my own history together again first."

"That's okay. I can wait. It's not like I'm going anywhere," she reminded him. They looked at each other, he grinned and made a face at her that made her giggle.

"Time for breakfast. I'll get something delivered." She immediately released his arm and stood up.

Chapter Twenty-Eight

After they ate, they spent the rest of the morning going through the boxes and sorting things out. It was hard work for him. So many memories.

"What's this? It looks pretty old," she asked him, holding up a clunky old-style tablet.

He wended his way through the maze of boxes and took the tablet from her. After examining it, he said, "You wouldn't recognize it. It's older than you are."

"You kept something *that* old? Why didn't you just transfer the data to a new tablet?"

"Why didn't I?" he asked himself quietly, trying to remember. He got it. "Because I didn't. Well, not on purpose. This was the tablet I used for work when I was in the Blerreon 4 PD. I was supposed to turn it in when I left them and joined Fleet. I remember getting ream… yelled at when I had to report that I lost it. It looks like Mel took it." He swore to himself; had she been pregnant *before* he left?

The girl was so excited, he tried his best to play along. They turned it on and waited impatiently for it to boot up. When it did, it felt like the floor dropped out from below them. There was nothing on the tablet. The girl let out a word that Kelley would have reprimanded her for under any other circumstance.

He wasn't ready to give up. Mel was neither cruel nor stupid. There was still something to be found; he knew it. He went through the tablet again. It was wiped, yes. In fact, it had been done by someone who knew what they were doing.

He tried to remember what he knew back then. He wasn't around; he had recently joined Fleet. He remembered agreeing to sell their apartment on Blerreon 4 because Mel was leaving for college. He and Mel kept in touch somewhat while she was in college, and not long after she graduated college, she married Hugo and they fell more out of touch.

He put himself in Mel's place and went through it again. Her brother leaves the moon, she gets or was pregnant but doesn't tell him. She swipes his PD tablet. She has the baby. She goes to college, a prestigious college, and graduates with honors, after which, she marries a man of means. How does a young woman do all that all by herself?

Simple answer: she doesn't. At some point, the father or his family finds out about the pregnancy. They can't convince her to abort but they do get her to agree to give up the baby and be collared. She gets her education paid for and never has to go back to that tiny moon where her parents died. A simple but solid hypothesis.

But why get him to find an empty tablet? And why his? Mel had had a tablet of her own. He got up and started walking around, trying to think.

The girl pulled her head out of her arms and looked at him.

"What are you doing?"

"I'm trying to think. There is something that we are missing," he told her.

"Like what? If she did leave me a message it got erased somehow." Her voice was strained with emotion.

"Yes! It was deleted. Professionally deleted. So that means they got a hold of it somehow. Maybe she had to give it to them. Maybe they were taking care of her while she was pregnant. She might have been watched by them. They wouldn't have let her keep any record of you. She would have known that. So, what does she do? How does she get a message out without their knowing *and* to where that message can be retrieved later, years later?"

He put the tablet down. "Which box did you get this from?"

She pointed to a box as she got to her feet.

He went over and looked inside. He found a small blanket that used to belong to Mel and a small tattoo gun that looked like a large pen. That was it.

A big box holding just three items: a tablet, a blanket, and a tattoo pen.

An erased tablet; if it was erased, it must have had something to erase. There had been a message. No, he told himself, it meant there *was* a message. Somewhere. If that was true, what was the point of his tablet versus hers? The tablets were similar in make and model except for the PD software. That's it! His tablet had special software that uploaded data in short, random bursts. The PD never wanted to lose evidence because someone lost or damaged their device. Whatever had been stored on the tablet had been uploaded somewhere before it was erased.

Blanket. Mel's blanket from when she was little. How little? A baby blanket. It was Mel's baby blanket. Both a clue and a gift to her daughter.

A tattoo pen. Tattoo pen? It wasn't professional quality; more like something the average person would use to tattoo their face. What would Mel tattoo that wouldn't have alarmed those watching her?

He twirled the pen in his fingers while he thought. As he did, he felt odd rough spots on the barrel that was otherwise smooth. He examined it more closely and held it under the light. Was something scratched into the pen? He could make out one word. It looked like a name. Whose name? He got his tablet and did a search.

Among the results was a listing for a company—a company that specialized in data storage.

"Now we are getting somewhere!" he said excitedly. The girl continued to watch him doubtfully. He handed her the blanket. "This was Mel's from when she was a baby. I think she meant it for you." She took it from him, holding it with awe.

He accessed the company's site and looked for accounts in Mel's name. He tried every variation of her name that he could think of but didn't find anything. Dammit.

"Even if you did find the account, why would the company give you access to her data?" she asked him from over his shoulder, holding the blanket to her chest.

"Good question!" He searched for his name. Several possible matches came up. He narrowed it down and selected the one he thought was correct, then entered in his bio information, as requested. Account holder verified. Yes!

The next screen asked him to remit his outstanding balance. It was a fair chunk of credits but not all that much given that the account had been opened over fifteen years ago. Had Mel been paying for this account all this time? He entered his credit information as requested.

While it processed, he checked his personal account balance. Fortunately, only his time with Mel was unpaid leave. He had been on assignment after that since both Tycor and Spectrum had been legitimate case work. He was relieved his balance wasn't so low. He tried not to think of all the expenses he would have very soon.

The screen beeped at him. The transaction was completed successfully and now it asked him to please enter his password.

He sighed. "All we have to do now is find the password." He held up the pen. "Mel wrote it down somewhere. Or she tattooed herself with it."

The girl shook her head. "Why would she tattoo herself? The account was in your name. The tablet was in a box she gave to you. You are the one who is meant to have the password."

"I wasn't there. I suppose she could have written it on something else and put it in one of these boxes." He looked around. It was a lot of stuff to go through.

She looked around the apartment. "What if you didn't keep it? It has to be something she felt sure you would never throw out."

"What would I keep?" He thought for a minute. "What if it's not what I would keep, but what I have now? What I would have to have to even look for the password?"

She stared at him, not understanding. He kept looking at her.

Then she got it. "Oh! Me? You think she wrote the password on me? No. I don't have any tattoos anywhere."

Kelley said, "We could try a UV light anyway." He just felt so sure that he was right. He had to keep going.

He took her to the GIS building, straight to the medical wing. She protested, saying they should keep looking into the boxes. He just gave her a general 'this way is better' response and kept going.

He found a doctor and asked her to do the exam. The doctor took the request well enough but had doubts as to whether a UV light would reflect anything given all the different variables. She was also skeptical as to whether a tattoo on a baby would have lasted until now.

The doctor insisted on having the pen analyzed. Kelley wasn't sure why; they knew what it was, but he agreed to the analysis.

It took a while. The girl, he really *had* to give her a name soon, was patient. She spent the time on her tablet, while he paced. He was antsy with anticipation.

A nurse finally came and took them back to one of the exam rooms where the doctor was waiting. The doctor asked him to take a seat in the chair and the girl to sit on the exam table. Kelley took that as a positive sign.

The doctor, Dr. Halleywell, reviewed the results of the analysis. The pen was there, completely taken apart and neatly arranged on a tray. The doctor explained that they should have found a needle cartridge inside the tattoo pen. What they found instead was a cartridge for a nebulizer.

They analyzed the nebulizer cartridge, with no results. Whatever it used to contain had long since evaporated and/or dissipated. Kelley and the girl groaned in unison.

The doctor continued her review. They were able to identify the type of cartridge. It was not a generic cartridge for the usual medications that are commonly used in nebulizers. It's was specially designed to hold nanites.

While she spoke, the doctor held up the cartridge and explained the different chambers and how the nanites would be mixed with the liquid that would be used as part of the delivery system, and when heated to a steam, the mixture would be inhaled by the patient.

Kelley and the girl looked at each, neither was particularly interested in the delivery system. They both wanted the doctor to get to the good part.

Dr. Halleywell went on to say the use of nanites was highly regulated in the Confederacy. Their use was usually restricted to the medical profession, closely-monitored research facilities, or government agencies. In this case, the lack of labeling that usually accompanies approved medical drugs and paraphernalia suggested that this cartridge came from a private facility; a facility that did not want the cartridge to be traced back to them.

The doctor paused and asked if there were any questions. Kelley asked, "If the cartridge came from a private facility, it would then follow that it was possible for it to have been purchased by a private citizen. Do you have any idea of the cost? I'm trying to get an idea of the type of citizen who could have purchased it."

Dr. Halleywell pulled up a graph on one of the monitors, usually used to display medical charts and such. She swiveled it so that Kelley could see it. She then explained at length how the costs would vary greatly depending on how reputable the facility was and the complexity of the nanite coding. From the graph, Kelley could see that the price ranges would have been very high for Mel, although he was also remembering that she had taken charge of selling their family apartment on Blerreon 4. She had told him at the time that she used the proceeds to fund her university education, which she wouldn't have had to do if she made a deal with the father's family. The credits from the sale may have gone somewhere else.

The girl interrupted his thoughts by asking, "So, what is the next step? How can nanites be detected?"

Dr. Halleywell said, "I would recommend we try a blood analysis first and see what that yields," she answered the girl, then turned to Kelley.

"I give you permission to draw her blood for nanite analysis, with the proviso that no genetic tests are conducted or made part of any file," Kelley responded.

The doctor readily agreed. Kelley suspected that the decoupling of Duine was in progress. This visit must have made the doctor very nervous. He also suspected that he didn't have much time to finalize her backstory. He didn't want Chief Belletor to have to contact him.

The blood draw was quick and painless. The doctor then asked them to leave, as it would take a while for the results to come back, especially if they did find the presence of nanites.

Kelley thanked the doctor for her time and assistance and left quickly. He was getting nervous at being in the gray area between personal and professional business. He had agreed to adopt the girl, who *had* been part of a GIS investigation. He was now using GIS resources for personal reasons. He was unsure when GIS would start charging him for the use of company resources.

The girl initially resisted leaving, she wanted to wait for the results, until Kelley whispered in her ear, "You're not here, remember?"

Chapter Twenty-Nine

They made it back to his now very cramped apartment without any problems. He let her look after herself while he focused on responding to his various messages. He was relieved that none of them were from Chief Belletor. One of the messages was the series of tests related to the team lead analyst position.

He found the tests interesting. Basically, he was given a set amount of information and asked to provide an assessment and list out the next steps. He worked until his door chime interrupted him. "Who could that be?"

The girl answered, "I ordered dinner. I got hungry."

He got to his feet and started for the door, asking her, "How? You don't have a credit stick."

"I contacted the same place you did for breakfast and told them to use the credit information from this morning," she answered.

Clever girl, he thought to himself, as he took the order from the drone.

He only then realized how late in the evening it was. "I'm sorry, I lost track of time. I'm glad you ordered something."

She nodded, her mouth full, as she ate hungrily. "No problem," she mumbled around the food. She looked inquiringly at his tablet, as she continued to eat.

"I'm almost done with their tests. After you finish eating, you should get some sleep and I'll finish up."

"Tomorrow, we need to start filling out the details of your past, like your name, your mother's name, all that stuff."

She frowned, swallowed slowly, and stopped eating.

"What's wrong, kid?" he asked her.

"Nothing," was the immediate response. He waited. "It's just I don't like having to make all that up. Isn't there anything we can use that's real?"

He felt the same way, but answered, "We have to finalize your history. GIS promised it would integrate you into a family and we have to make good on that promise. You can't stay in limbo like this. And I need to be able to call you something other than 'kid.'"

"I hope the nanites tell us something," she said, as if the nanites had already been verified.

"I do, too. We can start working on things like who your mother was to me and why she didn't tell me about you. We need to create an entirely fictional person. That's a lot right there."

She wasn't happy, but she agreed. At least she finished her dinner.

After she went to bed, he sent a message to Dr. Crane. He had missed a check-in and he wanted to apologize. To his surprise, Dr. Crane contacted him back on the vid. He asked for an update on Miss Arbith, as well as his progress with selecting a permanent post.

Kelley promised that they would be working on her past tomorrow. He took a deep breath and told Crane about his theory and how they were waiting on the results of the blood test.

Not surprisingly, Dr. Crane knew about it. This made it easier for Kelley to ask him about the costs. Crane agreed to authorize the test as an expense, provided this was the last one, and if Kelley got him the girl's biography for his review in the next two days. Kelley agreed. Crane still reminded him to tread carefully. Their research must not compromise the identity of the paternal family in any way.

Crane also indicated that he was pleased when Kelley had not included any mention of Mel's 'collar' in his proposal to the family.

Kelley made a face and answered, "Some things just cannot be changed. Mel made the agreement. It's not for me to try and fix things now. Sometimes what is in the past just has to stay in the past."

Crane did not have to be listening very closely to hear the tone in Kelley's voice. He gently prodded Kelley to explain.

Kelley briefly considered warning the doc that his answer could take a while. He didn't get a chance; it all just came out of him.

He talked about how trying to jettison his past had backfired and caught up with him. He talked about the collision of his past with the kid's desire to know about her history. And how important his history suddenly was to him and how the windfall of his possessions was now so important to him.

He said he was remembering what it was like to be part of a family and how much he missed it. He was getting used to the idea of being her father, but still struggling with all the details. He was starting to hope he got the team lead analyst job, but was nervous at the same time.

Crane listened to Kelley without interruption and didn't obviously check the time even once. He just said, "Kelley, when you make a breakthrough, you don't do it by halves, do you?"

Dr. Crane was appreciative of the update and assured Kelley that he was on the right track and to not rush things.

Crane also advised him to get some rest and to keep up the good work.

For the first time in what felt like a long time, Kelley relaxed. He really did appreciate Crane's reassurances. He went to bed on the temporary mattress feeling pretty good. His apartment was in chaos and nothing had really been decided, but he still felt good about it all. He wasn't sure why. Because he had chosen a direction? Because his present was joining up again with his past? Or because his life was moving forward in a good direction? He yawned and settled down. Whatever; as long as it felt good, it was enough for him.

Chapter Thirty

The next morning, he beat the kid to the shower. He was in the kitchen clearing the clutter so that it could be used as a kitchen when the kid joined him.

"Morning," she greeted him pleasantly enough.

He returned the greeting, and asked, "Do want some cereal for breakfast? I got some in this morning that I think you will like."

She agreed and sat down on a stool at the kitchen bar. He got her cereal together and pushed it over to her along with a glass of juice. He sat down next to her with his cereal and a fresh cup of coffee. As they ate, she looked at him and then back to her cereal a couple of times.

"What? Do you want to ask me something?" he asked her.

"Well." She hesitated but then continued. "Yes. Can I ask you about your stubble?"

He hadn't shaved that morning and consequently had a day's worth of a beard. Sort of. He had an idea of where she was going. He tried to answer her in an easy-carefree tone, "Sure. What about my beard?"

"Why is it only on one side of your face?"

Because I got blown up almost three years ago and half of my face is a prosthetic covered by fake skin, he thought to himself. Probably shouldn't put it that way though.

"Well, you know I was in Fleet, right?" He saw her hesitate, so he continued, "That is my Fleet dress uniform that is hanging over there. Anyway. I was in an explosion that did some damage to my face. I can't grow a beard on that side."

"Wow. That sounds pretty serious. Are you okay?"

"Yeah. I always preferred being clean-shaven, so no great loss," he said with a little smile. He knew that wasn't what she meant.

She gave him an odd look, but just nodded and went back to her bowl.

Curious, he asked, "Does it bother you? I mean, I never thought about it; it must look strange from your point of view."

"No. Not to me. Well, a little. It helps to know why. I'm sorry if I shouldn't have asked."

"It's okay. I'm not used to talking about it, but it's okay for you to ask." He wanted to tell her he was okay, and everything was fine, but he couldn't. That day and its aftermath was something that still ran deep with him.

She just nodded again and took their bowls to be washed.

They spent the day inside. Fortunately, she didn't mind being restricted to the apartment. He asked her to help put everything back into the boxes so that they could move around more easily.

Late in the afternoon, he received a notice of a classified communication. He took his tablet into the bedroom and closed the door. The message was from Dr. Halleywell who confirmed the presence of nanites in the subject's bloodstream. Analysis could not determine what they did or may have done. They appeared inert. The only interesting point was that they all had the same twenty-five-digit alpha-numeric code on them.

Kelley was so excited he almost kissed his tablet. He tapped a quick acknowledgment/thank you to the doc and practically ran back into the other room.

He opened the door and immediately collided with the kid who was just on the other side.

He helped her up and asked her if she was okay. She grumbled a yes, saying, "I know I shouldn't have been listening."

"No, you should *not* have been listening," he agreed sternly. "This can't happen again. I'm a GIS agent and I can't have my daughter breaking protocols every five minutes. This is the last time, do you understand, young lady?" He was serious, and she knew it.

"Yes, sir," she dutifully agreed. He kept staring at her sternly.

"Yes, sir. I understand I am not to listen in on communications or to snoop into anything that might be classified. I won't do it again," she elaborated. He thought she sounded sincere.

"Very well then. I'll take you at your word, this time." He relaxed his posture, so he wasn't so gruff. He wanted to add that the next time she listened at a door, she should ensure she stands to one side, for obvious reasons. He didn't as he didn't want to confuse her or weaken his previous order. If this was going to work, she really did have to observe certain boundaries.

Dr. Halleywell's message was text only, so he knew she hadn't heard anything.

He took a seat at the kitchen bar and gestured her to sit next to him. She came over while he accessed his data account again. He heard her inhale and hold it while she watched him paste in the password he had copied from the doc's report.

She let out a squeal as the screen blipped 'approved' and then 'data downloading'. She was practically bouncing on the stool and had a tight grip on his hand.

The screen finally appeared with a directory of data files. It looked like there were over two hundred separate video files in the directory.

He sorted the directory by date and tapped open the oldest one. Mel's face appeared. A young Mel. He paused the vid to let the girl process the image.

Mel and the kid looked very similar. Both had fine, pale skin and gray eyes. Mel at eighteen was a young woman and very pretty. Her hair was long and braided. The kid was still in her adolescence with some growing yet to do. Her hair was long as well, though she hadn't been doing much with it beyond washing it. Consequently, she looked like a young cub with a wild, unkempt mane of thick, curly hair.

Kelley wondered at the contribution of her father, given how much she favored her mother. But he reminded himself, Mel had favored their mother, too. Their father, Finn, was more evident when she spoke, especially with his mannerisms and turns of phrase.

"That is your Aunt, my sister. I knew her as Melvina Kelley or just Mel. She is married now and is known as Dr. Turner," he told her quietly. "Do you understand?"

She nodded quickly; it took a moment for her to be able to speak. "Yes, she is my Aunt. Your sister. Can I call her Aunt Mel?"

He smiled. "I guess so." He checked the time/date stamp on the file. "Mel was just eighteen at this time. Are you ready to hear what she has to say?"

"YEAH!" He tapped play.

And Mel spoke. It was obvious that she was making a video diary to herself. The image was mostly of her face and just a bit of her upper torso. Kelley thought he recognized the background as being the living room of the apartment they inherited from their parents. It was just general stuff that any young woman might have recorded. The kid looked disappointed.

"Wait and see. Remember, she was up against some well-connected people. She hadn't kept a diary before, but she started one now. Let's see where it goes."

They listened to several more entries. Kelley decided that Mel was getting used to talking to herself and keeping a journal. He wasn't the only Kelley who wasn't good at introspection, though in her case, he could see her getting used to it as the entries went on.

Finally, they came to an entry with a new backdrop. They could only see her face and neck. She looked the same except her eyes were more intense, like she was concentrating on what she was saying, and the words sounded rehearsed.

This Mel told herself she was happy with her new apartment; everything was so nice. As she gestured around the room, Kelley could see the implant incision on her neck. The kid paused the vid and looked at him.

He nodded. "At this point, she is in their care. We don't know the level of surveillance and its unlikely she does either."

"Why didn't she tell us anything before the collar was implanted?"

"I don't know, though I would guess that it's because it would have been in violation of their agreement. A simple polygraph would have revealed that. No, she has to be able to say that she didn't tell anyone about her liaison or the resulting pregnancy, ever," he reasoned.

"So, how did the vid entries get from the tablet to the data company?" the kid asked.

"I'm thinking Mel used the B4 PD software to transmit the data. It wouldn't have been highly advanced tech, but higher than they would have assumed she had access to. She gambled they wouldn't catch the data transfers." Kelley paused, remembering Alden's statement regarding his implants. What if Mel had done something similar?

It was getting late and they were both uncomfortable on the stools. She helped clear off the couch and they sat there and continued listening to the entries.

Mel started questioning who she was and where she was going. This led to her explaining to herself who she was and where she had come from. She started with her basic biography; mostly listing the facts such as her date of birth, the planet of origin, or moon, in her case. Kelley could tell she felt embarrassed and awkward talking about herself. Mel went on to explain in detail what she knew of the Kelley family history.

The girl was riveted to the screen and Kelley was interested at the genealogy refresher. It didn't hurt like he thought it would. Mel knew a lot more than he did about their family; generations back, in fact. Eventually, he got bored with all the details.

He called it a night and ordered the girl to bed despite her protests. He didn't feel mean; there was no way they could finish all of the entries in one sitting.

Chapter Thirty-One

He woke the next morning to the kid making breakfast, loudly. He groaned and yawned. His back started twinging even before he sat up. He had to remember to get some bed linens today, so he could move her out and get back to his own bed.

He didn't say anything; he just got up and shuffled his way to the facilities. After his shower, he went directly to the couch and logged in again. She brought over two bowls of cereal and sat down. When he didn't start the next entry, she looked at him. He looked back and held up his hand, as if he were holding a cup. She made a noise and scurried to the kitchen. A minute later, she was back with a hot cup of coffee. He took a sip and started the vid.

Mel continued with the genealogy lesson until she worked her way to their parent's generation. He started paying attention again. He learned some things he had not known, which helped to balance the ache of missing them.

He was surprised that there were several weeks of entries about him. She talked a lot about her big brother. He didn't think there was anything she didn't cover. Starting with stories from their childhood and through into their school years; it was both awkward and fascinating at the same time.

He was not only reminded of past events, but he also got to hear them from her point of view. It was evident that she loved him and looked up to him. His chest felt tight. He ached for the sister talking to him from the vid; he wanted to get up and contact her on Nibiru. However, he forced himself to stay put. He was too emotional, and he hadn't finished watching the entries. Besides, he wanted their next communication to be in person.

Mel was brief when it came to the loss of their parents. She dryly stated the facts; that their father had been killed in a mining accident and their mother had died less than a year later in a transportation collusion. She didn't try to make it look like she was making a diary entry; she looked tired.

He checked the log entry. She may have been about seven or eight months along in her pregnancy at this point.

Mel apparently decided that it was time to try and leave a message for her child. She first tried to look down and talk to her belly, but the collar would not let her address her child, even in the utero. When she had tried to say something about having children *in the future*, she couldn't finish her thought—the collar stopped her.

Eventually, after several other attempts, she abandoned the idea of trying to leave any sort of message. Instead, she recorded one sentence per entry.

I miss Garrett.

Fianna is my favorite name.

Tara is my second favorite name.

Love

You

Forgive

Me

The entries stopped for several weeks. The final entry was: Today.

The girl was crying. No, not the girl. Fianna. Fianna Tara Kelley was crying in his arms.

Chapter Thirty-Two

He let her cry for a long time, and then gently urged her to calm down. As she leaned back against the couch, he got up and brought her a blanket from the bed and a box of tissues. He made her a cup of tea and sat down again.

She wiped her eyes and blew her nose. After curling up in the blanket, she held the tea mug in both hands. He couldn't read her expression.

"You must be hungry, Fi. What can I get you? Soup and a sandwich?" he asked her.

"Huh? What did you say?" Fi asked.

"Hungry. You must be hungry. How about some soup, Fianna?" he repeated.

She looked at him. She had heard the entries, but it was evidently just starting to filter through. Then she lit up, like she had on the transport.

"She named me." She paused while it sunk in. "My name is Fianna. Fianna Tara Kelley." She said it so softly. Then she said it again, a little louder but more slowly, trying the name out. She set the tea mug down, thinking for a moment before taking a deep breath and stating, "My name is Fianna Tara Kelley." Then in a lighter tone, "But you can call me Fi."

Kelley, feeling like his heart was going to burst out of his chest, grabbed her in a big hug.

He then let her go, leaned back against the couch and said, "Yes. Go on. What else?"

"I go by Fi. My middle name is for my grandmother, Tara. I was born on..." she trailed off.

Kelley tapped the screen on the date of the last entry. Fortunately, the data company used galactic standard date/time stamps. "We know your date of birth. I can show you how to translate galactic standard time to any planet or moon's local time."

"Great!" she agreed happily.

"After that, do you feel up to helping me flesh out your biography?" He managed not to add that it was due to Crane. He also distracted Fi from realizing that if he read the time stamp correctly, her sixteenth birthday was coming up very soon.

Now that Fi was onboard, it was remarkably easy to draft up her new biography. One of the few points they did have a debate about was whether or not they should model her mother after Mel.

Kelley objected for several reasons, one of which was he really didn't want to refer to his sister as being a former girlfriend, even if it was all a pretense.

He reminded Fi that they would have to say her mother was dead. There wasn't going to be any possibility of finding her or contacting her. He also suggested it would be easier for her and Mel with Mel being just "Aunt Mel." Nothing else. There could never be anything more. He didn't want any confusion or blurring between her mother and Aunt Mel. Or worse, any attempts at being clever that would somehow trigger the collar.

Fi agreed, though he could see it was going to take time for her to come to terms with it. He wondered if meeting Aunt Mel would help or make things harder. He also wondered if talking to Dr. Crane might be a good idea.

After the Battle

Kelley reasoned he would have been nineteen or twenty when Fi was conceived. He wanted the woman to be someone he dated just after joining Fleet. They had been in basic training together and she didn't tell him about the baby because she didn't want to marry or leave Fleet. She placed the baby in an orphanage, as she had no living relatives. She was killed on a mission several years later.

The baby Fi grew up in an orphanage, not knowing about her parents. Most legitimate orphanages keep full profiles of their charges on record as they want the children to be found. These records are shared with legitimate representatives of the Confederacy, such as GIS. She was matched to him during their background check when he joined GIS and the rest is history.

Fi wanted to add more details, such as had he and her mother been in love, but Kelley insisted that they needed to keep it simple and plausible. He didn't like to admit it to Fi, but anybody who had known him back then would have known that he hadn't had any serious relationships.

He submitted the story to Dr. Crane who said he would review it and send it along to be finalized. It wouldn't take long for the necessary document trail to be generated and there were only a limited number of agencies that had to be brought into the loop. Crane advised Kelley to get ready for what came next.

Chapter Thirty-Three

Kelley and Fi spent the next couple of days completely boxing up his apartment. After that was done, he arranged for it all to be picked up by a transportation service.

Kelley was reasonably certain he was going to get a permanent assignment and move to whatever planet or moon it was on. He had narrowed it down to two posts—one that he wanted and one that wanted him. Either way, they weren't coming back here. The transport service would ship his belongings to the junction point and wait until he gave them the final destination.

Now, more than ever, Kelley wanted to get on a transport to Nibiru. He was confident Fi's background would be finalized before they landed, and he had kept Mel waiting long enough.

Dr. Crane, however, put a hold on their plans. Kelley asked Dr. Crane to talk with Fi about meeting her Aunt. Crane agreed that it was a good idea. Kelley assumed the sessions would take place via the vid, while they were en route to Nibiru; Dr. Crane, however, insisted their meetings be in person.

The first session went well enough; Kelley and the doctor discussed what could be done to prepare Mel in advance. Dr. Crane advised him to tell her as much as possible before they arrived and give her time to process the information in private. It was not a good idea to surprise her in any way.

Dr. Crane and Fi met privately for what Crane called a baseline assessment. The next session included them both where they acted out meeting with Mel. Kelley didn't need much coaching; he meant what he had said about the past being the past, as it related to Mel, at least.

Fi, however, wanted to know. She wanted to know her mother's story, she wanted to ask Mel questions. Reasonable, logical, justified, it didn't matter the type of question, it simply wasn't possible. Mel's past, and therefore Fi's past, was never going to be known. It was heartbreaking to watch Fi come to terms with that fact.

The three of them were in Dr. Crane's office. Fi crying, was curled up in the corner of the couch. Kelley, frustrated and hurting for Fi, sat silent and immobile in one of the chairs. Dr. Crane, exhausted after the emotionally draining session with Fi, sat in his desk chair, giving Kelley an inscrutable look.

Kelley ignored the look and stubbornly stayed silent.

Dr. Crane didn't try and be subtle. "Why aren't you saying anything to help Fi?"

Fi looked up, sniffling but alert, waiting for his response.

Kelley glared at Crane and damned him in his thoughts. He was trapped and he knew it. "Because I don't know what to say. I feel like a hypocrite. I can't tell Fi to let go of something she wants to know, what she *needs* to know, when I don't know how to do that myself."

He couldn't look at Fi, so he glared at Crane. Crane didn't say anything but maintained eye contact.

Fi asked, "You understand what I feel?"

Kelley hung his head and said, "I don't know. I know what it is like to have something taken from you, without your permission, and it changes everything, but you can't do squat about it. I know what it is like to be stonewalled. You know someone knows but they aren't talking. It's frustrating, it's unfair, it isn't right, and it doesn't matter how much you deserve to know, it just isn't going to happen."

Kelley ground his teeth. What he just said barely made any sense to himself. He knew he was mixing his and Fi's situations together, but he really didn't feel like explaining.

Crane said gently, "Can you tell Fi why you accept not knowing Mel's story? You are her brother and she didn't tell you. How are you okay with that?"

"Because she chose it. She got into a situation and she chose how she got out of it. I'm not saying it was easy, not at all. I'm sure it must have been very hard, but she did what she had to do. I am certain she did what she felt was best for Fi at the time; I don't doubt that."

"Mel and I both knew what the inside of Blerreon 4's orphanages were like. I am not excusing anything Spectrum did, but *you* were treated very well. You would not have gotten that kind of care anywhere else."

"She could have kept me," Fi said angrily.

Kelley shook his head. 'No, I don't think she could have. Between the pressure from the father's family and what she knew she would face on her own, no, she couldn't."

"We saw how tough it was for our mother when she was alone. She fought *so* hard for us, but we didn't do more than just survive."

"Fi, I know you have been through a lot with what Spectrum was doing to your friends, but I don't think Mel could have known what was going on. She placed you where she thought you would get first-rate care and a free education."

"I can respect her decisions and I can forgive her because I have a good idea of her sacrifices. I can love her because she's family. I took care of her when we were young, and she took care of me when I was injured; it's what a family does. I just want to be a family again."

Fi was crying again. He got up and she met him halfway. He held her until she was ready to let go.

Chapter Thirty-Four

Kelley and Fi had more sessions with Crane before the doc authorized their departure. After his last session, Kelley felt released and energized. Still no job and now no place to live, yet he felt like he was moving forward. He wasn't sure he found a direction yet, but he felt he was going down the right path.

He was on personal leave until he accepted a post. Even so, Crane had made it a point to say that he would be available to either him or Fi, if needed.

They boarded the transport liner as father and daughter, having received preliminary approval of her background. Fi was excited when she saw it was a luxury class transport. He had paid for a small suite of rooms and access to the ship's amenities.

He told the booking agent that he was celebrating his daughter's birthday and the crew responded beautifully. There were brightly colored decorations and a banner wishing her a Happy Birthday, as well as a small cake in their rooms when they arrived.

Fi was ecstatic. He had to take a guess on the cake flavor but Fi responded very well. She did admit to preferring a different flavor when asked, while at the same time she was very appreciative for the cake.

After the Battle

After that, she was hardly in their rooms. She took full advantage of the liner's facilities and tried everything she could.

He was surprised how easily they worked out a balance between spending time together, enjoying the ship's activities, and leaving her time to socialize with others closer to her own age. He, too, was able to socialize with others closer to his age, but he made sure he was discreet. He did not want a repeat of the moody Fi.

Her final biography was approved and sent to him while still en route, as expected. He read through it meticulously and noted the changes. Fi was difficult when he made her spend that evening in their rooms studying and rehearsing her bio. *Somehow,* she survived despite her predictions otherwise.

He was reasonable when she wanted to join in the final night's celebrations. He even agreed when she wanted a new dress for herself and a nice shirt for him. The celebration was a lot of fun. He danced with her a little and tried not to feel protective when she danced with others. And he was happy when she didn't make a fuss when he danced with others.

All in all, it was a good trip. They had a chance to get used to each other, in general, and to their new names of Fi and Dad. As an unexpected bonus, the ship's crew presented him with a file of pictures taken of them while onboard. He hadn't realized he had paid for that benefit but was very glad he did. Yes, most certainly a great trip. He just hoped everything would go nearly as well with Mel.

Chapter Thirty-Five

Fi was quiet from the time the liner landed until they arrived at Aunt Mel's house. Kelley could tell she was nervous, and he admitted to himself that he was, too.

They got out and walked to the door of the house without a word. They stood in front of the door for a minute while Kelley waited to make sure she was ready. He was about to ring the door chime when Mel opened the door.

Fi inhaled quickly in surprise with a small start. Mel smiled, perfectly calmly, and said, "Hello, Fianna. It's wonderful to meet you at last."

Fi was crying but was trying hard not to. Mel stepped towards her and gently pulled her close as she wrapped her arms around her. Fi stopped trying to hold it in and started sobbing, her head on Mel's shoulder.

Kelley stood by; protective in case someone tried to interrupt them, nervous about what Hugo and Brian would think, and on a razor's edge in case Fi blurted something out when she was so overwhelmed.

Mel, still calm, though her cheeks were wet with tears as well, took charge. She let Fi go, stepping back slightly as she cupped Fi's face in her hands. "Let me look at you, my niece. Don't say anything; just let me look at you a moment."

Fi gulped and sniffed, nodding her head. Mel advised her to take some deep breaths as she pulled out some tissues from her pocket and handed them to Fi.

Fi took a couple of breaths but looked to Kelley as if she was going to faint. He glanced at Mel, who saw it too. She guided Fi into the house, gesturing with her head for Kelley to follow them inside.

Kelley entered, closing the door, and looked around for Hugo or Brian. Mel took Fi through into the living room and sat her down on the couch.

"Your uncle Hugo and cousin Brian aren't here right now, but they will be back later this evening," she said to Fi, glancing briefly at Kelley. "Take your time. Have some water or tea, if you would like." The table in front of the couch had a variety of beverages and light edibles.

Mel went over to stand directly in front of her brother and father to her niece. They looked at each other intently, and then both stepped in at the same time to hug. They held each other tightly for a minute and then just let go without saying anything.

Mel sat down on the couch near Fi, and Kelley took a seat near a tray of small blueberry scones. He noted little cakes on a platter as well, and made a silent bet with himself that they were Fi's favorite.

Fi reached for a tea cup. Mel did as well, and then she took the pot and poured them both some tea. "Garrett, what would you like to drink?" Mel asked him.

Fi raised her eyebrows just a little at the use of his first name.

Garrett smiled back her. "It is my name even if only your Aunt Mel calls me by it. And I'll have some coffee, please."

Aunt Mel poured him a mug of coffee that smelled wonderful and tasted just as good.

He glanced at Mel as he held his hand over the scones. She nodded, saying, "Yes, please help yourself."

He did so, asking her "Did you remember they were my favorite or was it just a coincidence?" He popped the scone into his mouth whole.

"Garrett! Of course, I remembered!" She turned to Fi, "Your father, Garrett, doesn't eat sweets very much, but he does like blueberry scones."

Fi, still quiet, reached out for a scone. When Mel helped herself to a finger sandwich, Fi took one, too.

The three sat eating quietly, not saying too much, while Fi regained her poise. When Kelley saw her try one of the cakes, he asked her the flavor; he won his bet.

"Aunt Mel ..." she started very hesitant.

"Yes, Fi?

Fi hesitated. Kelley tensed, hoping she remembered the sessions with Dr. Crane.

"I just want to say that I love your scones. They are wonderful and I'm glad I got a chance to try them."

Mel just nodded and reached over to give Fi's hand a gentle squeeze. She cleared her throat and said, "And I'm glad you got a chance to try them, too." She paused, not letting go of Fi's hand. "You must forgive me for not giving them to you sooner."

That was cutting it close Kelley thought. He glared at Mel, who refused to look at him.

Fi turned her hand over to hold Mel's hand, "Aunt Mel, there is nothing to forgive, you are sharing the scones with me now."

Kelley squirmed in his seat. He understood what the two were saying but didn't like it. He didn't like how close they were getting, and he didn't like all this emotion being tied to his favorite dessert. Couldn't they love cakes or cookies, instead?

Mel and Fi looked at him and then at each other. They leaned in until their foreheads gently touched. Mel raised her chin and kissed Fi's forehead. Releasing Fi's hand, she got up and moved to the chair across from Kelley. "Relax, Garrett. We won't talk about pastries if it bothers you so much."

"Aunt Mel, can I use your bathroom, please?" Fi asked her.

Mel directed her accordingly. When they were alone, Mel asked him, "How are you two doing? Getting along all right?"

He assured her they were fine. He was telling her about their trip on the liner, when he was interrupted by the front door opening.

Mel was surprised. She immediately got to her feet, calling out, "Hello?"

Hugo, Mel's husband, strode into the room saying, "We're back."

Their son, Brian, trailing behind his father, was hesitant and worried. Brian, only eight years old, said, "I'm sorry, Mom; I know we're early."

Mel just nodded at him and then looked at Hugo for an explanation. She was clearly upset.

"What, honey? So we came back a little early. We just wanted to meet Garrett's mistake," he said, in a falsely jovial tone.

The atmosphere in the room went nuclear. Neither Mel or Kelley tried to hide their disgust at his remark. Kelley slowly looked Hugo up and down, sizing him up like the little worm he was, and just stared at him.

Hugo seemed to have expected a different reaction and now was at a loss as to what to say next. Brian at first looked between his father and his Uncle, but one glance at his mother told him she was the one he needed to worry about.

"How perfectly revolting of you, Hugo. Your lack of wit is breathtaking and only matched by your complete disrespect for my family." Mel's tone was wonderfully cutting without being overly emotional. She turned to Brian and said "Life happens to people who live it. Don't let yourself get caught up into judging other people. You will only stop yourself from living your life to its fullest."

Turning to Kelley she said in a formal tone, "Garrett. I apologize for my husband. His views about how worlds turn have gotten parochial over time. I am sorry."

Kelley stood up and faced her. "No need for you to apologize. You can't help the drivel of others."

He turned to Brian, "I think what your mother is saying is that while you should think first and act later, you should spend more time *doing* than thinking." Brian nodded as if he understood.

Kelley moved around the table and knelt down. "Can you give your Uncle Garrett a hug?" Brian, unsure, looked at his mom, who gave him an encouraging 'go on.' Brian ran over and gave Kelley a quick hug and then pulled away, eying the table full of sweets.

Mel sighed, "You shouldn't before lunch, but yes, you may. Take *one*." Brian dutifully took one and plopped himself on the couch.

Hugo still standing, was annoyed and hurt. "It isn't like she is even here."

"Fi. It's time to meet your relatives," Kelley said, facing the empty hallway just outside of the living room.

Fi came around the corner from the hallway. As she took in the room, she relaxed her shoulders, straightened her back, and made sure her head was up.

That's my girl, Kelley thought to himself. He gave her a quick nod and a wink of approval and encouragement.

Hugo spun around quickly, then stopped, gaping at Fi.

Even though she was just sixteen years old, the girl had presence. She had washed her face, so it wasn't as evident that she had been crying. She looked at Hugo then to Kelley, who mimed taking a deep, calming breath.

Fi did as suggested and said, "Good afternoon." She might have said more but ultimately decided against it.

Hugo, his manners forcing him to return the pleasantry in kind, said "Good afternoon. Fi, is it?"

"Yes. What would you like me to call you?" she asked him, her tone was polite enough.

He gaped at her. Once again, it seemed things were not going as Hugh thought they would. He started stammering and looked at Mel. Kelley wondered what he had expected to happen. For Fi to call him Uncle without his permission? So he could be angry at her presumption?

"And this is your cousin, Brian," Mel told Fi. Fi walked away from Hugo and sat down next to Brian saying. "Hello, Brian. I'm Fi." Brian looked at her and shyly said 'hi.'

She asked him if he liked to play games, and when he said yes, Fi asked Mel if they could go play a game. Mel agreed and suggested going outside to the backyard. Fi stood up and asked Brian if he could show her to the backyard. Brian got off the couch and taking Fi's hand, led her through the house, presumably to the backyard.

Mel and Kelley exchanged a 'how adorable' look, and then both sat down. Mel refreshed his coffee and poured herself another cup of tea.

"Hugo, please come sit down," Mel said to him.

Hugo did so, taking the chair on the other side of the table, opposite Kelly. He gave Kelley a look that suggested to Kelley that he was in Hugo's usual seat.

Kelley waited; he could see Mel was thinking. She had anticipated having more time with him and Fi before Hugo and Brian complicated things.

"I want to take Fi shopping," she said in a 'change in plan' kind of tone.

"That sounds nice; I think she would like that. And I'm sure the three of us will have a nice visit," Kelley said amicably.

"You are leaving?" Hugo's voice was strained. He was worried about being alone with Kelley.

"Yes. I wanted you to spend the day with Brian and come home to a nice dinner. I don't know why you are back so early. Brian is fine," Mel answered him.

Hugo didn't say anything. Mel got up and went towards the back of the house. Kelley followed her. She was about to call the kids inside but watched them through the window instead. Kelley stood with her and watched them, too.

"How about this? We leave the kids to play while we clean up the living room and get lunch ready?" she suggested.

Kelley said that was fine by him and asked how he could help. She told him what to do; she might never have been in the military, but she knew how to give orders. Mel still reminded him of their mother when she was in the kitchen.

It was curious to him that the memories and reminders of his parents weren't so painful now. Maybe things were changing.

Chapter Thirty-Six

After lunch, Mel and Fi left to go shopping. Hugo suddenly realized that he had 'something important' to do for work. Kelley, who was going to use a similar excuse himself, played along.

Brian was curious about his Uncle G. He snuck out of his room where he was supposed to be playing quietly to where Kelley was sitting. He asked him what he was doing.

Kelley said nothing much and asked if he wanted to play. Brian answered in the affirmative. Kelley ended up spending the rest of the day with his nephew. They played a little, but Brian was fascinated by Kelley's ability to fix stuff.

It started by Kelley showing him how to put a wheel back on one of his toys and escalated from there. To Brian, taking something that wasn't working and making it work again was better than play. Kelley wondered at the number of broken things the family had, but it did pass the time.

When Mel and Fi finally came back they found Kelley at the kitchen table with Brian on his lap, showing him the proper way to use a screwdriver.

He saw Fi and did a double take. She had gotten a haircut. "Wow," he said in admiration. "That look really suits you." She still had long hair, but it was styled and under control, making a dramatic difference to her overall look.

Fi, smiling happily, said, "Thanks, Dad." When he looked at the bag in her hand, she blushed.

"Nothing for you to see, Garrett. Just a little lingerie for my favorite niece," Mel said.

Kelley, who did not have any interest in his daughter's lingerie other than being glad *he* didn't have to buy it, changed the subject. "We've had quite the afternoon, haven't we, Brian?"

Brian said yeah and happily told Mel everything that they had fixed and how he had helped Uncle G.

"I think you have an engineer here," he told Mel.

She grinned and picked Brian up for a hug. "Are you going to be an engineer someday, my little man?" she asked him, giving him a tickle. He giggled and said, "Yeah".

Mel put him down and asked Fi, "Would you please keep an eye on your cousin? I want to talk to Garrett for a little while."

"Yes, of course. Glad to," Fi didn't hesitate in answering.

Mel said that as it was getting dark, they should go to Brian's room to play. After they left, Mel took Kelley to her office at the back of the house. Once inside, he saw that she locked the door.

He took a seat at what looked like one of the dining room chairs. He assumed the desk chair was Mel's.

She sat down in the desk chair and picked up her tablet. She opened her mouth to speak but Kelley stopped her.

"Mel, what is with the secrecy? It's not going to help things with Hugo and there is no need for it now, is there? I mean, what needed to be said or implied has been, hasn't it?"

"I know today didn't go as planned, but it still went very well, don't you think?"

Mel said, "Today was phenomenal. Better than I ever, ever thought it would be. I don't quite agree with you that everything has been said. In many ways, it's just beginning.

185

But, yes, I understand what you meant. I don't have to hide my relationship with my niece, or my brother, for that matter, from Hugo."

"I didn't like his coming home so early, especially after he promised to take Brian to meet up with his friends, which is another point of contention with us, by the way. But this is not about secrecy, it's about privacy."

"I have some items of our parents that I kept. You said a long time ago that you didn't want anything. I wondered if you wanted to look through them now?" She wasn't pressuring him; just asking.

He was silent for a time while he processed what she said.

"I do have some stuff of theirs but, sure, I'll take a look. Maybe I can find something for Fi. She would like to have something of her grandparents. Especially now that I'm looking to get us a house; we'll have somewhere to put it all."

"And while I do that, why don't you take a look at the pictures of us on the liner and see if there is anything you want?"

She took his tablet and started looking at the pictures. He got up and moved to where a table had been set up against the wall. A variety of objects were laid out. Some things he recognized, others he did not. Mel downloaded the entire file of pictures onto her tablet and came over to him.

"All of them?" he asked her. "I'm sure there are a lot you don't want." She just shrugged.

More memories; more pain, but less than before. Or maybe he was just dealing with it differently. "Hey, do you have any pictures of Mom and Dad?" he asked her suddenly.

"It's about time you asked," she said with a tone. Going over to her desk, she opened a drawer and took out a memory stick. She handed it to him saying, "There are too many to transfer by tap."

He thanked her as he put the stick in his pocket and went back to the items on the table. They talked about what was there for a while. He now appreciated her foresight about privacy.

"I'd like Dad's diploma, if that is okay." Their father had had a degree in mining engineering.

Mel, surprised said, "Sure. Are you finally thinking of getting your degree someday?"

"Actually, I have a criminology degree, sis," he told her with a bit of attitude in his tone. "Do you think they let anyone into GIS? I have all the requisites. I was in Fleet for thirteen years. I did more with my time than shoot things or get shot at. A lot more actually."

Mel made an effort to close her mouth, but immediately opened it again to say, "I am truly sorry, Garrett. I should not have made such an assumption. I never knew what you did. I didn't think you could talk about it, so I didn't ask."

He shrugged. "It's okay, I guess. I'm sorry, too. I could have made more of an effort to tell you or to even keep in touch. It's just that you and I had such different lives."

She nodded in agreement, and just said," Yes."

Looking down, he picked up a wood carving, a little larger than the size of his hand. was something their mother used to do. There were no natural growing trees on Blerreon 4, but sometimes their father, Finn, managed to find pieces while he was off on a job. He would sneak them back for Tara and she would carve the odd pieces into something beautiful.

"Can I take this, too?"

"Yes, but it's not as good as some of her other ones. I have more if you want to choose one of them as a keepsake."

"No, thanks. I like this one. I remember her talking to me while she was carving it."

Mel took it from him and wrapped it and the diploma ready for travel.

After the Battle

He looked at the remaining items on the table. Without knowing their history, they were just old things that were ready to be thrown away. He had no idea what Fi would treasure as a keepsake.

"Help me out here. Would Fi want of these things?" he asked Mel.

"No, probably not. This was more for you than for her. Well, except for this. You can give it to her after you leave here," she said, giving him a small box from her desk.

He opened it and saw a necklace. The stone was peridot and it was Mel's. Their father had given it to her and now she apparently wanted to give it to her daughter.

He closed the box and just nodded. That was a conversation for a time and a place where Mel was not present. Kelley would tell Fi the necklace came from her mother and Fi would understand. For everyone else, 'mother' would mean Emma Rayan, the mother they created for Fi. For Mel, this was too close and would probably trigger the collar. He would have to give the necklace to Fi 'from her mother' when Mel wasn't around. He was grateful Mel hadn't risked giving it to Fi herself. He again appreciated the need for privacy. Hugo would have questioned why Mel was giving that particular necklace to a new-found niece.

Kelley was suddenly very tired. It was getting late and it had been a long and very emotionally draining day. He looked at Mel and saw she was drained, too.

"One last thing, I promise. You know I appreciated your taking Fi and my side earlier, and I know your marriage is none of my business, but he is your husband. I can't help but see..."

"Stop," Mel said quietly but firmly. "Since you know so much, you should also know I understand a wife's loyalty to her husband. Garrett, what is going on between Hugo and I has been in the works for some time. What you see now isn't the beginning of our problems. It *is* making them more evident, yes but, it isn't in any way the cause." She paused for a moment then continued. "Hugo and I want different things now than we did before. We have different ways of looking at the world. If anything, Brian is the cause. We have different ideas of how he should be raised."

"Garrett, I need you to understand that whatever happens between Hugo and I, and to our marriage, it has *nothing* to do with you or Fi. And whatever happens, Brian and I will be fine. I can take care of us. You will have enough to do taking care of you and Fi. It's okay. I will be okay. Got it?"

"Okay, okay. Got it. I get it," he assured her.

Chapter Thirty-Seven

They left Mel's office and went back to the kitchen to find Hugo at the stove banging pans, an exasperated Fi sitting at the table, and a worried Brian on a chair on his knees facing backward.

"There you are. Finally! Were you ever going to feed your son his dinner?" Hugo asked Mel.

"Yes," Mel answered simply, without emotion.

Mel and Garrett looked at each other. Kelley said to Fi, "Time for us to say goodbye, if we are going to make our flight."

Fi only hesitated briefly. He was sure she didn't want to leave her Aunt and cousin, but she too had had a long day. She stood up and gave Brian a hug, saying "Goodbye, little cousin."

He squirmed, saying goodbye Fi in a sad, small voice. "Hey, it's okay. We can always talk over the vid," she assured him. Brian brightened up a little and said, "Okay."

Kelley smiled, a warm feeling in his chest. It was as if they had known each other for a long time and hadn't just met.

Fi kissed his forehead and then went straight over to Mel, past Hugo, and gave her a big hug, saying, "Goodbye, Aunt Mel."

Mel returned the hug, saying "It's not goodbye. We will see each other again. I'm your Aunt. I'm here if you ever want to talk." Mel kissed Fi on the cheek.

As they stepped apart, Kelley immediately stepped in and gave Mel a hug. "See you later, sis. Thanks for everything. I'll look into a communication portal once Fi and I know where we'll be at so we can all keep in touch."

"See you around, little man," he said to Brian. Brian stood on the chair, arms reaching up towards his Uncle G. The two hugged. Brian told him, "I had fun today." Kelley assured him that he did, too.

He turned quickly to Hugo and grabbed his hand, shaking it strongly, his other hand on Hugo's arm. "Thank you, Hugo. We had a great time. We have to do it again," he almost gushed in his fake exuberance.

Fi followed his lead, saying, "Thank you, Uncle Hugo. You have a lovely house. It was very nice to meet you."

Hugo, caught off guard and overwhelmed, stammered thank you a couple of times.

Kelley nodded at him curtly, then he and Fi gathered up their things and headed for the door. Mel followed, carrying Brian with her.

They stayed in the doorway as Kelly and Fi got into their land transport and left; everyone was waving goodbye.

As soon as they were out of sight of the house, Fi leaned back in her seat and let out a loud, relieved sigh, her chest heaving as she breathed, releasing the pent up emotions.

"I know. I feel the same, too," Kelley told her.

They drove in silence for a while until Fi asked, "Where are we going?"

"To the Port. The plan was we would spend the entire day at your Aunt Mel's, have dinner, and stay the night at a hotel. We were thinking of maybe going somewhere tomorrow morning and catching a flight sometime tomorrow afternoon.

After the Battle

As you know, plans changed. The way Hugo behaved from the beginning told us a fun, relaxed time was not going to happen."

"I appreciate you not reacting to him, by the way. That was very mature of you. You had a reason to be upset with him; I'm proud of you for being the bigger person."

She mumbled, "Thank you." "I've never thought of myself as a mistake. Is that what people think of orphans?"

Kelley adjusted his thinking quickly. Hugo had been referring to her being conceived outside of any formal agreement between the mating couple. Fi had grown up in a place where the children had been wanted very much; just not in a legal or ethical way.

"Your Uncle Hugo has a different way of thinking and of looking at things. Honestly, whatever his opinions are, he has a right to have them, just as we have a right to *our* views and opinions. You will find many people have views and opinions that are different from yours. Sometimes that is a good thing, sometimes it isn't."

She gave a tired grunt of agreement at his words of wisdom. Suddenly decisive, she said, "I think he's a giant windbag."

Kelley would have scolded her, but he had to keep himself from laughing. She went on before he got himself under control.

"I mean, we get back from shopping and he is nowhere to be seen. How rude is that? Then later, Brian and I are just playing a game, when Uncle Hugo comes in, all upset, demanding to know what we are doing. He practically yelled at us to go downstairs."

"Then, he storms through the kitchen, opening cabinet doors and slamming them closed, like he has no idea where anything is in his own kitchen. I offered to help, but he didn't like that, so I didn't say anything more. Brian tried to help; he

192

seemed to have more of a clue than *Uncle* Hugo did. I was so glad when you and Aunt Mel came back."

"I get it. As I said, you have a right to your own opinion, however, I would like you to keep in mind that he is your Aunt's husband and Brian's father. We should treat him with respect," Kelley counseled her.

"Yes, sir," she reluctantly agreed.

"Good. Thank you. Let's get to the Port and see what flights are available and if we can get something to eat. Nibiru isn't a hub; we'll have to take what we can get."

Kelley managed to get them to the Port. In the land transport, he went from tired and emotionally drained to outright exhausted. He expected the meeting between Mel and Fi to be difficult; he had prepared himself for that. He just hadn't anticipated how sticky the day had been.

Nothing went as it should have. One thing happening after another. The initial meeting, Hugo busting things up, change of plans, dramatic haircut, lingerie, playing nanny fix it with his nephew, his parents' stuff, Mel's necklace, and now a complete change of itinerary on an empty stomach. He didn't know why he was feeling like this. The day had gone really well. Maybe he just needed time to absorb it all.

Once inside the Port, he reviewed their options at a self-serve kiosk. Fi leaned in, peering at the screen, wanting to see, too. "What about that one?" she asked, pointing to a flight.

"Well, it's a flight with very limited facilities. It will be very cramped in comparison to anything you have seen so far." Though he liked the price—it was half the cost of the flight he had currently reserved—he didn't feel right about suggesting it.

"But it leaves in just two hours. And the travel time to Visnia is only four days from here. I think we can manage," she insisted.

"Okay. I'm too tired to argue." The thought of getting prone in two hours was just too tempting.

They managed to get through the Port security, find food, and get to their gate just in time. They were the last ones to board, but they made it.

He saw she was surprised looking at their quarters. It was barely big enough to be called a room. One side of the room was a wall with recessed space for their baggage and the opposite side was recessed with sleeping bunks. The wall in the middle had a very small table and two chairs. Over the table was a food dispenser. Next to the table was a door to the toilet and shower, which were very close together in the little room. She would be okay; it would be a tight fit for him.

The ship had practically no space for socializing or leisure activities. Passengers were expected to spend the trip in their quarters.

She looked around; it didn't take long. "If you put your stuff in the higher luggage berth, I can get to my stuff easier and without needing to bother you. I will take the upper sleeping bunk, if that is okay with you."

Her suggestions were perfectly logical, and he wanted the lower berth, as he suspected she already knew. He stowed their stuff and got into his berth. If he hadn't, there wouldn't have been much room for her to move around.

She pulled out a bag of toiletries and a nightshirt from her luggage and disappeared into the facilities.

A short time later, she came out to find him already asleep, clothes still on.

She stuffed her toiletries back into her luggage as quietly as possible and climbed up to her berth. It wasn't so bad. It wasn't as nice as the luxury line, but it was clean. She got comfortable and fell asleep herself.

Chapter Thirty-Eight

Kelley woke at the sound of a tablet alarm going off. "Fi, turn off your tablet," he grumbled up towards her berth.

"Um. Shouldn't we be getting up now anyway? I mean, if we are going to try and acclimate to local time?" she answered sleepily.

He looked over at the wall of his berth. As he thought, there were no controls for setting such an alarm. "How did you figure the sleep schedule?"

"I woke up a couple of hours ago and had trouble getting back to sleep. I tried to work out the math using what you showed me on the liner," she answered; the tablet suddenly appearing from above. She must have been leaning over and holding it down to him.

He took the tablet and got out of bed, mindful not to catch his head on the upper berth. He couldn't think lying down on so little sleep. He sat at the table and reviewed her calculations.

"I'm impressed. You're close; just a couple of minor points." He stood up and showed her where her formula needed revision. He went to the food dispenser and got them a couple of nutrient packs. "Here. It's goopy and doesn't taste much like anything, but this stuff will give your body what it needs to help it acclimate. We don't have as much time on this trip as we did on the liner."

She took the packet, opened it, and tried some. She made a face, but ate some more before saying, "If all goes well, this will be the last trip for a long time, won't it?"

He nodded and grunted agreement as his mouth was full. He swallowed and said, "If all goes well."

They got through the next couple of days without fighting, but it was close; the last day was decidedly tense. This time, they were the first ones off when the ship landed.

Fi's mood changed dramatically when she got her first look at Visnia. Leaving the Visnia Port in the rented land transport, she opened the window and relaxed against the seat, breathing in the planet made air.

Kelley grinned and opened all the windows. He was relaxing too, after being released from their tight quarters. He tapped the transport's center console to bring up one of the local entertainment channels at random. They listened to the music as he drove.

After a time, he said, "Okay. Let's talk. We're headed for the GIS branch office for my interview. I managed to get it moved up. We were supposed to land two days from now, if you remember. The longer the interview goes, the better, I think. What would you like to do while I'm doing that?" he asked her.

"Well, assuming you get the job, I'll have to start school in a couple of months. Right? That is what you said?" She wanted confirmation because she was not used to school having semesters. At the orphanage, they had been taught every day, year-round.

He confirmed she was correct, so she went on, "Well, we haven't figured out what level or grade, I'm in, have we?"

"No, you're right. There are still a couple of things we need to get settled," he answered, starting to catch on.

"Since we'll be at GIS, can't I take the aptitude tests today? And shouldn't I check in with Dr. Crane? He made me promise that I would tell him about the meeting with Aunt Mel."

"Do you feel ready to take the tests? You just got on the planet. It would be okay if you wanted to take a day or two to rest or study."

She shrugged. "I'm as ready as I'm going to be. I want to get them done."

He gave a little shrug himself. "Suit yourself." He contacted GIS using the voice-activated commands of the transport's communication module. He arranged for the tests and a private area for her to take them in and wait for him afterwards.

When they arrived at the GIS facility, he got out, stretched and looked around. Nice. The main building was large without being intimidating. It looked efficiently designed while being aesthetically pleasing. The campus itself was beautiful. Open space, lots of growing things, bushes, trees, and such.

Inside, Kelley identified himself to the receptionist and verified his credentials at the scanner. Fi signed in and was given a temporary visitor badge. The formalities completed, a young agent stepped forward and introduced himself, saying he was sent to escort Fi to the testing area.

After confirming the location, so he could find her later, they went their separate ways, each wishing each other good luck.

Kelley walked around the building. He was early for his interview and he wanted to get an idea of the place. The atmosphere was very relaxed compared to the military posts he had been used to. The inside was as efficient as the outside had indicated. The furnishings were not new but were well-maintained and pleasantly colored. All in all, it was kind of nice.

After the Battle

After his initial recon, he made his way to the area designated for his interview. When he got there, the door was closed. There was no door chime to request entry. He opened the door and half-entered, looking around. The room was large, laid out like a bull-pen. There were three workstations and a large monitor that covered most of the back wall. For a society that had gone paperless centuries before, this office still managed to look cluttered and disorganized. The general atmosphere of the room was busy.

There were three agents in the room. There was a human male, a female Sialia, and an Actaia. The Actaia surprised him because he or she was on land. They all looked busy. He didn't know at what. The monitor had many things on it and there was no way of knowing what they were focused on.

He gave the Agents an amiable, "Good morning." They looked at him. After a moment, he continued, "I'm Agent Kelley. I was told to report to this location to interview with Senior Agent Ibbota." Still nothing. He came in and closed the door.

He saw a chair at the corner of the Actaia's desk and the only unoccupied seat in the room. He crossed the room towards the chair, but his attention was on the monitor. He thought he saw an open communication channel icon that had been minimized.

He turned the chair to face the monitor but did not sit. He stood facing the monitor and addressed it saying, "Good afternoon. Is now a good time to meet with you, Senior Agent Ibbota?"

The monitor went black for a moment and then came back with the image of Senior Agent Ibbota. Presumably, it was Agent Ibbota. The person on the monitor matched the badge picture he had found in the GIS directory close enough; as close as anyone matches their badge image.

"Yes, Agent Kelley. Now is a good time," Ibbota said. As he didn't indicate he should sit, Kelley remained standing.

Ibbota was an older male. A cross of one or more non-human species, probably. He said, "Well, I've read your file. I also liked your line of inquiry based on the data I sent you. You've got a good way of thinking. You would fit in well around here."

Kelley acknowledged the tacit compliment but did not say anything.

Ibbota waited a moment, and then asked, "So, do you have any questions for me or the team?"

Kelley turned so that the monitor was on his right, with the team in front of him or to his left.

He nodded amicably at the agents but did not repeat his salutation.

"I have read your files and I know your names, length of service, and current position. Agent Khatin, would you tell me briefly what it is that you are currently working on?"

Khatin, Nicholas Khatin, looked startled but answered him. Kelley had to keep Khatin from straying into too much detail and his objectives were vague.

"Agent Rahla Duma, same question." He was direct, but not curt.

Duma, more prepared for having gone after Khatin, answered him more succinctly, but her list was equally long.

Agent Ahanu Qinhana did not wait to be asked. She, from the timbre of her voice, reported to him quickly and concisely. More importantly, her list was short, and her hypothesis was focused.

"Thank you, Agent Qinhana. I look forward to hearing more about your investigations," he told her. She nodded pleasantly in agreement.

"How long have you been on land?" he asked her.

"Seven Visnia days."

The answer surprised him. "Why so long? Is this a temporary assignment for you?" Actaia's were a brilliant species. They also preferred to live and work in the water. Highly analytical yet intuitive, they excelled in many professions that required more intellect than physical activity. They could, as Agent Qinhana was demonstrating, live out of water for short periods of time.

"No, I want to stay here, but my residence hasn't been cleared by security. It can't be flooded until it has been cleared," she answered.

Kelley looked at Ibbotta still on the monitor. Ibbotta merely answered, "These things take time."

Kelley attempted to keep his face neutral. He did not want to criticize his superior and possible new boss, however, Qinhana's residence clearance should have been a priority.

"What do you think of the team, Agent Kelley?" Ibbotta asked him.

"I think they are good analysts, based on the bios provided. I would limit the number of their cases and focus on fewer areas, with more defined objectives. I would also have them work together as well as individually."

"Their current skillsets appear to be adequate. I would need more time to assess before being able to provide anything further."

"Agent Ibbotta, while you are here, so to speak, would you contact Security about Agent Qinhana's clearance?" he finished.

"That is the job of her Team Leader, Agent Kelley," Ibbotta answered. "I'll leave it to you, shall I?"

Kelley was stunned for a full second, then answered. "Yes, sir. You can leave it to me."

"Excellent. I will update Interspecies Resources and you can get with them to work out the details. Good day, all."

The monitor went dark. A moment later the previous busy screen came back.

They all looked at him. "Okay, then. You two," referring to Duma and Khatin, "as you were, please. Agent Qinhana, bring up your security request."

Chapter Thirty-Nine

Kelley had never appreciated the difficulty in rehydrating an Actaia after it had been dry for over seven days.

Sorting through Agent Qinhana's residence security approvals was tiresome, though not complicated. The site visits had already been done, it was just a matter of getting various parties to sign off.

After getting the Security's approval, the next step was to flood of her residence. It was more complicated than just pumping water into the approved living quarters. The water had to be ionized and infused with nutrients. And, of course, the nutrients had to be specific to Qinhana's metabolism.

Kelley tapped a quick message to Fi as he escorted Qinhana to Medical. Fi's reply was terse; an unhappy face emoji. Unsure what that meant, he promised her he would be there as soon as he could.

He expected to leave Qinhana with the doctors to get prepped for rehydration while he arranged the flooding. He wasn't entirely sure what a rehydration entailed for the individual Actaia, but he presumed the doctors would, or at least Qinhana would; he was wrong on both counts.

The doctor in-charge was kind and professional but as Kelley watched him, it became apparent something was wrong. The doctor was hesitant and seemed to be doing research on his tablet. Kelley asked the doctor how many rehydrations had he done. The doctor admitted this was his first one but he had everything under control. Qinhana turned to him, clearly afraid. He told her to stay calm. He excused himself saying he would be back and left to find a place to make a private call.

Fortunately, Dr. Crane answered. From his expression, he was clearly irritated with Kelley.

"Agent Kelley. I really must ask you to respect some boundaries. I am not your personal therapist. I have many duties and many other patients to see to. And I have a personal life, you know," Crane said.

"Sir. Please. Please listen. One of my Actaia agents has been on land for over seven days. The medical staff here have never done a rehydration before. The doctor in-charge won't ask for help and I don't know how to go over his head. I know you are a medical doctor as well as a psychiatrist, aren't you? Could you please point me in the right direction, sir?" Kelley pleaded.

Crane's face changed from irritated to grave while Kelley spoke. "Of course. Certainly. A rehydration after so long is tricky, even if you know what you are doing. If it isn't done properly, the Agent could go into shock or experience other complications, potentially fatal." Crane started typing quickly and asked Kelley to verify the Agent's location and other particulars. Crane then told him to return to his agent and wait with her.

Kelley went back to find the doctor trying to persuade Qinhana to go with him. She was refusing and was visibly upset.

"Doctor. Stop a moment, please." Kelley was stern but not rude. "Let me talk with my agent; I'm sure I can calm things down."

The doctor hesitated but relented when he realized Kelley wasn't actually asking.

Kelley told Qinhana that reinforcements were on the way and asked her to keep calm. She agreed to sit but remained tense.

While they waited, he asked her to tell him about becoming a GIS agent and why she chose this post. Just like any new recruit, she was young and wanted to try new things. She wanted to have adventures and was full of romantic idealism. Like him, she was fresh out of training, but with none of his life experiences. She had liked the idea of being the first Actaia in this Branch of GIS but hadn't appreciated the downside of being the first.

The doctor approached, looking officious, and demanded that Qinhana come with him as he didn't have all night.

"Then you are free to go home, Doctor Fowler," a disembodied voice said. "A rehydration takes time and if you are unwilling to take the time to do the procedure properly, you are excused."

Dr. Fowler worked his jaw and glared at the nursing staff, who shook their heads in denial.

The voice continued speaking. From what Kelley understood, the doctor, Senior Medical Officer Jagadis Vad, was assuming command of the medical suite due to the medical necessity. The staff present acknowledged the transfer of authority with alacrity.

When Dr. Fowler looked like he was going to leave, Kelley suggested, "Stay. Stay and learn how to do a rehydration."

Dr. Fowler hesitated before swallowing his pride and agreeing as well.

Dr. Vad informed Kelley that the procedure would take several days and suggested that he leave. Agent Qinhana was greatly relieved. She thanked him and assured him that it was okay if he left.

Kelley told her to take all the time she needed to get acclimated, and that they would talk later. He asked Dr. Vad to please keep him informed and to notify him immediately if they needed anything. After Dr. Vad acknowledged his request, he was only too glad to leave.

He made his way back to Fi but didn't rush. His head was swimming and he felt overwhelmed in a way he hadn't felt when he was in the military. He wasn't sure why. Fleet was more dangerous in certain respects, but he had taken for granted how much had been taken care of for him—food, housing, medical care; things that now he had to take care of for himself and others.

He was unsure about being a father and Team Leader, if it meant rushing back and forth between the two and handling the non-stop issues. In Fleet, there was a lot of downtime in between missions. Here, there wasn't a clear direction of a mission to prep and execute. He had to build everything from the ground up.

That team, his team, was going to need a lot of work to get into shape. And Fi, he was almost scared to find out what had upset her in the short time they had been apart.

He stopped in a quiet part of a hallway to take several deep breaths. He closed his eyes and tried to focus. He reminded himself that leading a team was nothing new; the goals were different that was all. He also reminded himself that he got the job—the job he wanted! The pay was great, the location was great, especially for Fi. Things were going great.

Okay. He told himself he felt better. He resumed his way to Fi at a brisk pace. His tablet buzzed as it received a message. It was from Fi wondering where he was. He sighed. *I can do this*, he told himself.

Chapter Forty

Kelley found Fi curled up in a desk chair, looking upset and moody. He checked the time. It had been several hours, but it wasn't that late. "I'm back; ready to get some dinner?" His tone was deliberately light.

She shook her head. "I'm not hungry."

"Really? I'm hungry. Why aren't you?" he asked gently.

"Because I failed!" she burst out. "I'm a failure." She gestured vaguely towards her tablet. This reminded him that he had received several messages that he hadn't read.

He ignored the message from Mel and tapped on the one labeled, Assessment Results. The results surprised him, not because she failed, but because she hadn't. In fact, she excelled in math, science, technology, and literature; even outpacing her peers. He did see that she had done poorly in history, local and general, as well as civics.

"Hey! The results are great, Fi!"

She stubbornly refused to answer or even look at him.

"Fi," he stated firmly.

No response.

"Fianna Tara Kelley. Look at me, young lady," he stated in a more authoritative tone.

She turned towards him, still looking moody.

"Your results *are* great. You shouldn't let what didn't go right overshadow what did. It's an assessment. It is telling you where you need to focus. C'mon. 'The orphanage' wasn't going to teach you history. They were hardly going to give you an idea of the size or diversity of the universe, or the history of other planets that you were never going to see; certainly not their revolutions and revolts. That might give the older children ideas. And Civics. Surely you can understand why *they* were not going to teach you Confederate citizenship rights and responsibilities?"

"Yes, but what happens now? I was supposed to start school this fall." She sounded so desperate.

"I don't think this will stop you. It *may* complicate which grade to put you in. You are above average for your age in most fields of study. We could get you a tutor for history and civics to get you caught up. We can probably even work with a school counselor or someone like that and arrange for a study plan over the summer, if you would like."

"Really? You'll get me a tutor?" she said hopefully.

"Sure thing. It will be okay." He was smiling to reassure her, but also at the thought of a teenager wanting to study over the summer. "Just leave some time to meet the neighbors."

She was starting to smile at the first part, but then looked at him confused at the second.

"Meet the neighbors? Oh! We're staying? You got the job?"

When he nodded, she squealed happily and threw her arms around him for a hug, saying "I knew you would!"

"Yes, you did." He hugged her back briefly. "Are you okay, now? I really would like to get some dinner."

She just said "Sure," as she got up and collected her tablet. "The interview must have been really involved to take so long."

He gave a half shrug, "Yes and no. Let's just say a Team Lead has a lot of responsibilities. Did you give Dr. Crane an update like he wanted?"

"No. I forgot we were supposed to land later in the week. I think he was on vacation or something. He told me to call back then. He was a little short with me."

I bet he was, Kelley thought to himself. He must have called Crane not too long after she had. He felt a little better knowing why Crane had been so cranky.

They found a restaurant where they could eat and relax. During dinner, Kelley checked his tablet periodically for any updates on Agent Qinhana. Fi located a nearby residence hotel where they could stay until they found something permanent. Over dessert, they searched for places for sale in the area.

Kelley had had a variety of different residences over the years, mostly apartments and mostly on military bases. This would be his first home since leaving Blerreon 4. He wasn't sure what he wanted and was okay with Fi taking the lead, at least for a little while, but he did contact several of the local real estate agencies, too. He wanted their expertise, especially with what school districts were better than others.

He wondered if GIS had any sort of onboarding protocols. Fleet had been very good with getting the families of its soldiers settled in new locations; well, as far as he had been told. Still, he wondered if GIS had anything similar. He sent a message to IR briefly outlining his situation and what, if anything, was available.

After dinner, Fi found an open grocery store and insisted they pick up a few things. It was late, but she was all excited about his job and being able to stay on Visnia.

Chapter Forty-One

The next morning, he was up and out early for a run. When he got back to the residence hotel, Fi was in the kitchen. The smell of fresh coffee was in the air.

"Good morning. Are you into drinking coffee, Fi?" he asked her.

"Good morning!" she said brightly. "No, I made it for you. You know I like tea."

He thanked her and got himself a cup. As he did, he noted a lot of food on the counter. "What's up?"

"I'm trying to figure out how to make breakfast. I mean, a real breakfast, not just pour cereal into a bowl," she answered. "I never really got into cooking while I was at Sp... the orphanage."

He nodded. "Good catch. You'll get used to it soon enough. And I'll show you how to make breakfast, if you are okay clearing up. I want to get into the office early today."

She agreed, so he showed her how to make a simple, hot breakfast of eggs and bacon. She made him promise to show her more the next day. She was always so eager to learn everything she could.

He wanted to get himself cleaned up, but he made time to talk to her about what she could and could not do while he was at work. She could go out if she wanted to, but she had to be mindful. This wasn't the orphanage with highly secured grounds. He reminded her that not everyone was as nice as they wanted you to think.

She dutifully promised him she would be careful.

On his way to the office, he made note of the public transit options along the way. He wondered if he should get a place more outside the city and take public transport into work.

When his tablet buzzed, he tapped to put it through the transport vehicle. It was Crane.

"Good morning, Dr. Crane. I'm glad you called. I want to apologize for our bothering you while you were on vacation. Our itinerary changed unexpectedly, and we lost track of what day it was space time versus local time. We are both sorry to have intruded on your personal time."

"Thank you. I appreciate your apology." Crane paused briefly then continued, "Now it's my turn to apologize. I should not have lost my temper. I forgot how new you are to GIS and how inexperienced you are when it comes to its processes and procedures. And you certainly had a reason to call me. I hope the agent is doing well?" Crane was genuinely concerned.

"Yes, according to the last update, she is in the first phase of transition and the doctor says she is stable and doing well. Her residence was fully flooded as of 0300 this morning. They are going to start testing this morning."

Kelley saw the entrance to the Branch parking lot and started to wrap up the call. He thanked Crane for his help and promised to figure out the proper protocols as soon as possible. He didn't want to mention his new job; he didn't want to go through it all right now.

Fortunately, Crane didn't press him. Instead, Crane assured him that he would get the hang of things very soon. Also, he wanted Kelley to know that it was okay to contact him if the situation warranted it. He, Crane, trusted Kelly to know when that was. Crane signed off saying they would talk again soon.

Kelley entered the building through the main entrance and scanned his credentials at the security gate near the reception area. There was a loud ping and the scanner displayed a message for him to see the receptionist. The same message was being repeated audibly, as well.

He looked around. No one seemed upset and the guards stayed at their post. He approached the desk and identified himself to the receptionist.

She smiled pleasantly and asked him to wait; someone was coming to see him.

A few minutes later, a rather large female hybrid came over and introduced herself as Interspecies Resources Specialist Dana Hildebrand, and asked him to follow her to the training room. She started walking away before he could protest.

As they walked, she told him that normally agents go through orientation after getting out of training. She made it clear that she did not approve of him going straight out into the field. That he was managing just fine didn't seem to make a difference to her.

As they entered the training room, she continued on saying now he had been assigned a permanent post *and* put straight to work, without IR being *properly* notified and without Branch orientation. She was *very* displeased.

Kelley hung tightly on to his patience. He couldn't help but wonder if Crane had put a word in her ear. He also tried not to think Hildebrand was responsible for the Qinhana snafu. He had no basis to suppose that she did, but Specialist Hildebrand was a lot to take first thing in the morning, and her manner grated on him.

He ignored the seat she indicated when it seemed to him that she was going to start some sort of a lecture. Instead, he politely pulled out a chair for her on the side of the table, rather than the end, where he did not want her, saying, "Specialist Hildebrand, I appreciate that your time is as valuable as mine. Would you start by giving me an overview of what you would like to accomplish today, please?"

She took the seat, a bit put-off by his manner. He took the seat next to her and gave her his full attention.

"Agent Kelley, you haven't been listening. I have been trying to tell you that you haven't been through orientation."

He interrupted before she could go on, "Yes, I understand that, but how much of the orientation is available through online, self-paced training modules?"

"I was getting to that, but very well." She proceeded to list the multitude of courses that were available. He paid attention and made sure he understood which ones were required and where they could be located.

Once the baseline requirements had been established, he asked her for a *brief* overview.

"I would have done that already, if you had let me," she told him.

"In quite some detail, I'm sure. Specialist Hildebrand, I would prefer that you refrain from giving me the same lecture that you would give a raw trainee with no work experience. I have an idea of how large organizations operate. I'm sure GIS has its own protocols, but I doubt they are very different from what I'm used to. A brief overview would give me more of an orientation than an in-depth lecture with no baseline understanding," he said, his tone even and unemotional.

Agent Hildebrand's eyes widened briefly in surprise, and then narrowed as she regarded him. Without any further preamble, she launched into a concise overview; neatly and logically laying out GIS's overall structure.

He asked questions and she responded. She was intelligent, and it did not take her long to appreciate Kelley's approach. She was also very informative. Her draconian manner waned when she found him to be receptive and interested in what she was trying to teach him.

He couldn't be sure, but he felt like they had accomplished more in an hour than they would have had she lectured him for the entire morning.

He unintentionally broke their rapport when he looked at his tablet for an update on Qinhana. Agent Hildebrand coolly told him she did not take kindly to being disrespected. She snippily reminded him that he still had to read the training materials and take the self-study courses.

With no trace of apology, Kelley calmly informed her that he was monitoring the medical status of one of his agents.

Knowing he had only been assigned yesterday, she gave him a dubious look and asked for more information. He gave her a concise recap, making sure to keep his tone civil.

To her credit, Hildebrand was appalled at Agent Qinhana's situation and immediately asked how she was handling the transition. When he informed her Qinhana had successfully passed the first stage and was into the second, she breathed a sigh of relief and a prayer of thanks.

To his surprise, she apologized for IR's deplorable oversight. She assured him that this was not the way GIS at this Branch, or in general, treated its agents and she would see to it that a formal inquiry was opened to *thoroughly* review the incident.

She looked at him almost belligerently, as if she expected resistance to a formal inquiry.

He nodded curtly. "I will be available if you need me, otherwise I would appreciate being kept informed as to the results."

She, in return, nodded in agreement and looked at him with something that might have been respect.

He decided to ask, "Did you expect me to argue?"

"Yes," she answered simply. "I am usually asked if an inquiry is really necessary or told not to bother. And during the inquiry, I get very little cooperation.

"You seem to be different; if you meant what you said."

"I did. I understand the need for a formal inquiry, and I intend to cooperate fully. I will speak with Agent Qinhana, when she is able, and if it is necessary, make sure that she understands as well."

Agent Hildebrand thanked him and then suggested a brief break.

When they resumed, she reviewed the responsibilities of his new position in detail. She started to get into the differences between reporting to his immediate supervisor versus his managerial reporting responsibilities to IR. She stopped herself and gave him a brief rundown of his quarterly and annual deliverables to IR instead.

He had a few questions, including wanting to know the latitude for training his agents. Hildebrand answered him but also reminded him that it was only his second day; perhaps he should get to know his agents before suggesting improvements. He assured her he would.

She gave him the full set of forms and disclosure statements for his review and signature. They ended the morning by finalizing the details of his salary and syncing his tablet to the Branch network. As she stood up to leave, she asked him to come back after lunch to complete his onboarding.

Kelley attempted to disagree. He wanted to come back the next day so he could spend a few hours with his team. Hildebrand firmly maintained her position and told him to report to her office at 2100 hours. She might as well as said, dismissed.

After lunch, he reported to her office, wondering what they had left to go over. She took him on a tour of the Branch office and grounds, fully explaining each department as well the site's amenities such as a workout center and around the clock cafeteria.

Back in her office, she reviewed his submitted expenses from his two temporary assignments and informed him what the Branch would expect to see when he submitted the rest of his expenses to them. She reminded him to get those expenses in timely. When he asked what expenses she was referring to, she had him run through everything he spent from leaving the Pagnol system to today. He found out that he could request reimbursement for a fair amount of credits, not everything, but some travel and other expenses were covered as it was related to his permanent posting and relocation to Visnia.

He was practically twitching in the effort to contain his excitement, when Agent Hildebrand asked him about his recent IR query regarding onboarding and if she had already answered his question.

"Well, as you are probably aware, I am here with my daughter. I am anxious to get us settled into permanent quarters. I also need to get her schooling arranged. I was wondering what GIS had available to help me with any of that."

Hildebrand just stared at him. He looked back politely.

Finally, she said, "You just arrived on Visnia. Don't you want a few days to settle in and look around? You will feel the effects of a new planetary timezone very soon."

"I was in the military. I am used to new timezones and still know the best ways to acclimate to them. Which isn't to say I'm not tired, but you asked, so I thought I could at least get an idea of what is available," he replied, imperturbably.

She sighed and stifled a yawn. He hadn't realized it had been a long day for her. They had been working since early morning and it was late in the afternoon now.

"I'm sorry. You must have other duties and I have been monopolizing your time all day."

She gave a dismissive gesture, "It is quite all right, Agent Kelley. Getting new agents settled is part of my job. However, I could use a bit of a break."

"Why don't we meet in the west side of the cafeteria in about fifteen minutes?" he suggested.

Hildebrand nodded. "Yes. Excellent suggestion."

They met as arranged in the cafeteria; he had coffee and she had tea and a light snack. She was surprised that Fi had already taken her assessment exams but let it go. Kelley hoped she was getting used to him. She reviewed Fi's scores and wanted to know more about the anomalous results. Kelley politely but firmly stopped her. He assured her that the scores weren't mistakes and asked again about the local schools.

"I suppose you want me to skip the lecture about all the different schools and how wonderfully Fi would fit into any one of them, and just give you the bottom line?" she asked him, wryly.

"Please. It would save us both a lot of time and effort."

"Very well. With the understanding that this is just my opinion, which doesn't relieve you of the responsibility of doing your own research, I will."

"Of course."

"The schools in this area like to think they are unique and offer different curriculums, but truth be told, there isn't much to tell them apart. They are all accredited, fine schools. It would largely come down to what neighborhood you want to live in. However, your daughter is highly intelligent and appears to be equally motivated."

"I believe she would find most of the schools here very rigid and somewhat restrictive. Rote learning does not encourage individuality or personal growth. She would be expected to fit into *their* expectations."

She paused. He sensed a but or a however coming, so he just nodded for her to continue.

216

"However, there is one school where I think she would excel—Verbier Polytechnique. It has *very* high academic standards, and they also encourage each students' individual talents and career pursuits."

Kelley called up Verbier on his tablet. It was truly a *very* prestigious institute of education. Not only did the potential student have to meet certain academic requirements, there was also a rigorous interview process.

The happy feeling he had when he learned he was due a large sum of credits left him as he saw Verbier's tuition fees.

He decided to leave the subject of schools and ask Hildebrand about the surrounding neighborhoods. She showed him a link on the Branch website that compared the neighborhoods using a variety of metrics.

He suddenly hit a wall of fatigue at the thought of doing any more work today. He thanked Agent Hildebrand profusely for all her help and indicated he should be getting back to Fi.

She let him go after telling him to take things slow and not to burn himself out by doing too much, too soon. "Yeah. Yeah."

Chapter Forty-Two

He made it back to the hotel and dragged himself up to their rooms. Inside, he again found Fi in the kitchen. She was making something, probably dinner, by the smell. As he got closer, he could hear a voice but couldn't see anyone other than Fi.

When she saw him, she smiled and said, "Book pause." The voice stopped. "Hey, Dad, how was your first day?" Before he could answer, she went on. "You look tired. Want to try some stew? I found a recipe online that didn't look too difficult. I guess it tastes okay," she finished, sounding doubtful.

He leaned over the counter and tasted the stew from the spoon she was holding out. "Um. Not bad."

Before he could thank her for making dinner, she said, "Eh. It's okay. It doesn't taste bad, but it doesn't taste good either."

"Needs more flavor, that's all." He walked into the kitchen and washed his hands. "What have you been doing all day?"

Fi responded with a flood of information; he was only able to absorb the general gist of it all. She went for a run and then spent most of the day online. He got a full rundown on everything she looked into; from books on Civics to the nearby schools, houses, and finally dinner recipes.

He listened to her while he added more spices to the stew and stirred the pot. She continued as they set the table and started to eat. He finished two bowls in the time she took to eat one.

She was quiet as they cleaned up the kitchen. Afterwards, he sat on the couch, his head back. She joined him, sitting on the opposite end with her feet on the couch. After a minute, he roused himself and went to get his tablet.

"Are you going to work tonight?" she asked him.

"No. I mean, I do have to monitor one of my agents, but I wanted to talk to you about schools and stuff."

She gave him a doubtful look. "Do we have to? I mean, we only just got here."

"The Interspecies Resource Specialist said something similar. Why not now?" he asked her.

"You look so tired. Why do we have to do everything all at once?"

"Well, I just want to get everything settled so I can relax," he told her.

She gave him another look that he didn't understand. Fortunately, she said, "We're fine. I'm fine, you're fine. Your agent is fine. You should relax *now*."

The couch was pretty comfortable. He took off his shoes. "I suppose I could read some of my orientation material. What are you going to do?"

"I'll read some more about civics." She stood up, which seemed to him to be a contradiction, and went into the kitchen to get herself a cup of tea. When she came back, she had a mug of tea in one hand, a bottle of beer for him in the other, and a bag of cookies under her arm. She set the beer down in front of him, and the tea and cookies at the other end of the table, before getting comfortable on the other end of the couch.

After the Battle

"Hey. Share, please," he said, nodding at the cookies. She stuck a cookie in her mouth and pushed the bag down.

He settled himself and tried to concentrate on his orientation assignments. He woke up suddenly a while later. He was still on the couch, his neck stiff, and Fi was trying to put a blanket over him.

He thanked her, trying not to sound as gruff as he felt. Dammit, he should be taking care of her, not the other way around.

Chapter Forty-Three

It didn't get easier for him over the next several weeks. It was difficult adjusting to the pace of his new life when he was trying to be a father and the head of a team. Either one he was confident he could do, but juggling both was the problem. He couldn't get his team into shape and be a good Dad to Fi.

He felt hamstrung at work. On the positive side, he completed his orientation deliverables and submitted his expenses in record time. Agent Qinhana was finally immersed in her quarters and assured him she was doing well.

On the flip side, his agents were working on too many leads and working on them individually. Duma was young and took directions well. Khatin, however, was more resistant and believed he could do it all on his own. Qinhana did too, except she was close to being right. He was training them to focus on less and work together more to get better results.

As Team Lead, he received the intelligence feeds available for his assigned area of the Sector. It was a lot to go through every day. In addition to his three agents, he was also permitted to reach out to any active agent anywhere for specific intel, as needed. He liked that a lot, but at the same time, it was difficult because it was a switch for him. He had been the one on-site, running down intel for others. At GIS, he was on the receiving side. He was now the unknown stooge asking for intel from the teams that he used to think did the 'real' work.

His team was a work in progress, and he was swamped with the sheer amount of intel to absorb, but it was also stimulating. Being on this side of the ops, and finding leads and building cases was more interesting than he had anticipated.

When a lead became a fully developed case, he was required to hand it over to one of the investigative teams. That team would work with the local law enforcement or relevant agency or entity, as required. Kelley was getting into the case building, but still had a way to go with completely accepting the handoff. He felt that he should be putting in more hours at the office, however, he could not.

There was Fi to see to. She was adjusting to Visnia and her new life better than he was. He wanted to spend more time with her and didn't like leaving her alone all day.

He set up the communication portal with Mel, as promised. Inter-planetary communication had really come a long way. The fees weren't so bad as he and Mel agreed to share the expense. Kelley made sure that they each had private connections within the portal, which Mel and Fi both appreciated.

He also got his head around Verbier Polytechnique, tuition and all. When he and Fi sat down to talk about schools, he wasn't surprised that she preferred Verbier to the others. He was surprised that she was initially reluctant to admit it. Once he convinced her that Verbier was the school he wanted her to go to, she was ecstatic.

He wasn't thrilled at their protocols. There were meetings, school tours, and of course, assessment tests. *Verbier's* assessment tests; GIS's were not good enough. Kelley chafed at waiting to see if Fi was accepted. He just wanted a decision so they could get on. Fi, bless her, took it all in stride.

He couldn't bring himself to talk to Fi about anything other than her immediate future. College, fields of study, jobs, careers, none of that seemed to matter if he couldn't get her to finish her mandatory schooling.

On his days off, they went around to various neighborhoods and got acclimated to the area. They enjoyed getting out. He liked going places with her, even when she shopped for clothes. Now that they knew they were going to live on an open-air planet and not a temperature-controlled moon, it was time to get her a wider selection of things to wear.

He engaged a realtor who showed them various residences, but he couldn't decide until he knew if he had to factor in the tuition fees or not.

He complained to Crane that it was all wait, no hurry. He just wanted to get *moving*. Crane counseled patience and advised him to relax and savor each day. Kelley, new to parenting, didn't appreciate the advice.

Fi wanted to go with him on the days when he went to work early to workout in the gym. It was what she had done while they were on the liner. Conversely, he didn't want her to. He wanted more time with her, but it was not that. He needed the downtime to clear his head and prep for the day.

He suggested she get a membership at a local facility with a good selection of equipment and a variety of classes. He was relieved when Fi took the suggestion well. She located a facility near public transport and immediately signed up for kickboxing.

Crane supported his suggestion, saying it was good for Fi. It got her out of the hotel and interacting socially, independent of him.

All was good, or at least nothing was wrong, yet he was restless and irritated but he didn't know why.

Chapter Forty-Four

In their next session, Crane asked him to talk about these feelings, but Kelley was reluctant. "Why? It's no big deal. Nothing is wrong after all. It will work out *eventually*. It has to."

Crane disagreed, shaking his head. "Agent Kelly, no it does not. You are going through a transition, a pretty big one, and nothing is going to work itself out. I recommend a considered approach the same way you would have decided on a line of attack."

Kelley ignored the military reference, civilians rarely got it right, and asked, "What 'transition' am I going through?"

Crane gave him the list. "You are adjusting to life as a civilian. You are integrating yourself back into a family dynamic emotionally with Mel and Fi. And you should not underestimate the effort of cohabitating with a young daughter after years of single living."

Kelley reluctantly agreed that it was a lot. "What do you advise?"

"Can you tell me what you liked about Fleet? I mean, not just why you enlisted, but why you had stayed? What was really important to you?" Crane asked.

"Why?"

"If you can identify what exactly it was that mattered to you, it might make it easier for you to relate and find parallels in your current post. It is easier to find what you are looking for if you know what was lost."

"C'mon, doc. I'm not that lost," Kelley objected. "I don't need a deep dive into my soul. I kind of like my job; you were right, okay? It's better than the boring desk job I thought it would be."

"You have a sense of purpose here at GIS?" Crane challenged him.

The question made Kelley stop and think. He could see that comparing his current situation against what he really wanted, what he needed, was going to take time.

"Okay, I get it. I'm not sure about a sense of purpose. I can say that it's not such a bad fit. There are differences between what I did in Fleet and what I do now, but I *like* my job. I like digging in, sniffing out leads, and developing a case. It appeals to me, a different part of me, which in itself is sort of interesting. And there is less physical training." He added the last part as a weak attempt at humor.

Crane ignored his attempt, asking, "And outside of work? Do you like your family?"

"I love them. I love Mel and Fi, and Brian, too. I like being part of a family again. But, it's just…," he trailed off.

"But?" Crane prompted gently.

"BUT, I'm angry. I'm angry about what had happened to me after the explosion and the disgraceful way I was treated. I chose to retire, but it's not like I had much of a choice."

"What do I feel? Betrayed. I feel betrayed. I want to know how they could do that to me. If nothing else, I want to know more about the explosion; I want to know what happened and why." He stopped; a big, heavy ball of anger was sitting on his chest.

Crane was silent for a time before asking quietly, "What are you going to do?"

"There is nothing I can do. I know that." As he shrugged, he felt how tight his neck muscles were. "That is what I need to deal with, isn't it?"

"You aren't going to use GIS resources to find 'them'?" Crane asked, his tone even.

Surprised, he said, "No, of course not. I never thought about doing that."

"So then, how are you dealing with your anger? What is your plan?" Crane asked.

"Anger management? You think I have anger management issues? Look, I have known plenty of soldiers who had anger issues. I saw how a lot of them dealt with it by drinking, fighting, or whoring. It doesn't lead anywhere good, I know that."

"Do you think I need anger management? I mean, I don't think I'm at any boiling point, or anything like that," Kelley said.

"Good to know. And I'm glad we are at a place to able to talk about it."

Kelley frankly didn't see how talking about it helped at all. He would have preferred *doing* something, but he didn't want to argue with the doc. He was leery about being branded as 'angry' or 'argumentative.'

"Talking is doing, you know," Crane told him, as if he had heard his thoughts.

"If you say so."

"I do. How often did you tell a fellow soldier to get their head on right, for whatever reason?"

He shrugged again, "I didn't keep count. More than once."

"Any why did you tell them that?" Crane pressed.

"Because going into an op without being focused can lead to mistakes and even to getting yourself or others killed."

"Why is it any less important to get your head on straight when you are not under fire? Can't not being focused lead to mistakes in your life at any time? It's your life you want to pull off here, not just one op. It's your life and how you choose to live it that we are trying to get straight."

Kelley didn't hide his expression. "Yes, I know. I started out by saying I know my life isn't all that bad, if you recall. It's just that… Well." He stopped, unsure of what he was trying to say.

"Go on, Garrett," Crane urged.

"It is my life. And it is going pretty well, dammit. There is a lot I like about it. I know I'm just going to have to accept that I may never know what happened. It is just that it, it isn't right. Nothing is right. How can everything be going so well when everything is wrong. The explosion was wrong, the investigation was wrong." He stopped again, his throat unexpectedly tight, his hands clenched into fists.

Crane nodded. "It's hard. Letting go of the anger won't make the past right, but it just may help getting things right with your life now."

"I want to, sounds nice and all, but I don't know if I can let it go."

"Start small. I am only asking you to work on dealing with your anger, and not the need to find out what happened."

"There is a difference?"

"Yes," Crane said simply.

"How?"

"I will help you."

Chapter Forty-Five

Such a small decision took an incredible amount of work to pull off. In his opinion, it was counter-intuitive to bring his anger to the front instead of pushing it down or ignoring it. But with Crane's guidance, bringing it forward and addressing it did seem to make it less—like chipping away at a mountain. But Crane was pleased with his progress and that was enough for him, for now.

Kelley was surprised by the events of the next few weeks. Things started to fall into place. His team started to gel and Fi was accepted into Verbier. She was even placed a year ahead for a girl her age.

He didn't believe his decision had anything to do with those events, but he was living his life better. He was more relaxed; it was possible his team was responding to that. Fi had gotten herself into Verbier, though he had aced his interview with them.

He and Fi found a place to live that they both liked. He was relieved to be out of the hotel and finally settled into permanent quarters. Okay, maybe seeing things differently played a part, he admitted privately. He had liked the place previously, but he had been daunted by the amount of work that it needed.

From the outset, they both liked the neighborhood. It was nice without being ritzy or too upscale for their tastes or credit limit. The area had a nice mix of retail stores, eateries, and residential units. Public transport was within walking distance from almost everywhere. There was urban development with a decided bucolic accent and Fi had taken to it immediately.

Kelley gave Fi the option of a house with a yard, like Mel's, but she had preferred to be in the middle of the city. This suited Kelley; having grown up on a moon without natural greenery, having a yard to take care of now did not appeal to him.

He wanted something to own, not rent. He was paying for storage on the stuff that had arrived via transport and he was only going to move all one final time.

Where they ended up was perfect. The building was beautiful with a lot of interesting architectural details. It was crescent-shaped with three sections; the left and right sections each had their own entrances and were like any other apartment building with multiple units per floor. The middle section had one single-level unit per floor. These were also crescent-shaped, with the main living area/kitchen in the center and bedrooms on either side. The front midpoint of the crescent was the elevator shaft that opened into a small foyer before the main doors of the unit. Guests would need permission before the elevator would take them to a specific floor.

The midsection of the crescent was the heart of the unit with the kitchen in the center and the living and dining rooms on either side. The design was very specious, though with little natural light except from the skylights. The two bedrooms each had windows on the side facing the street. The master suite had a private full bath and a walk-in closet. The second full bath was accessible from the second bedroom as well as the main living area. Both bedrooms were generous in size.

After the Battle

Normally, Kelley, a first-time home buyer, would have found it difficult to manage both tuition and the mortgage on such a unit, however, the owner was unable to find a buyer. There was a fire in the unit and though the fire suppression safety features engaged, there was significant damage. Repair bots were expensive, and possibly more than the unit was worth. The owner was off-world and just wanted out.

Kelley grew up in a family where they did their own work without bots; he could do the repairs. The renovations were limited to the main living area so both bedrooms were habitable. It seemed like a great opportunity.

He talked it over with Fi. He made sure she understood what they would be getting into. The renovation would take several weeks at least, as repairs could only be done after he got home or on his days off. He wasn't surprised when Fi said to buy it. That girl was game for anything.

Game or not, Kelley did not want her home all day, all by herself in such an environment. He asked if she would consider getting a part-time job. He said that it would give her an opportunity to get out and meet people, and whatever she earned would be hers to spend as she pleased. She agreed, if he would agree to let her study at night.

After being accepted at Verbier, they had met with a counselor who gave Fi a study plan to bolster her weaker academic areas. Knowing her commitment to her academics, Kelley solemnly agreed to her condition.

Chapter Forty-Six

The rest of the summer passed in a pleasant blur with no drama to mark the days. They were always busy between his work, her work, renovations, studying, and settling in, but it was interesting, challenging, and sometimes plain fun.

The first thing he did after closing on their new place was to paint Fi's room. While the paint was drying, he took her to lunch and had her choose bedroom furniture. He was used to living out of boxes, but he wanted better for his daughter.

It took them a while to settle in, but a more relaxed Kelley was able to be content with the progress. Every day saw a little more get done, a box got unpacked or a wall sanded smooth; it was fine.

Decorating was new to him; he hadn't anticipated the level of detail he was expected to care about. He wasn't sure how much of it was Mel and how much was Fi, but he was certain they were collaborating. He didn't argue; Fi was happy and the place looked great.

Late in the fall, they were in the living room after dinner, when the wall panel beeped, telling them they had a visitor in the lobby.

Kelley was surprised to see Dr. Crane's face on the monitor. Crane had not told him of the visit. Kelley tapped accept, got up, and walked to the door.

Fi, barely looking up from her tablet, asked, "Who is it?"

Kelley didn't reply, he just opened the door. "Dr. Crane, what a surprise." His tone didn't sound surprised. "Come in, please."

Crane entered, looking around, and said, "Thank you. Very nice place you have here." He saw Fi and said, "Hello, Fi! How are you?"

Fi was wary. "Um. Fine, thank you." She looked at Kelley.

He gave a little shrug in return. "No, I didn't know he was coming." To Crane, "But you are welcome, nonetheless. Can I get you anything to drink? Coffee? Tea?"

Crane, glancing at Kelley's coffee mug on the table, said, "Coffee? If you have any left?"

Kelley nodded and poured him a cup. Crane declined any additives and sipped at it as Kelley showed him around.

When Kelley asked Fi to show Dr. Crane her room, she looked nervous and said, "I wasn't expecting visitors."

The room wasn't pristine, but it was close, so Kelley didn't understand her reluctance. He had been in group quarters a good part of his life and didn't see the fuss. Crane was more compassionate of a young woman's feeling of privacy and didn't enter the room; he just looked around briefly.

Kelley invited Crane to sit down. As he did, Fi asked him, "What's going on?" Her tone wasn't hostile; just direct.

Crane glanced at Kelley, who answered, "I think it's called a site visit. Dr. Crane is checking in with us to make sure we are okay."

"To make sure *we* are okay?" she repeated dubiously.

"It's all right, Fi. What if we weren't and didn't tell them? They have to verify. What if I was hurting you? Would you know where to go to get help?"

"You would never hurt me," she immediately stated protectively.

"You're right, I wouldn't; but you have also just told Dr. Crane, you probably wouldn't tell him if I was or even if I was just doing a lousy job of parenting. More the reason for him to come and check things out for himself."

He turned to Crane, "Fi or me, first?"

"Fi," Crane answered simply.

Kelley picked up his tablet as he got to his feet. "Fi, really, it's okay. Talk with Dr. Crane. Be nice. Be honest. I'll be in my room until you need me." He went into his room and closed the door.

About an hour later, there was a knock on his door. Kelley called out an amiable, "It's open."

Crane opened the door and stood on the threshold. Kelley got up from his desk, asking "Is it my turn?"

Crane gave him a wry smile and gestured for Kelley to proceed him into the main room. Fi was on the couch, looking more interested than nervous.

"Fi, please go to your room. We need to be able to talk in private." Kelley told her.

She got up, looking like she was going to say something, until she caught the stern look on his face. She went to her room and quietly shut the door.

"Would you like anything else to drink before we get started?" Kelley asked Crane. Seeing Crane hesitate, he added, "Or eat? Have you eaten since arriving on Visnia?"

When Crane admitted he had not, Kelley went to the kitchen. Crane sat at the table and the two talked while Kelley cooked, and then while Crane ate. For a check-up interview the atmosphere was very relaxed.

When Crane finished both his food and his questions, Kelley said, "Look, I know you can't speak about what you and Fi talked, but is there anything you can say that I should know?"

"Like what? Is there something you are expecting me to tell you?" Crane answered.

"Well, overall I think she's fine. She doesn't get out much though. She should be spending more time with kids her own age. I suppose starting school will help with that."

Crane nodded. "Getting a job helped, too, but there is no need to rush or push her. She has been through a lot, it's okay to let her take her time."

Kelley just nodded before getting up to finish clearing the dishes.

Crane waited a short while before asking, "So are you ready for her to be more social and to start dating?"

Kelley gave an automatic, "Sure." Then followed it up with, "Maybe. Yes." Crane just watched him and didn't say anything.

"I am okay with her dating. Mostly. I hadn't really thought about it. Is that normal?"

"Perfectly normal for a father. What about you? Are you ready to start dating?"

"Me? I'm fine. I'm fine in that area, thanks." Kelley shrugged off the question.

"I'm not talking about getting yourself taken care of sexually. I mean, dating as in a relationship with someone—a long-term relationship."

"I can see you haven't given it much thought," Crane continued at seeing the derisive look on Kelley's face. "Whatever your reasons were in the past for not pursuing a relationship, perhaps you should reconsider them now. Your circumstances have changed. You have a permanent assignment here and you just told me you plan to stay for the foreseeable future."

Kelley looked to see if Fi's bedroom door was still closed, and then he answered honestly, "But I like the way things are now. Why should I change if it's working for me?"

"Have you given any thought as to why you choose not to have long-term relationships?" Crane asked.

Kelley groaned and stopped himself from rolling his eyes. Not more introspection; he thought he was done with all that.

"I like just having fun. I like not caring. I mean, I'm nice; I'm not an ass or anything like that."

"I understand. From what I have been told, you can be quite charming." Crane tried to reassure him but failed. Kelley wasn't sure what disturbed him more, that Crane called him charming or that he had checked up on him to that extent.

"I've taken your advice or at least tried to take your advice so far, Doc, because it was for Fi, but I don't know about this."

Crane regarded him, "You are saying you care more for Fi than you do for your own wellbeing?"

Kelley ignored the implication and said, "Yes, because my being is well enough, thanks."

"Well enough? So, you agree you have been holding back?" Crane continued before Kelley could respond, "And examining yourself in this area would be for Fi. She will learn from your behavior. Is your current dating dynamic something you would want Fi to emulate?"

The question hit him like a punch to his gut. That was a clear 'no' without reservation.

He groaned again, this time in resignation. "I will put some thought into it," he promised Crane.

"Good. I'm sure it won't be as hard as you make out. What about your sister? She has been married for over ten years, hasn't she? Perhaps she can help as well."

Ah. He didn't want to tell Mel's secrets, even to Crane. "She might not be the best role model in this particular area. She…" He paused, trying to think how to put it. "She may be more closed off than I am," he said finally.

Crane was surprised but only said, "I see." He didn't ask Kelley for more details.

After the Battle

The two talked a while longer. Crane finished by giving Kelley specific questions to ask himself. Then, he asked for Fi to come back in the room.

Crane wound down the interview by asking if either of them had any questions. They both said no. Seeing that Fi was trying to hide a yawn, Crane decided it was time to go. They ended the evening with Kelley thanking Crane for coming and Crane thanking him for dinner. When everyone was sufficiently thanked, Crane left.

Chapter Forty-Seven

Kelley thought about what Crane said over the next several days, but he still had reservations.

One night, he and Fi had a video chat with Brian and Mel to wish Brian a happy ninth birthday and watch him open the presents they had sent. Brian was very happy with his gifts and dutifully said thank you after Mel gently reminded him.

The four talked for a while, and then Brian excused himself to go play with his new toys. The three of them continued talking, mostly about Fi starting school. Everyone was relaxed and enjoying catching up.

Hugo was abruptly heard in the background, complaining about Kelley's gift of a set of age-inappropriate tools. Hugo's voice was faint, but they could make out that he was sneering about manual labor and threatening to throw the tools away. Brian howled in protest, not his present from Uncle G!

Mel excused herself quickly, flicking the privacy lock on as she left. Their screen went dark and the sound was off.

Fi rolled her eyes and said, "Why does she stay with such a windbag?"

"I don't know," Kelley answered, shaking his head. He had his suspicions but said, "It's Mel's decision though."

When Mel came back, she found Fi and Kelley drinking tea and eating a snack. "So, where were we?" she asked them.

"You were reminding me to have fun in school and not to work too hard," Fi answered. "I have to go now, though. I have to study. Love you, Aunt Mel. Bye!" Fi got up and went to her room.

"Love you, too!" Mel called out before looking back to Kelley. "So, did she hear me or not?"

He laughed. "To her it isn't work." He stopped talking and just looked at her. She returned his gaze steadily, almost daring him to bring up Hugo.

"Can you go somewhere private, sis? I want to talk to you about a session I had with Crane."

Mel arched her eyebrows in surprise but agreed. The image bounced as she went into her office.

After she was seated, Kelley told her about Crane's latest suggestion for him to think about serious dating. He also gave her a brief rundown of the reasons why he didn't feel the need to change the status quo. When he was done, he sat back and waited for her to comment.

And comment she did. As expected, she was all for him to reflect and do some really deep soul searching. She expounded at length about how he was only scratching the surface of his emotional depth and how much he had to offer if he would just open himself up to the possibility. There was so much he was missing, etc. There was more but he was having a hard time taking in all her sage advice.

Finally, she stopped talking. Her face told him she was prepared to attack whatever argument he came up with. However, he didn't argue.

"I will, if you will."

Mel's jaw dropped in shock. He continued, "Everything you told me applies to you just as much as it does to me."

"I get it. You had reasons for marrying him. Good reasons, I'm sure. Reasons that are none of my business. Just like I have my reasons for running around like I do."

"It works for us. No harm, no foul, why change?"

He paused, trying to gauge her reaction but her face might as well have been made of stone. He checked to see if their connection was still intact.

"I'm just saying that neither of us is wrong. And we are both fine. I just think it's time for us to do better," he ended quietly. He gave her a similar look to the one she had given him, like he would attack any argument she presented.

First, she swore at him, venting some of her frustration. He didn't react; just waited. She got up and paced; he could see her moving around her office from time to time as she moved in and out of his field of vision.

Finally, she sat down with a thump and glared at him. He knew what she was feeling.

"What do you tell your patients when they have to deal with stuff?" he asked her.

Mel was surprised but didn't say anything; she just looked at him warily. He continued "I mean it. I don't like introspection. It's tedious. It takes a lot of work to move an inch. It's slow. Moving through mud is faster and more fun."

"I know I'm going to do this and I'm asking you, Dr. Turner, do you have any suggestion for me, to make it easier?"

She considered his question. "Well, I'm not sure what I tell them. I will say that it's not going to be the same platitudes after today," she replied drolly.

"It's going to be difficult for me because of Brian. It's going to be difficult for Brian," she said.

"Dr. Crane told me that I should change my behavior so Fi doesn't pick up my bad habits. Does any of that emulating stuff apply to you and Brian?"

She nodded. "Ultimately, eventually, yes. Though I would rather not discuss it in detail with you right now," she told him.

"Hey, I understand. You know I do." He paused, then said, "Before when you said all that stuff about why I should do all that soul ripping introspection, was it because you thought I would be better for it? Happier?"

"*Yes*. I truly think you would be a happier person." Mel was very much in earnest.

"I'm willing to try. You and Crane have been right so far. And I really don't want to think of Fi behaving like that."

"But you need to know that I truly believe you would be happier, too. I remember you before I left B4; you had a spark then that you don't have now. We both know why. I lost my light, too. I see that same light, that spark of life in Fi, just like you probably see in Brian. I just can't help but want you to get yours back."

"You know, some days I feel like I'm getting mine back. If I can, I *know* you can, too. You know what I mean?" He felt awkward talking like this to his sister and worried he wasn't making much sense.

Mel sniffed and wiped her eyes, her nose red as she tried not to cry. She nodded and cleared her throat. "Yes, I understand." She paused and wiped her eyes again. "Hell, I'm game if you are." She gave him a wry, half-smile.

He smiled back, his own eyes watering up. "Love you."

"Love you, too." They ended the call at that.

Chapter Forty-Eight

"School dance? You just started school, how can you be having a dance so soon?" Kelley demanded of Fi.

"It's mid-term already. And why not? You are always telling me I should be more social," she replied.

"Yes, I am. And I agree that dance is fun, but this isn't just a dance. It's a formal, *cotillion* kind of dance."

Fi started to explain the history behind the gala's timing and the alignment of cultures and seasonal dates, but he stopped her. He decided he didn't really need to know the *why* to deal with it.

Things had been going well, so well that fate had decided that they should celebrate with a ball and that he, Kelley, should be chosen by the parents of Fi's friends to take the girls dress shopping. He was scrupulous at being at all the school's various meetings, but he missed the one where he was nominated as chauffer to a gaggle of teenage girls. Women. Teenage women, he corrected himself.

He pulled himself together. "Okay, let's make a plan. Give me the particulars. Go."

He made her give him all the details, how many girls, how many shops, their objectives, the whole deal. He also contacted each of the parents and checked in with each of them, where he learned that the objective was different for each girl.

After the Battle

Tami could buy a dress only if it was within a certain credit limit. Patrice could only look and hold a dress, but she could not buy without her mother's approval. Dridel's father said she also could buy a dress only if it wasn't too suggestive.

Kelley then contacted each of the shops to verify their operating hours. He was informed that they preferred appointments. They could come in without an appointment but they would have to fend for themselves, and the staff would be focused on the clients that had made an appointment.

He worked with Fi to set up a chart of their appointments. He initially wanted to canvas eight different shops over two days, however, Fi convinced him that four shops were enough, if they could go to all of them before they made their choice. So, he suggested making appointments at four shops twice over two days. They would see everything on day one and go back and make a choice on day two.

The shops, or boutiques, were very accommodating. They appreciated his effort and even advised him to remind the girls to bring shoes similar to the ones they would be wearing and to also be wearing appropriate foundation. He let Fi pass along the foundation tip to her friends.

The first day went well. Kelley stayed in the background and let the girls work with the boutique staff. The staff was very attentive and presented them with many choices and offered helpful suggestions. He saw other customers impatiently trying to get their attention. He suggested to the girls that they should ask that their top favorites be held for just one day. The boutiques agreed for one day only, and if the dress wasn't purchased it went back out for general sale.

At the end of the day, he took Fi out to dinner after taking her friends home. He was tired and didn't feel like cooking. Fi must have been just as tired but was still talking excitedly. She was impressed that he had taken notes and knew which dress was from which boutique.

He was finishing his second beer, when Fi turned suddenly, saying, "Isn't that Agent Sof...ow!" Fi yelped in pain as Kelley pinched her. He gave her a stern look, shaking his head no.

He whispered a firm, 'stay here' to Fi, as he got up and went over to Agent Sofia Deleon, who was seated at a nearby table, having dinner with a companion. He expressed surprise at seeing her again, apologized for intruding during their meal, and asked how she was doing. After she amicably replied, he asked if she would like to be introduced to his daughter.

Deleon was taking the interruption well and seemed to understand his tacit request. She got up and came with him to his table, where he made it a point to introduce Fi, his daughter, to Agent Deleon, whom she had never previously met. Fi got it and played along, though she did make a point of rubbing her arm where he had pinched her.

Apparently, Agent Deleon was on Visnia on temporary assignment and would be at the Branch for several months. She went back to her table after telling Kelley that she was happy to have run into him and that she hoped to see him again.

Kelley, relieved that the impromptu meeting was over, paid their bill. He intended to go home and get into bed. He wanted some rack time before the dress hunt continued early the next day. Fi, however, was now talking excitedly about meeting Agent Deleon and asking him if he didn't agree how nice she looked.

He didn't get her line of thought until she asked him if he was going to ask Agent Sofia out on a date. He managed to avoid the question by saying he would have to check GIS's policies on Agent fraternization.

Chapter Forty-Nine

Kelley started the next day by taking the girls to breakfast. He had them talk about which dresses they liked and reminded them that the dresses they put on hold yesterday would be released this afternoon. His notes from the day before and the direction from their parents came in handy in getting them to narrow down their choices.

Tami bought her dress at the first shop. She was thrilled they had gone early enough to find a dress she *adored* that was still available in her size and within her price limit.

Patrice convinced each of the four boutiques to hold one dress each for an additional day so her mother could review them. Kelley was impressed at her negotiation skills.

Dridel had to be convinced to not buy a particularly low-cut gown. Kelley advised her that while she could buy it, she would most likely be told to return it, and by then, her second favorite might be gone. The boutique assistant came to his aid and told Dridel that the more conservative gown allowed her more freedom of movement and she would be less likely to fall out of it. She also said that accessories would go a long way to spicing up her overall look. Kelley didn't need to hear talk about falling out of anywhere, but he appreciated the assist.

Fi was torn between two stunning gowns, each beautiful in completely different ways. The white dress was elegant; she wasn't just beautiful in it, she was breathtaking. The red one was just as beautiful, and it was more fun, sassy without being trampy. She decided to go with the red one.

Now that the major purchases were completed, the girls went off by themselves to shop for accessories. Kelley was grateful for the respite. The four of them had talked non-stop for almost two days.

He went to a nearby bistro for a snack. While eating, the girls' conversations kept buzzing around his brain until a thought occurred to him. He turned it over in his head several times and told himself he was being foolish. No good; the thought stayed put. He finished up and went back to the dress shop to purchase the white dress.

Chapter Fifty

The evening of the gala arrived. Fi was more excited than nervous. She had her hair and nails done, and now, stepping out of her bedroom, she looked amazing; decidedly beautiful and with the confidence of someone who was ready to take on the world.

This gala was very different from the school dances Kelley remembered on Blerreon 4. For whatever reason, Verbier Polytechnique was hosting a cross between a coming-out ball and a school-wide mixer where parents were expected to attend. It was *the* social event of the season for school kids and their parents. Kelley was so glad Fi's tuition was being put to good use.

Whatever. It was, what it was. Fi hadn't let him slack off on getting his own attire for the evening. He hadn't put so much care into getting dressed since the last time he put on his dress uniform. The tuxedo fit fine, though he still felt strange. He wasn't dreading the evening; it was probably going to be a good time; he just had a nagging feeling that made him tense.

They arrived at the hotel where it was difficult not to get swept up in all the excitement. The hotel was lavishly beautiful and elegantly decorated for the event.

The evening's events started with a cocktail meet and greet, followed by a formal sit-down dinner, and finished with dancing in the grand ballroom.

Fi was radiant. Kelley would have felt compelled to give the evening his best shot just to make her happy, however, it didn't take much effort for him to get into the ambiance of it all. It was easy to socialize and chat with Fi's friends and their parents. Fi also made sure they joined the queue to get professional pictures taken of them separately and together. He was having a good time but had nothing stronger than soda water to drink.

Kelley was on alert; he couldn't help it. The thought he had the day they bought Fi's dress was still there. Because he was watching for anything unusual, he did see a girl glare maliciously at Fi. She eyed Fi up and down, like she hated her, before turning and walking away. He noted her dress and hair color, so he could ask Fi about her, but didn't get the chance for a quiet word before the hotel staff announced the dining room was open.

The dinner went well. They were seated with Fi's friends and their parents. Everyone got along and the conversation was light and relaxed. The other parents made it a point to thank Kelley for taking the girls dress shopping and raised a glass to him in gratitude. The food was delicious without being overly rich. He allowed himself wine with dinner. He kept a discreet watch but did not see the girl who glared at Fi anywhere nearby.

After dinner was over, the ladies excused themselves to freshen up. Kelley and the other gentlemen waited for them at the entrance to the ballroom. The facilities were located down a hallway, to the right of the ballroom entrance. Kelley had a good view down the hallway but wasn't close enough when he caught sight of the girl again.

She was moving towards Fi with a large glass in her hand. Kelley couldn't shout without attracting the attention of everyone moving into the ballroom. He interrupted Dridel's father, saying "Watch." They all turned to look and saw the

247

girl deliberately walk into Fi and pour the glass of dark liquid down her front, from shoulder to thigh.

There was an immediate scene. The girls were angry, and the mothers were torn between their own anger and trying to control their daughters. When Kelley got there, he heard the girl protest that it had been an accident, in a prove-it tone of voice.

The mothers hadn't seen it coming, so they couldn't be sure it wasn't. They were upset, but they wanted to see what they could do to help Fi. The long, ugly stain down the length of her dress was obvious. The rest of the men caught up and tried to intervene. The arguing flared up again as they stated they had seen her do it deliberately.

Kelley stared hard at the girl and told her that they would be taking this matter to the headmistress, in a tone that cut through the commotion. They all turned to him, gaping mutely. Kelley continued in a quietly authoritative tone and told them that he and Fi would join them in the ballroom shortly. They continued to gape as he took Fi by arm and led her away. She was shaking as she followed him. He glanced over at her to see how she was doing while they walked; she was still angry and looked like she might start to cry.

"Don't cry. It will be all right. Just don't cry," he told her, as he urged her to move faster as they got away from the general crowd.

"Why not?" she snapped angrily, gesturing to her dress.

"Because Fortune favors the Kelley who is prepared," he told her evenly. They reached the front desk of the hotel, where he presented a claim check ticket and asked that his parcel be retrieved at once.

Fi stared at him. At least she wasn't crying.

Fortunately, the front desk staff person quickly came back with a garment bag and handed it to Kelley. Kelley handed it to Fi saying, "I'll explain later. Just go. Clean yourself up and get dressed. This evening is still yours, just take it."

Fi considered her options, head down, while taking deep breaths. She sniffed, making Kelley wonder if she could do it. When she looked up, her eyes were glistening with tears but she kind of shook herself, sniffed again, and seemed to pull herself together.

"I love you," is all she managed to choke out.

"I love you, too. Now get going. Show them what you are made of. I'll see you in the ballroom, okay?"

She nodded once and hurried off to the facilities near the front desk.

He walked quickly back to the ballroom where he took a moment to gather the scene. He noted that the other parents were in conference with the headmistress. He didn't go over to them; instead, he looked for one of the professional photographers. He found one who was packing up his equipment; the rest had already departed. Kelley had a quiet discussion with him and discreetly passed him a few credits.

A few minutes later, Fi entered the ballroom. She had pulled her hair down and styled it to better suit the dress she was now wearing. She had removed some of the jewelry that had accented the red dress in favor of a more simple, elegant look. She was wearing her mother's pendant, which looked lovely with the white dress.

Head up, shoulders back, she strode into the ballroom like a princess. He went over and gallantly offered her his arm. She accepted with a sweet smile, eyes radiant. He led her straight to the dance floor. He wanted her seen, so he was a bit flashy and even twirled her once or twice. As the dress flared out, she seemed to relax and get back into the spirit of the evening.

When the music ended, he told her to go find her friends and have a good time. She just nodded. She didn't get too far before she was asked to dance. He kept going.

The headmistress was still in conversation with the parents. He thanked them for their help and encouraged them to go find their daughters and to enjoy the evening. As they walked away, Kelley and the headmistress moved off in the opposite direction, talking quietly.

The headmistress had seen Fi's entrance. It was certainly hard to miss. They agreed that there didn't need to be a scene here tonight. The girl didn't actually break any rules and the event didn't happen on school grounds. The headmistress thought the act was deplorable, but at the same time, was uncertain what disciplinary actions could be levied against her.

Kelley suggested to the headmistress that he give her the stained dress and that she should give it to the girl's parents, explain what had happened, and say that they would be responsible for getting it cleaned or replaced. The headmistress agreed. Then she surprised him by asking him to dance. He, in turn, agreed.

Kelley was very relieved that the rest of the evening passed uneventfully. Now that he wasn't on high alert, he enjoyed himself even more than before. And from what he could tell, so did Fi. They even stepped out to have their pictures taken again with the new dress. Kelley had felt it important to capture the second dress in pictures. He made a mental note to make sure Mel got a copy of Fi in the dress with the necklace, especially since it was Mel who had told him to put it in the garment bag.

It was very late by the time they left. Neither spoke much on the way home and both went straight to bed when they got there.

Chapter Fifty-One

The next morning, Kelley got up late and still was awake before Fi, which was unusual. He was feeling pretty good and decided to go for a run. When he got back, he found Fi awake, but still in her pajamas. He gave her a cheery good morning. She returned the good morning, which turned into a yawn.

"Quite an evening, huh?" he asked her.

"Yes! I'm looking at some of the pictures now."

He just nodded and started to make breakfast.

"So, how did you know Angelic was going to ruin my dress?"

He shrugged. "I didn't. It just seemed to be a likely outcome from the data presented to me."

"I listened to you four talking for two days. It wasn't just about finding a dress; I heard there was a lot of *competition* to find the best dress."

"I also heard Tami say while you were buying the red dress that she thought you beat one of the other girls to it. Dridel mentioned how jealous and mean Angelic had been in grade school."

"Patrice asked if you all had heard about the school project that had taken first place over Angelic's team and how it had been broken, but nobody knew who had done it."

"Therefore, it seemed likely that she would try something. I hoped she wouldn't, but you were more than fabulous in that dress. You stood out and attracted a lot of attention, the attention I think Angelic was used to getting."

When he finished, Fi looked at him in awe. "You really are a good analyst to come to that conclusion from what you heard."

"Call it a hunch. Nothing more than that, really."

"But you had another dress there. And even with matching shoes!"

"Your Aunt Mel helped me with that stuff. But you know, it was you who had to pull it together. You had to get past a moment when you had every right to be upset and angry. You had to get yourself cleaned up and dressed all over again. Not only did you do it, but you also did it in less than ten minutes. *That* was impressive."

Fi shrugged. "As you said, I could cry over a ruined dress and lose the evening, or I could get into a new dress and get back in there. It seemed like an easy choice."

"Adapting isn't easy, you know. It's a skill that not everyone learns. You would be surprised how many get stuck and don't move on to a new dress, or whatever, and don't get back in there," he told her.

"Is this like some sort of a life metaphor, then?"

He gave a light chuckle, "I don't think I'm that deep a person. I'm just really glad that you didn't let that girl ruin the night. It was too good an evening to let get away."

"It was the best time ever! Take a look at these pictures." She eagerly took him through a slew of pictures the kids had taken and shared with each other.

"You know, you looked like you were having a pretty good time, too," she said in a tone that made him wonder what was coming next.

He had been watching out for Fi; not her classmates. He looked again at the pictures and only saw himself dancing or talking with various people; nothing bad or embarrassing.

"Yes, I had a good time," he admitted, a little warily. She nodded like she had gotten him to agree to some important point. "When you get a chance, please transfer me copies of the pictures, okay?"

As she did, she asked him, "So, does that mean you are going to ask Agent Sofia out on a date?"

He blinked. It took him a moment to process her leaps in reasoning. "Deleon isn't interested in me," he protested.

"*Sofia* is very much into you and was even on Tycor," she argued.

Part of Kelley hoped not because that would have been a breach of GIS protocols for a Team Lead to get personally involved with one her underlings. Another part of him said she hadn't and reminded him that they were more or less peers now. "Okay," he told Fi, "I will ask her out."

Fi squealed happily and hugged him like he had done something amazing.

She looked up at him and said, "Thank you for everything. You are such a great dad, Dad."

"Ah, you make it easy; you are an amazing daughter." He felt that came out awkwardly. "I love you, Fi."

She hugged him again and said, "I love you, too." She smiled as she scurried off to her room.

Awkward or not, he felt all warm and fuzzy. Then, he realized she left him with all the breakfast dishes. "Get back here!"

Chapter Fifty-Two

"I don't know why everyone makes such a big thing about dating," Kelley told Dr. Crane.

"I gather things are going well with Agent Deleon."

"I think so. It's been about a month since we started seeing each other. Fi is fine, Sofia is fine, I'm fine."

Crane noted that Kelley didn't mention his sister but he let it go and asked, "Do you two have many things in common?"

"I suppose so. Or are you asking if we go out or just stay in her bedroom all the time?"

"Yes. You mentioned previously that you didn't take my advice to wait on the physical side of the relationship."

Kelley shrugged. "I would have, but she didn't want to. I don't think she likes to wait on anything, but yes, we go out occasionally."

"Do you talk, I mean, do you really connect with her as a person?" Crane pressed.

Silence.

Crane elected to wait him out and assumed a patient expression.

"We do talk. Just not about everything." Kelley sounded mildly defensive.

"What can't you talk about? Politics? Work? Kids?" Crane probed.

Kelley squirmed. "It's not like that. There aren't taboo topics in general. It is just one case. She is working on a case apart from her assigned workload and she won't talk about it. In fact, she is very careful to not let me know anything about it."

"Does this bother you?" Crane kept probing.

"I don't know why, but yes. It's not like I don't have clearance. In fact, I have a higher level of clearance than she does. Why do I care? I don't expect her to tell me everything. I don't want her to tell me *everything*. We really haven't known each other that long. I haven't told her everything either." Kelley was defensive and now he was rationalizing.

"Does she ask?"

"No."

Ah. "Are you in love with her?" Crane asked, his tone even.

"No. I don't know why. I should be falling for her. She is everything someone could want in a partner. Smart, funny, good-looking, fun to be with..." Kelley's voice trailed off like that wasn't the rest of the sentence. Crane did not press that particular point.

"I mean, I care." Kelley continued. "I care about her. I would be upset if something happened to her, but...I don't know. I don't think I love her."

Crane peered at him. "You don't *think* you love her?"

"It's not like I've been in love a lot and know the feeling."

"True. Or it could be as simple as she isn't a good match for you. Or perhaps, you know that she is on temporary assignment and don't want to risk deeper emotions."

Kelley's expression indicated disagreement, but he didn't reply.

"What is your question?" Crane asked him.

"Is it all right to end the relationship?"

"You are asking me for permission to end your personal relationship?" Crane asked, genuinely surprised.

"Yes. Everyone was making such a big deal about me dating. You, Fi, and even Mel wanted me to settle down. I don't want everyone to be upset." Kelley was in earnest.

"Yes, but we wouldn't want you to stay in a relationship you don't want to be in. Speaking for myself, I did not think you would make a lasting bond with the first woman you dated. I simply wanted you to explore dating versus single encounters."

"As for Fi and Mel, I suggest you talk with them and find out what they have to say for themselves," Crane advised.

Chapter Fifty-Three

After their session ended, Kelley made his way to Sofia's for dinner. Fi was out on a date of her own, so his evening was free. He parked at the far end of the lot, hoping the walk to her place would help get his head together.

As she let him in, he noted she was still wearing a work blouse but had put on comfortable pants in place of her usual business slacks. This indicated that she didn't have amorous plans in mind, which was good.

He didn't see or smell anything cooking, which bothered him. She had invited him for dinner and hadn't said they would order in, and she wasn't even dressed to go out. His bad for assuming. She had probably lost track of time, again, working on a case. Probably 'the' case. She would probably try and wheedle him into cooking for them. Wouldn't be the first time. *Would be the last time though*, he thought to himself.

Sofia was, in fact, apologizing to him for having lost track of time as she was working on a case.

He moved several garments from the couch and sat down. Sofia was good at organizing her cases but not her apartment.

"I don't suppose you want to tell me about the case?" he asked her. He was going through the motions, expecting her to decline, again.

"I could use your help." She was tired and her tone told him she was frustrated. "I've hit another dead end and I can't find a way around it." She sat down next to him and took a sip of her beer. He was too surprised at the reversal to say anything, though he wouldn't have minded a beer for himself.

She went on, "I've done some checking on you, Garrett, and you're a pretty good analyst. I would be glad of your help." She snuggled up to him and said in a suggestive tone, "I would even make it worth your while."

"You checked up on me? Couldn't you have just asked me?"

"What's the difference?" She got up and started going back towards her office. He wasn't sure if she missed his implication or ignored it. He followed her, intending to tell her the difference, but his irritation left him as soon as he saw the inside of her office.

Her office was practically empty, with barely any furniture, and all the surfaces were white and flat. In the center of the room was a document projector. The machine had never been on previously, but it was on now and projecting images over every available space. Case notes, pictures, timelines, suspect lists; her entire virtual file was on display.

"What is this case you are working on?" he asked, as he scanned the room. It would take some time to absorb it all.

"I'll give you the highlights. I took this case over from another agent a little over three years ago. When he started the case, it was as simple as the sale of contraband on one planet, but it got bigger. He started seeing a network of illegal goods being bought and sold across several worlds. He could get to the local small fry but could never move up the chain to those in charge. I took over the case and have been working on it ever since."

"What I need your help with is finding a way to the next level. I've had leads. I get the local movers, but I can't get them to tell me who they report to. They plead out, do their time, and I never see them again."

"There has to be something else here. I can find enough to make connections that indicate a network, but if you go through it all, maybe you will be able to find *someone* that links them all together." When she finished, she was practically pleading for his help.

Kelley took a deep breath. He went to her apartment intending to break up with her. He had only become increasingly annoyed with her since he got there. He put a finger on what was bothering him. He felt like he was being used.

She wasn't being open with him about the case; she was only telling him a fraction of the case now because she wanted his help.

He heard several holes in her synopsis that despite himself, he wanted to ask her about. Almost. What he didn't see anywhere, on any of the displayed images, was one document that had a case number on it. Neither Sofia nor this 'other agent' had ever gotten the case sanctioned by GIS. It looked like the entire case was off-book.

He turned to her and said 'no' in a flat tone.

She was taken aback and said in a nasty tone, "I guess I shouldn't be surprised that you won't help me. It's okay with you to come over here and just get a little honey and then leave when there is any real work to be done."

Dammit, damn you, dammit it all, he swore to himself. He could not believe he was facing a seasoned agent with multi-galaxy case experience. How did she win her cases with such emotion and leaps in logic?

"First, it's you who is treating me like a toy to be played with when you feel like it. Second, you made damn sure to keep me at arms-length and well out of this case; that is until *you* thought of a way to use me there, too."

"Then, you give me a synopsis that is so full of holes that it's ridiculous. And finally, it's an unsanctioned case. Were you going to tell me that?"

"GIS gives their agents a certain amount of leeway when they are developing a case, but in three years you have never had enough to get this case approved?"

"And yet, you have the brass to get mad at me when I won't help on your snipe hunt, just because you ask me with the promise of sex? Ever think of dangling facts or evidence in front of me? How about a little spicy predication?" Kelley said angrily, glaring at her as he finished.

She glared back at first, while she tried to come up with something to counter him. Failing that, she turned away in frustration.

If she starts crying, I'm out of here, Kelley promised himself.

Sofia turned back to him and said, in a trembling voice, "Garrett, please." Her lip quivered. She was about to say more but stopped as Kelley turned on his heel and walked out.

"Garrett! Wait!" she yelled after him, no longer trembling.

He was out of the apartment and halfway to his transport when she caught up with him. "Garrett, wait. I'm sorry."

He stopped only because she sounded somewhat sincere.

"Do you want my help on this 'case' of yours?" he asked her.

"Yes. I'm not getting anywhere on my own." She stopped when he gave her a look. "What? I do want your help."

"I am going to get some dinner. If you want, I will come back, and you can tell me *everything* about this lead you have been following. I mean everything. No more games. Can you do that?"

She was peeved at him for calling it a lead, not a case. "It's a case and I'll tell you what you want to know," she answered grudgingly.

"Then you shouldn't have any problems logging it in and getting it approved." Even now she was still being cagy. When she shook her head, he said, "Fine. Then I won't help you. I won't be a party to whatever you have going on." He stepped around her and continued to walk to his transport.

Sofia ran up and grabbed his arm. "You don't understand. I can't. Bringing this through official channels is what got Donni killed."

She was utterly serious. She really believed what she was saying. He was skeptical; how could bringing a case through channels be dangerous?

"Help me understand. Tell me everything," he said softly, gently gripping her arm.

"I will. Please come back inside."

He hesitated. "Do you have anything to eat in there? Be honest."

"Yes, you just have to make it. Or we could order in."

Chapter Fifty-Four

Kelley got back to his place with dinner and the case file. He was feeling pretty good for a man who had just broken up with his girlfriend.

He tried to listen to her. He really had given it his best shot. She was so biased, he doubted her ability to present the facts of the investigation. And she didn't like him questioning her. How was he supposed to find anything new if she didn't let him question her assumptions?

He decided to tell her it would be better if they didn't continue to see each other and work on the case together, instead of telling her that he wanted out of the relationship because of the many things he didn't like about it.

Sofia readily agreed to the breakup. That she preferred his analytical expertise instead of him personally stung a little, but it didn't shock him.

It soon became clear it was going to be an exercise in hell to review the case with her and that he wasn't getting dinner any time soon. He asked for a complete copy of her files and told her he would get back to her after he had reviewed her 'case'.

Sofia was just as annoyed with him as he was with her, so she agreed to that, too. It appeared as if she copied everything, but he doubted it. She solemnly handed him the data stick, telling him to promise her that he wouldn't bring the case to his boss; it was just too risky.

He promised with perfect truth that he would not take the case to his boss, which was true. His team had enough solid leads to work on. He wasn't going to give them this one, especially as it was from his ex.

He loaded the data onto the GIS network under his name as a preliminary review, unsubstantiated allegations case. He knew Sofia was going to render him an extra orifice when she found out, but he was *not* going to go along with any off-book investigation.

He was still reviewing and sorting through the data when Fi got home, several hours later. He noted that she was dutifully within her curfew. She was a good kid; she never gave him cause to worry about her.

"Hey, Dad, you're home early. Everything okay with you and Sofia?" Fi asked him, flopping down on the couch.

"Hey, Fi. Well. Since you asked, I asked her if we could take a break for a while." He waited for a reaction.

"Is Sofia okay with that?" Fi asked.

He snorted involuntarily. "Sofia is fine with it, especially since I agreed to help her on a snipe hunt she's been working on her own."

Fi's eyes widened in surprise at his tone but wisely didn't remark on it, just asked, "You? You're working on an unsanctioned case? Is there anything you can tell me about it?"

"My part isn't unsanctioned. I've entered it into the logs as a prelim. And I would appreciate it if you didn't say anything to Sofia. She wouldn't like *her* case in the GIS database; she wouldn't like even you *knowing* about it."

Fi was amused. "You got it, Dad."

"Are you okay with me breaking up with Sofia?" he asked her.

She shrugged, "Why wouldn't I be?"

"You made such a big thing about me starting to date."

"Yes, I wanted you to *start* dating. I didn't think you would stop with the first woman you asked out. You're not going to call it quits, are you?"

"On dating, in general? No. I just don't think Sofia and I are a good match." He switched topics by asking, "Why are you home so early? Is everything okay with you and Alexis?"

"Yeah. I just felt like coming home." She pulled off her shoes and didn't say anything else. She looked sad.

"Are you still upset about Sage?" She only nodded in reply.

A classmate and friend of Fi had been raped the previous week. The police were not hopeful that the assailant was going to be found.

"How is she doing?"

"I don't know. She's doing okay then she's not doing okay. She's scared then she's angry." Fi sat back hard into the couch in frustration.

"It's a lot for Sage to process. Listen to her and give her time. Just be her friend."

Fi suddenly sat straight up, animated, "That's just it. I feel like I should be doing more."

"I understand how you feel, but you can't." Something flickered across Fi's face for just a moment.

"But you can't, can you?" he asked, looking at her intently.

She held his gaze for a full two seconds, before caving in. She wanted to tell him. "I think she knows who it was but won't tell the police for some reason."

"Okay. Then, it's a matter you need to take up with her or her parents or maybe even the police. I can't help; GIS has no authority or jurisdiction. And neither do you, Fi." He wasn't sure why he added the last part; she was just so restless.

"I know. That's why I'm upset. I just want to do *something* to help."

He put an arm around her and pulled her close for a hug. "I know."

Chapter Fifty-Five

After four days of review, Kelley had only scratched the surface of what was in Sofia's files. There was years' worth of data to sort through and analyze.

One fact stood out fairly quickly; all the moons or planets that were suspected to be part of the alleged contraband network were worlds where Fleet had bases.

If Fleet personnel were suspects, this was a Fleet investigation. GIS would have limited involvement, if any. Fleet was more than capable in dealing with local PDs and setting up joint investigations, where and when it wanted them.

The Spectrum case had no military connection as far as the allegations went. There, GIS had, and as the case was still being sorted out, still had, a role in oversight and coordination with the many entities that were involved.

Kelley knew he needed to talk to Sofia about handing the case over to Fleet's legal branch, but he wasn't looking forward to it.

The thing was, it was a pretty good case, all things considered. Sofia did know her job and she and whoever this Donni person was, did have predication. In Kelley's opinion, they had kept hitting dead ends because the culprit or culprits would disappear behind Fleet's shadow; more the reason for Fleet to be lead on any investigation.

He couldn't figure out why neither of them had taken the case to Fleet from the beginning, or why Sofia was so intent on keeping her investigation quiet. The case was getting stale, if not outright cold after three years.

He had to talk to Sofia. He had read through enough of the background on the case and gathered his fortitude; he was ready to hear her side of the story. He contacted her and they agreed to meet at her place. He was fine with that but made sure to eat before he got there.

When she let him in, he noted she was still in her work clothes except that she had her oversized, soft slippers on her feet.

He stayed standing, preferring to let her direct him. He didn't want to make assumptions that would make her feel uncomfortable. She gestured for him to take a seat on the couch as she sat down on the opposite end, facing him. He sat on the edge, facing her.

Sofia was both wary and expectant. He had an idea why. It was fairly obvious to him now that his former military service was the reason why she did and did not want him involved in the case.

She wanted his analytical skills to further her case and his knowledge of military channels to get *around* the Fleet protocols. She didn't want his opinions or his advice on how to work *with* Fleet. He spent a good two hours in the gym working through his feelings when he had realized that.

"Talk to me. Tell me why you think this isn't a Fleet investigation. Help me understand, please." His tone was soft, not demanding.

She took a deep breath and started to tell him the ways she thought they could get jurisdiction. He stopped her, shaking his head. "That is how, not why. *Why* is it so important to you to make this a GIS case?" His voice was even and firm.

Sofia looked at him like he was an idiot. "Why? Because Fleet will just cover it all up and not do anything." Her tone, in contrast, was sneering and practically hostile.

Kelley looked down at the floor, like he lost something. He picked up his patience, took a deep breath and let it out slowly. "Why do you think Fleet won't investigate?"

"When Donni went missing, they denied everything. They said they had no record of him. They were lying!" she said angrily.

"Donni is missing? That is new information. It doesn't explain why Donni's case, and now your case, was never listed with GIS."

"How does that matter? Donni just didn't. I think he was tired of doing all the work and never getting any credit."

Kelley's head started to ache at such childish reasoning. He did not practice office politics and made sure his team didn't either. He understood GIS protocols that stated a lead would be worked, or a case assigned, to wherever or to whomever it was best suited.

When he first got the job as Team Lead, he initially had difficulty with handing cases over to the investigative teams because he was both qualified and used to doing that kind of work; it had nothing to do with getting the credit.

"If Donni didn't have a sanctioned GIS case, what was he doing at Fleet? He couldn't have been asking for a joint investigation."

Sofia dropped her eyes and squirmed. "I don't know."

"Yes, you do," his voice was hard.

"No, I really don't know. Not for sure. I think he was going to get information. He didn't tell me."

"If it was an unofficial meeting, why do you find it so hard to believe that Fleet would have no record of him?"

Sofia gaped at him. "They had no record of him signing in or…" She stopped herself midsentence. "I'm not even sure he told me which base he was really going to. He was so protective of me."

He believed her and didn't criticize. Now that she was finally seeing through some of her own assumptions, he didn't want to antagonize her. Instead, he persuaded her to tell him about her and Donni.

Sofia talked for some time. She started from the time she began dating Donni, just as she graduated GIS agent training, to when she had last seen him.

After listening to her, it was clear to Kelley that Sofia had idolized Donni and equally clear that he had used her. In his opinion, Donni had taken advantage of the young, naive agent she had been.

Kelley was glad that he and Sofia had ended their personal relationship. He doubted she would have been so open about her and Donni if they had still been a couple.

The evening ended with them on good terms. He promised her that he would think about her proposal if she would consider the benefits of turning the case over to Fleet. She agreed and even hugged him goodbye.

When he got home, he immediately pulled up Agent Donavan (Donni) Kendell's GIS service profile. He wanted to get a more objective understanding of the man from an unbiased source.

Kelley didn't get past Donni's picture. It was the same face; the same man that had been standing next to him, on his right, in the elevator, in a Lieutenant's uniform, the day the bomb went off.

Chapter Fifty-Six

Kelley stared, gaping at the screen for a full five seconds, before starting to swear at the picture. Furious, he got up, pacing agitatedly around his room, still swearing. He wanted his mind to work, but it was stuck on that twerp's face.

That IDIOT had been the target. Kelley was sure of that. Donni was the reason for everything that had happened to him. He was glad Donni was dead; his being dead saved him the trouble of hunting him down.

He jumped at the unexpected knock on his door. He heard Fi's voice saying, "Dad? Dad, are you all right?"

It was a huge effort to pull himself together. Well, enough to go over and open the door. Fi didn't look in, she didn't back away, in fact, she stood perfectly still in front of him.

"Is everything okay?" she was trying to sound calm, but she was worried, even scared.

Kelley took a deep breath and let it out again in a rush, shaking his head. He wasn't going to lie to her. "Not really. I just got some unexpected intel that hit me really hard." He stopped, words were getting jumbled in his head and not making it to his mouth.

"Can you talk to me about it?"

He shook his head.

"Okay." She paused. "I'll make some tea and leave it on the table, in case you want some." Another pause. "It's during the

270

day where Dr. Crane is." Then, she gave him an awkward little nod, turned, and walked towards the kitchen.

He closed the door and leaned against it, eyes closed, and waited. Eventually, he heard the whistle of the tea kettle. A short time later, he heard Fi's soft footsteps approach his door. He stayed still and silent. He heard her walk away. He opened his door and made sure she had gone back to her room.

He got the tea, fortified it with a shot, took a swig from the bottle, and took the mug back to his room.

He contacted Crane's office and asked if the doc was available. When he was told Crane was busy all day, he told the receptionist to tell Crane that he knew who was responsible for the bomb, which wasn't true; he just knew the target of the attack, but he thought that would get Crane's attention.

It did. He was sipping on his tea when Crane's face appeared on the screen.

"Agent Kelley? You say you know who set the bomb?" Crane was decidedly calm.

Kelley tried to bring Crane up to speed. As he heard himself speak, he realized he was nearly incoherent. Damnit, this wasn't his first briefing. He stopped and apologized.

"I understand. It's a lot to process. Take your time." Crane was reassuring and patient.

On the second attempt, Kelley was able to give Crane the short version.

"And you now believe the man next to you in the elevator was Agent Kendell. Tell me what you think happened."

"I think Donni was sniffing around and got on someone's radar. He was lured onto the Fleet base with the promise of intel. Donni basically walked himself right into someone's crosshairs." Kelley stated his opinion very decisively.

"That is quite a leap. A logical leap, granted, but a leap you don't usually make," Crane said.

"It's a sound premise," Kelley started defensively. "Oh, are you trying to say that I'm upset and making false accusations?"

Crane gave a non-committal shrug. "I would not expect you to be objective, given your personal involvement."

"Do you think I'm mistaken?"

Crane didn't answer right away. He tapped on his tablet and then paused to read something. "It seems Agent Kendell was rather ordinary looking. You haven't been seeing his ghost in others of the same general description, so I am not assuming you are mistaken. It is rather an extraordinary coincidence, though, wouldn't you say?"

"I wasn't looking for a connection. I was looking into a lead given to me by a fellow agent," Kelley said. He was relieved his brain was starting to function again; his logical side was kicking in to answer Crane's questions.

"An agent with whom you have a close relationship?"

"Had. Yes, she and I had an intimate relationship. She asked for my help on something she was working on. I was reviewing the case she took on after Agent Kendell went missing."

"Which case is this?" Crane asked.

Kelley gave him the prelim case number and asked, "Do you think I'm doing anything inappropriate?"

Crane shook his head. "No, not yet, but you are skirting the line. I am concerned you will be very shortly. It's good that you logged it into the system." Crane had noticed the brand new prelim ID number.

"As a working theory, you hypothesize that Agent Kendell was the target and you were simply collateral damage. Do you recall why you were on base that day? Why you were in that particular elevator at that particular time?"

Kelley shook his head slowly. "No, I don't remember. My memory of that day is spotty; clear in some places, not in others."

"You cannot rule out that you were a target as well?" Crane asked him.

Kelley inhaled, starting to get the warning Crane was trying to convey. "No, I cannot rule that possibility out."

"Explosions don't happen very often *inside* a Fleet base. Yet you told me, in your opinion, the investigation was closed without an adequate explanation, did you not?"

"Yes. You're saying there is a lot I still don't know?"

Dr. Crane nodded with certainty. "Yes, I am saying there is a lot you don't know. And I am saying you should tread carefully. If you are right, someone killed a GIS agent with a bomb inside a military base and got away with it. Wouldn't that take someone in a position of authority? Someone of rank and position?"

"If you were a target, you got yourself out of harm's way by leaving Fleet. If you go back, they may still consider you a threat."

"I agree there is predication for an investigation at this point, but I do not recommend that you be involved in it. Not you or Agent Deleon. You both are too close."

Kelley was silent for a time as he considered Dr. Crane's advice. Then he nodded. "I understand what you are saying. Thank you for speaking with me today. I really appreciate your taking the time to help me work through... all this."

"That is quite all right. I'm glad you called and that I could be of some assistance."

After the call ended, Kelley laid down on his bed, his head buzzing with emotion and a barrage of questions. Eventually, he calmed down enough to review the situation. A short time later, a thought struck him. He got up to type a message to Crane, asking him to verify a couple of things.

After the Battle

As he got back into bed, he realized the irony. He had been derisive of Donni for hiding the case and not working it with others through proper channels. Now he was faced with a somewhat similar situation—find the answers he needed himself or turn the case over to others, outside of GIS, as protocols dictated.

It didn't take long to reach the obvious conclusion. He knew what the right answer was, if the question was as simple as who should work on the case. The question was, did he trust Fleet to do justice to the case, *to do him justice?*

In the end, he decided there was no way around but through. Where he needed to get to, to reconcile his past, led back through Fleet, and wherever the end of the case left him was where he would be, and he would have to deal with that once and for all. He knew he was going to turn the case over to Fleet for investigation.

Chapter Fifty-Seven

The next morning, Fi came into the kitchen to find Kelley up and dressed, making her favorite breakfast.

"Morning," she said tentatively.

"Morning. I hope you are hungry. I've got a lot of food here."

Fi just sat down without saying anything.

"Look, I'm sorry I scared you last night. I was upset. I'm doing better this morning."

Fi started eating and asked, "Can you tell me about it?"

"Wish I could, Fi. It's part of an open investigation, or it will be after I talk to someone this morning, so I can't say anything. I did take your advice and I talked to Dr. Crane. He helped."

She visibly relaxed. "Okay. Maybe you will be able to tell me after it's over."

He smiled. "I will, if I can. Are you going to be okay today? Got anything going on?"

"No, just the usual school stuff. Nothing exciting."

They finished breakfast and he saw her off to school before going into work. Once there, he headed for the gym, instead of the team bullpen.

He waited until he saw Agent Azizi Nandi, Branch head of the Legal department, approach the entrance to the gym, dressed in workout clothes.

"Agent Nandi? Do you have a minute, please, sir?"

"Agent Kelley. Good morning. Can it wait? I'm just about to start my morning workout."

"No, sir. It's better if you are informed sooner than later."

The Branch head wasn't sure if he should be concerned or merely intrigued, but he agreed, and they went to his office.

Kelley gave Agent Nandi a full and concise report regarding the contraband case and his and Agent Kendell's potential involvement. When questioned, he was completely candid.

When he finished with his questions, Agent Nandi said, "I appreciate your bringing this to my attention. Do you have a recommendation as to what to do next?"

"Yes, sir. I think GIS needs to present our evidence to Fleet so that, if they agree, they can open an investigation," Kelley immediately answered.

"Are you going to present the case to Fleet, Agent Kelley?"

"No, sir. I'm a witness or at least involved in the case. Someone else needs to take point. I was hoping you would assign someone."

"Agent Deleon?"

"No, sir." He paused briefly. He didn't want to say that in his opinion she didn't have the necessary detachment to deal with a Fleet legal team, nor did he want to stress her personal involvement. "I think it would be better for the case if another agent was Lead."

Agent Nandi nodded. "I can do that. Anything else?"

"Yes, sir. As I believe you understand, if my concerns have grounds, then even giving the case to Fleet is going to be tricky. We need to get it to the right people without alarming or alerting the wrong people, so to speak."

"I can help you there. I will discuss the matter with Chief Belletor and see what can be arranged. In the meantime, I need you and Agent Deleon to stand down. No further involvement without going through channels, understood?"

"Yes, sir. Thank you, sir." Kelley stood up to leave. "I will speak to Agent Deleon immediately."

As he left, he thought he heard a barely audible 'good luck.'

Chapter Fifty-Eight

Kelley needed all the luck he could get. Predictably, Sofia went ballistic when he told her that not only was the case official, it was officially out of her hands. She was furious and yelled at him for betraying her trust and for going behind her back, as well as over her head.

He stoically weathered the barrage. He calmly reiterated the many reasons why this was a Fleet case. He also impressed on her how much they needed someone like the Chief to be the liaison and intermediary in getting the information to the right people in Fleet.

He patiently reminded her that they were both too close; their involvement would complicate, if not compromise, the case. Her stubbornness in refusing to accept that simple but irrefutable fact was annoying. She also ignored the part where he had been blown up because of Donni. He tried not to be upset; she was barely able to process the fact that Donni was really dead.

He was grateful when his device chimed, indicating an incoming contact. It was Verbier. Sofia was now angry that he wasn't listening to her when she was talking to him. He ignored her by turning his back as he answered the call.

He listened for a minute before saying he would be there immediately.

When Sofia tried to tell him they weren't done yet, he said, "Fi's hurt. I have to go." He expected her to understand and move out of his way.

However, she stubbornly said, "No, not until I'm done telling you what I think of you."

He got in close but didn't touch her. "Fi is hurt. I am going. Now move." His tone was ice-cold, his eyes fixed on hers.

Sofia seemed to shrink. She still didn't move but because she was stunned. Perhaps she remembered that he didn't always have a desk job. He brushed past her on his way out.

Chapter Fifty-Nine

He arrived at Verbier in record time and headed to the school's medical suite at a quick pace.

He identified himself to the woman at the desk and asked to see Fi. She led him through the door next to her desk that led to a small hallway with what looked like offices or storage on the left, and three partitioned medical beds on the right.

Fi, it seemed, was in the one on the end. As he passed the first bed, Kelley could hear sounds of a male groaning, presumably in pain. He ignored him and continued down to the end. There was no door to knock on, so he cautiously pulled the curtain back a little saying, "Fi, it's me, your Dad."

She was seated on the medical bed, her shirt covered in blood. She had an arm around her ribs and a bruise on her face that was already starting to swell.

"Hey, Dad. Come on in," she spoke very softly, but clearly.

"What happened to you, kid? You look like you've been in a fight," he said going over to her.

She nodded and was about to speak when the school nurse came in, snapping the curtain wide open. "Mr. Kelley, at last. Perhaps you will authorize us to provide medical treatment to your daughter?" The nurse reminded him of IR Specialist Hildebrand in manner, though the two looked nothing alike.

Confused, he turned to Fi, who only said, "I can explain." She looked meaningfully from him to the nurse and back.

"If I could have a moment with my daughter, please?" he asked the nurse politely. She didn't say anything as she left, snapping the curtain closed.

He pulled a chair over, close to Fi's bed and sat down.

She tried to take a deep breath, found that it hurt, and then said very quietly, "Sage's attacker is a student. He was leaving Visnia. I had to do something."

Kelley's jaw dropped as he tried to take in what she was saying. Fi went on, "I'm sorry. I know now is a really bad time and all."

He held up a hand to stop her. "Fi, it's okay. Don't worry about that. Just connect the dots for me between Sage, her attacker, and why you refused to let the nurse clean you up. Am I correct in thinking the boy two beds down is her alleged assailant and you two got into it?" He was also keeping his voice low.

She nodded and looked down at her bloody shirt. "DNA sample."

Kelley's head snapped up and he sat back abruptly. He glared angrily at her but didn't say anything.

Finally, he leaned back in close and said, "You are not the police, Fi. What were you thinking starting a fight with a fellow student?"

"Please listen. Sage went to the police with her parents and told them who it was. The police tried to question him, but his family wouldn't let them. They are trying to get a warrant for a DNA sample, but it won't be in time. I heard him saying he was being transferred to another school off-world." Fi looked pleadingly at him.

He looked back at her thinking, most girls plead with their father to get them their own transport, not to help them provide evidence in a rape case.

"And you couldn't get his beverage container or gym shirt?" he asked her, only slightly sarcastically.

"Not without being seen," she answered simply.

"This is going to be ugly, Fi. I don't think you are going to understand how ugly until it's too late."

"When we go to the police, his parents are going to assume the worst and will most likely bring charges against you. You'll probably end the semester with this still not resolved."

"I also don't think you appreciate the long-term impact. You will have a record for fighting at school and a record with the Visnia police that you will have to live with. We aren't going to leave like we did Tycor or Pagnol."

She hung her head for a minute considering his caution. When she looked up, the pleading look was gone. "I want to do this."

Chapter Sixty

And so it began. Kelley had the nurse bag Fi's hands and accompany them to the local police station, where Fi told her story three times. Once to the front desk, again to the detective assigned to Sage's case, and again for the detective and prosecuting attorney.

After the second time, they took Fi back to collect the physical evidence, with Kelley's permission. They took her shirt, swabbed her hands and under her fingernails, and even combed through her hair.

They let her wash up and gave her a PD tee shirt, but they only gave her an adhesive bandage for medical care.

After the third interview, they were left alone in an interrogation room while the police interviewed the school nurse. Kelley left briefly to get himself a cup of coffee and a bottle of water for Fi.

"How are you holding up?" he asked her softly, mindful of the security cameras.

"I'm tired and hungry. I just want to lie down." She sounded drained.

"And it hurts, I'm sure." He rubbed her back gently. "It's been a long night, but you are doing great, kid." He smiled at her. "Where did you learn to give evidence like that? You kids watch too many vid shows," he said only slightly mockingly.

She looked at him for a long moment, then seemed to get his caution because she said, "No, I read too many civics books last summer." He grinned briefly and mouthed 'good girl.'

She went on to say, "What happens now?"

He sighed. "Theoretically, if they have a clean sample, they may apply for an expedited warrant, now that you told them their suspect is a flight risk. So, they need to obtain a warrant, the sample from the suspect, and if the sample matches the one taken from Sage, they will build a case for the prosecution. Assuming his father can't quash it."

"And that is going to take time, isn't it?"

"Yep," he answered her simply but not unsympathetically.

"And his parents will be filing charges against me for assaulting their son?"

"Well, I'm not so sure. I had assumed you picked a fight with him, but I underestimated you, kid. It sounds like you got him to throw the first punch." He gave her a look of respect.

Fi was about to answer when the detective came in and told them they could go but to be available, if needed.

Kelley took Fi to an urgent care center to get her ribs x-rayed and some pain medication. She was going to be feeling the ribs real soon, even if they weren't broken.

Fortunately, they were not broken, just bruised. They both were questioned by the facility staff who wanted to make sure Kelley wasn't beating his daughter.

On the way home, he brushed aside her apologies for getting him suspected of abuse. When they got there, she was too tired to eat and went straight to bed.

Over his late-night dinner, he read Crane's reply to his message yesterday, which only said to contact him immediately.

Before doing that, Kelley sent a message to IR informing them of Fi's fight at school, in case they were contacted by the Visnia police, the boy's father, or the local urgent care center. That done, he got himself a drink and initiated a vid call to Dr. Crane.

"Agent Kelly. I hope you can explain your inquiry. You should know that I will not be a party to any unauthorized activities." Crane was particularly severe this evening.

Kelley straightened his spine to present a more formal posture and replied, "Certainly not, sir. That was not my intention. Also, when I sent the inquiry last night, I had not yet presented my findings to Agent Nandi. He ordered me to stand down this morning. As such, I will understand if you don't wish to answer me now."

"Agent Nandi? You went straight to your Branch head?" Crane asked.

"I would have gone to Chief Belletor if I didn't think it would be outside the chain of command," Kelley replied honestly.

Crane shook his head briefly before sighing in resignation. "At any rate, what is important is that you are keeping yourself above reproach."

"Given that, do you wish to withdraw your question to me?"

"No, sir. I would like to know approximately how many agents had Fleet experience prior to joining GIS, and out of them, how many are in a position to access intel as I do." Kelley paused briefly, before continuing, "I want to know if it was a coincidence that Agent Deleon and I found each other." He paused again before saying softly, "It's important to *me*; I'm not working any case."

Crane regarded him a moment before asking in a strangely neutral tone, "Is this a formal inquiry?"

Kelley's jaw dropped in surprise at the question. Then he thought he understood. *Damn office politics.* To him, Crane's question indicated that it wasn't a coincidence and now Crane was asking if he was taking it further.

"No, sir. This is a session between a doctor and his patient. Deleon has to be one of the very few people in all of the known planets to have any answers about what happened to me. And she and I cross paths, not once, but twice in my first year at GIS. I can't take that at face value. I have to ask, was our meeting a coincidence?"

"This is serious, Garrett. There is only so much doctor-patient confidentiality will cover. What if she was involved?"

"Involved in the bombing? Why do think she was involved in that?" Kelley asked. "What did you find?"

Crane's eyebrows arched in surprise at Kelley's calm demeanor. "I spoke to her previous supervisor. She lobbied to get the Visnia assignment. She wanted to be where you were, wouldn't you say?"

"It's *possible*, yes, but that alone doesn't mean she was involved with the bombing. Do you have anything else? What about the Tycor assignment?"

"No, I don't have anything else," Crane admitted. "The Tycor assignment appears to be a random meeting. So, based on what you know of her, you don't suspect she had any involvement with the bombing or Agent Kendell's death?"

"Not at all." Answering Crane's questioning look, Kelley continued. "I do know her. I worked with her on the Tycor case and I did get to know her outside of work. Now that I know about Donni almost everything makes sense."

"I believe she was involved with Donni and nothing else. She loved him and would do anything for him, including finding out what happened to him. She doesn't just want to know; she needs to know, it's everything to her."

"However, what doesn't make sense is, if she wanted to get to me, to use me in some way, why did she take so long to ask for my help?"

Crane disagreed, saying, "It was only a month into your relationship. That isn't much time to wait before asking a fellow agent to breach protocols and provide sensitive intel."

"And I don't think you appreciate all the complexities. From a psychological point of view, based on what I know of the agent, I would hypothesis that she didn't necessarily *want* to ask for your help. Her psych profile indicates a highly-driven person with obsessive tendencies. She may have known she needed your help but waited to ask until all other avenues had been exhausted."

"How many other agents could have given her access to what she wanted?" Kelley pressed Crane to answer his original question.

"Actually, only you. Of the agents that have Fleet experience, you are the only viable option. The others are either retired or too senior for her to have access to, or too junior to be of any use."

"So, I was worth going after. I think this lends weight to my hypothesis that she was only working an off-book case by any means possible."

Crane was not convinced, but at the same time, he knew his limitations. He agreed to leave any conduct reviews or investigations to the appropriate departments. He also sternly reminded Kelley that after this session, he was to follow Agent Nandi's orders and stand down—no working on the case. Only after Kelley dutifully agreed was he was able to end the call with Crane and get into bed.

He wanted to sleep but finding the Donni connection to the explosion and then Fi's fight and ensuing crusade for justice was too much. Either of the two events would have been more than enough for him to handle, but both together should have leveled him. He was amazed they didn't.

It was really sinking in that he had found a very promising lead into the bombing and that he had been ordered not to pursue it. If it wasn't for Fi, doing nothing would have been *very* difficult.

She needed him right now and it was important to him to be there for her. He reminded himself that he had chosen to hand off the case, and now, he had to trust Nandi's judgement and believe that the agent assigned would prepare the case for Fleet justly.

Exhausted in both body and mind, he finally got some sleep.

Chapter Sixty-One

The next morning, Kelley was up at his usual time, despite going to bed so late. He sent a message to his team telling them he would be working from home the next several days taking care of his daughter. He also sent a message to Mel to bring her up to speed and ask for her help over the next couple of months.

He knew Fi had finally woken up when he heard a long groan from her room. He grabbed the pain meds, some water, and knocked on her door.

He entered when he heard a muffled 'come in.' Fi was in bed, eyes closed, face in the pillow, swollen side up. "Morning, my little crusader."

Fi just grunted.

"Here. Take your pain meds. You'll feel a lot better," he said with compassion.

She sat up slowly. "I'm sore in places that didn't get hit."

He nodded as he handed her the pills and water. "Yep. That's the way it works."

After swallowing the pills, she looked at him and said, "And you used to do this for a living?"

"Not every day, no." He went on briskly before she could respond. "Do you think you can get yourself cleaned up while I make breakfast, or would you rather stay in bed and let me bring you something?"

"Eh. I'll get up," she said making a face, wincing as she did.

He left her to it. Later that morning, he got a message from Mel essentially saying, like father, like daughter. He found her remark to be ironic, if not unfounded, all things considered. Mel also mentioned that she and Hugo were in counseling, but she would make time for Fi.

Fi's situation took time to resolve, as Kelley predicted, and he was grateful to have Mel's help over the next several months. Fi, overly hardworking to begin with, was determined to prove she could handle the trial and her studies to the point of obsession. She ended her first semester with high honors, but it took a toll on her health. Mel was able to reach Fi in a way Kelley couldn't, and she helped her find some semblance of balance.

Verbier, while strongly disapproving of students fighting, ultimately declined to formally reprimand either student. Kelley suspected the father put pressure on the school to not sully his son's record, and Verbier, to its credit, wasn't going to discipline only one party.

In addition, Verbier's own review into the fight confirmed the boy threw the first punch. Kelley was impressed at the high quality of Verbier's investigation. From what he read in the transcripts from the student interviews, the other students thought the boy was a major jerk, that he deserved it, and they were glad he got what was coming to him. The students who witnessed the fight were impressed with how Fi fought the older boy.

Kelley watched the fight that had been partially captured by one of the school's security cameras. He was astounded at how much Fi had learned during their sessions in the gym. He hoped that the vid and the transcripts wouldn't find their way too far outside of Verbier, but at the same time, he was proud; Fi had taken the kid apart.

Soon after the fight, Kelley and Mr. Batcheler, the boy's father, were called down to the police station when Mr. Batcheler pressed them to bring charges against Fi. Apparently, in addition to some cuts and bruises, Fi had broken his son's nose and wrist.

The two fathers met with a police mediator, accompanied by their respective legal counsels. Kelley had hired an attorney recommended to him by GIS IR. The attorney reminded Mr. Batcheler that his son threw the first punch, on a lower classman who was shorter and twenty pounds lighter than him. The attorney wisely left out that the kid still got his head handed to him. Taking the offensive, he further indicated that it was Mr. Kelley who should pursue charges for the battery of his daughter.

Not surprisingly, Mr. Batcheler didn't want that. What was strange was how quickly Batcheler's attorney folded. There was no more talk about bringing charges against Fi and the attorney even offered to pay for Fi's medical expenses, if she would sign a non-disclosure agreement. Kelley knew without being told that an NDA could severely hamper the police's investigation into the rape charges.

Kelley rejected the offer, which inflamed Mr. Batcheler all over again. Batcheler's attorney had to calm his client before mediations could resume. In the end, both sides essentially agreed to call it a draw—no charges would be filed against either student.

Kelley felt the skirmish over criminal charges had been a test. He knew the Batcheler family wasn't done with Fi yet. They were gearing up for the trial—the trial where the prosecution's case rested on the DNA evidence pulled from the fight.

Chapter Sixty-Two

The trial of Visnia v. Batcheler was moved up at the father's urging as his son needed to migrate off Visnia to attend another school of some prestigious reputation next semester.

The defense was unaware of Fi's past experiences with the legal system. They also underestimated her resolve and Kelley's ability to anticipate and prepare.

The prosecuting attorney took the lead, certainly, in preparing Fi for the stand. Kelley ran her through several mock cross-examinations, as well. He did not want any trip-ups when it came to her 'integrated' past.

She took trial prep like a pro. She stayed focused and listened to the prosecutor's assistant's advice. She didn't complain that her friends were off on fabulous vacations or that she was missing out on the mid-term break.

Fi handled the mock crosses with Kelley well. He focused on tripping her up verbally and catching any inconsistencies or hesitations. He let the prosecutor's staff fill her in on the 'rougher' side of a cross-examination.

When the trial began, the defense took the position that it was not their client; he had been somewhere else.

Kelley thought, with the DNA evidence, they would admit to the encounter and argue that it had been consensual. Since it wasn't their client, the defense went easy on Sage, in that, they agreed that she had been assaulted. They were rough on her when they attempted to raise doubts that she knew who had attacked her. Sage was shaky but poised during her testimony; she was in tears after cross-examination.

The defense now turned their guns towards Fi. It seemed evident their plan was to discredit the DNA evidence.

Little, sweet-looking Fianna took the stand. She was completely healed by the time of the trial, yet frail-looking due to the loss of weight from overwork during the weeks leading up to the trial.

During prep, Kelley got the impression that between the two girls, Fi and Sage, Fi was the stronger one. If the defense was going to go after either of them, the prosecutor wanted it to be Fi. Kelley didn't argue with the tactic and neither did Fi. They just planned accordingly.

The defense made the mistake of thinking they could easily trip Fi up and find a way to dispute the chain of events that brought the blood sample to the police, or in its handling that allowed it to become contaminated in some way.

Once she gave her testimony, Fi stuck to it and never wavered. The defense hammered at her for two hours, but there were only so many ways to ask the same questions. The prosecutor eventually called on the judge to intervene and she did so. As the defense was not able to ask any new or relevant questions, the witness was allowed to step down.

With the DNA evidence tying the defendant to the victim, the jury found him guilty.

Chapter Sixty-Three

For Kelley, Fi and the trial was a welcome distraction while the assigned GIS team put the 'Donni' case together. Even then, waiting and doing nothing wouldn't have been easy. Fortunately, it wasn't all wait and see.

After the GIS team completed their initial review, they called him in to debrief him as to his involvement with the case. They also interviewed Deleon. It didn't take Agent Franklin, lawyer and team lead, long to figure out it was best if they kept Deleon separated from Kelley. She was holding onto her grudge against him very tightly.

Agent Deleon was also very forthright with her opinions on how the case should be presented and by whom. These opinions were not shared by Agent Franklin or the other members of the team.

In fact, the team wanted Kelley to be the main relator. They said his name was on the prelim, so it made sense for him to present the case to Fleet and provide them with the overview.

Kelley knew this was complete space slag. They wanted him because of his experience with Fleet protocols and because they assumed Fleet would find the case more credible coming from one of their honorable discharged officers. Apparently, his connection to the case was not a concern.

On top of everything else, Kelley had difficulties coming to terms with Deleon's behavior now, in contrast with how she had been on Tycor. She was off the wall crazy. On Tycor, she had been poised, logical, and every bit a formidable attorney. She was nothing like that when it came to Donni's case.

He still had feelings for Sofia, not that he wanted to get back together with her, but it didn't feel right to stand by and do nothing while she did a better job at damaging her career and overall credibility than being an asset on the case.

Her relationship with Kendell wasn't an issue; it was how she handled things after he went missing. GIS had so far declined to pursue the fact that she had evidence regarding a fellow agent's disappearance, but failed to bring it to anyone's attention. Nor did they reprimand her for working a case off-book for three years. Frankly, Kelley wondered what they were waiting on.

He knew the assignment that brought her to Visnia was over. She was still there only because of the Donni case, now officially known as Investigation 2621-KD/KG-Trafficking-Sector 3 & 4.

After a bad meeting, where she had been both rude and dismissive, he took her aside for a private discussion. He suggested that perhaps it would be better to work with the team, to achieve her objectives, and not against them. He told her she was a good agent and usually very good at reading a room, but…He wasn't able to say anything further as she ripped into him.

She snidely reminded him that they were only here at all because he had betrayed her by bringing GIS into Donni's case, and not only that, he was so incredibly stupid for thinking handing *her* case over to Fleet was a good idea. She finished by saying when she wanted his help, she would ask for it. She flipped him off as she flounced away.

After that, he no longer intervened on her behalf during meetings or attempted to buffer her behavior. He talked to Crane about it though.

Crane listened to his concerns, then said, "Agent Kelley, please keep in mind that you can only help those who want to be helped. My colleagues have tried to reach out to Agent Deleon, several times, in fact. She has declined or rebuffed their offers of assistance."

"But her behavior is hurting her career."

"Yes." Crane agreed simply; he didn't even attempt to soft pedal his response.

Kelley decided to fish around a little since Crane was so forthcoming. "Why hasn't GIS taken any disciplinary actions against or even reprimanded Deleon for her past and/or current behavior?"

Crane regarded him for a moment, then answered, "Fleet will ask for the backgrounds of all the agents involved in the case. It would damage our credibility if one of the agents had multiple disciplinary actions for misconduct, would it not?"

"You can be assured that IR will be in touch with Agent Deleon in due time; perhaps soon after the case is presented to Fleet."

Kelley didn't try to hide his expression of amazement. He was impressed; he wouldn't have thought GIS that devious. They were making sure the case got handed off in the best possible light and he deeply appreciated that.

In due course, Kelley briefed the investigative team on what to expect when they arrived at the Fleet base and what would happen during the hearing. When Deleon made comments, Franklin asked her to leave. When Deleon protested that she couldn't do that, Franklin proved that she could.

Chapter Sixty-Four

Kelley was now managing his analysis team, and since being named as its relator, was putting a lot of hours into the Trafficking case. This meant his time with Fi was limited.

The Batcheler trial was over and Fi was in school and back to being her usual overachieving self; all her health issues behind her. Now that the date for the Fleet hearing was set, Kelley decided it was time to sit down and talk with her.

He explained he would be very busy for the next couple of weeks, and then, he would be going off-world to present the team's finding to Fleet on their base on Rivne-O-35.

"I understand. I promise to help with dinner and chores and always do my homework," Fi said. "I'm glad to know it's a case you have been working on," she added.

"I appreciate your help, Fi, though you already do your chores and your homework. Why are you glad it's a case?"

"Could I come with you?" she asked, not answering his question.

"No, Fi. Not this case. Besides, I wouldn't want you to miss school."

"What makes this case so different? I mean, other than you are presenting a case to Fleet, in person?"

"Maybe they just want me because of my military background," he suggested.

"Yeah. I understand. You can't tell me. I won't keep asking."

Curious he asked, "Why do you think this is different from any other case?"

"I'm not sure. You are different. Ever since that night you had a meltdown in your room. And you have been working *really* hard. You don't look like you have been sleeping all that well since then, either. I've been worried about you."

"It could mean I'm just stressed at work or have issues with my ex-girlfriend," he deflected quickly. He had no idea she had noticed any change in him or that she was worried.

"Yes, it *could*. But you haven't denied you are working on something *really* important to you," she countered.

He sighed; he didn't want to talk about it, but he didn't want to lie to her either. He decided he owed her the truth. "This case is personal. It has to do with something that happened to me several years back."

"The explosion?"

He had forgotten he had told her anything about the explosion and just nodded.

"And they are letting you work the case?" she asked, more surprised than prying.

"Extenuating circumstances. And my involvement is limited and strictly monitored. Can we talk about your being alone while I'm gone?"

"Hey, don't worry about me. I'm going to be seventeen; I can take care of myself," she reminded him, breezily.

"I don't doubt that," he assured her. That she would be seventeen was precisely the reason why he was worried about leaving her without any supervision. "I just don't want anything to happen to you, kid."

She smiled and moved closer to give him a hug. "I'll be okay. I hope everything goes well and that you will be okay, too."

They left it at that. A couple of days later, Mel contacted him at work. He tried to tell her to call back after work hours, but she said she may have information about one of his cases. He set his jaw and asked what Fi had told her.

"Only that you were going off-world to present a case to Fleet that had something to do with some explosion you were in," she said.

"And you are calling me at work because…?"

"I wanted to know if Iaso gave you anything when you left."

Iaso was the private facility where he had done his rehab after the explosion.

He closed his eyes briefly and pulled in a deep breath. "No, no they did not."

"You should check with them. Also, I'm coming to stay with Fi while you are gone. Hugo and I are formally separated. And, if it comes up, yes, I would be willing to testify." Then, she ended the connection before he could respond or react.

He talked with Franklin and told her of the possibility that Iaso may have something of relevance to the case. She drafted a letter for him to sign, which gave GIS the authority to ask Iaso for any such evidence and to take possession of it on his behalf. He signed it, hoping it would prove useful.

Chapter Sixty-Five

As it got closer to the hearing, Kelley found himself getting energized in the way he used to before a mission. He focused on his prep work at the expense of everything else. He wasn't so much impatient at roadblocks, just highly motivated to push through them. Fortunately, Fi was sensible and gave him space. Deleon did not. She pressured him one too many times to let her speak at the hearing.

He went to Franklin and said flat out that he didn't want Deleon at the hearing. He found her both annoying and distracting and she would be a liability when he presented their evidence.

Franklin didn't argue with him, though it had been decided previously that it might appear they were hiding something if she wasn't there. Deleon had had the case for three years; they were concerned Fleet would want to question her. Franklin said, if asked, she would tell Fleet that Deleon was personally involved and too emotional to be present at the initial hearing. GIS would make her available at a later date, if necessary.

Just how much Deleon had exasperated Franklin became apparent when Franklin didn't even make a pretense of giving Deleon something case-related to work on. Franklin simply told Deleon she wasn't going and that she had been re-assigned to the Records Office. The rest of the team stood in a united front of stony silence until Deleon stormed out.

On the day of the hearing, the team arrived at the base on Rivne-O-35. Kelley was ready for anything. He was dressed in a business suit having chosen not to wear his uniform.

Once they went through security, they were shown into the hearing room and told they had twenty minutes to prepare before the hearing convened.

When the tribunal consisting of three generals arrived with their entourage of support staff, there was a brief round of introductions and the team was sworn in. Kelley had done his best to warn them, yet the team looked unsettled by the sophisticated monitoring and surveillance Fleet used in its court proceedings, in both the hearing room and on those individuals present. The monitoring was voluntary for civilians, of course, but it was all or nothing. The individuals agreed to the monitoring or they didn't stay. The monitors were so sensitive that they often picked up when someone was tense with an urge to urinate.

That Kelley was not in uniform did not go unnoticed by the brass presiding over the hearing, though only one general commented.

Kelley began by thanking the tribunal, then immediately launched into presenting the allegations without any unnecessary preamble. After laying the groundwork and stating the evidence supporting the allegations, he drilled down and outlined the evidence in more detail.

Having completed the overview, he stopped and asked for questions. The monitors showed his team was nervous and tense. They had argued previously that he should review the evidence in much more detail and provide presentation handouts in addition to the case packets.

Kelley disagreed and reminded them that this was a Fleet hearing where the purpose was to convince the tribunal that there was a case within Fleet jurisdiction. If the tribunal agreed, the next step would be for GIS to review their evidence in detail with the appropriate Fleet investigators.

The floor open, two of the three generals started with their questions. They had Kelley review the premise again and then moved into testing the strength of the evidence supporting the allegations. They pulled apart what GIS called facts indicating Fleet personnel were involved, and reviewed every shred of evidence for soundness.

His team remained tense and nervous, but Kelley was calm. He was back in his element where reporting to the brass was nothing new. He didn't take their questions personally. In fact, he was pleased; they were asking good questions, pertinent and material. Kelley answered fully and elaborated where they wanted him to.

General Paine, however, went directly for the weakest point of the case. He bluntly stated, "Your allegations tying the trafficking to the Tydfil CF48 base bombing are based on hearsay."

"At the moment, yes, sir," Kelley responded evenly. "However, we may have evidence that will link the two without a doubt.

"As you may know, after the Tydfil CF48 base bombing, an investigation was initiated that was closed soon after, with the results sealed. What you may not know is that evidence that was initially bagged and tagged was later deemed as my personal effects and given to my sister at the time of my discharge. She was acting on my behalf being my next of kin, as I was incapacitated at the time."

"I am speaking of the uniform I was wearing at the time of the explosion. My uniform was sealed in an evidence bag by Fleet investigators immediately after the explosion and kept in their possession until my discharge."

"My sister took possession of the sealed bag and sent it along with me when she transferred me to the Iaso rehabilitation facility. Iaso, a highly regarded facility, has been keeping it in their possession since. GIS agents were recently sent to Iaso at the direction of Agent Franklin, where they confirmed the uniform is still there, sealed and in appropriate storage."

"While they had the authority to take possession of it, it was deemed that, should Fleet choose to investigate, it would be better if Fleet personnel took the uniform and tested it themselves. GIS is ready to provide Agent Kendell's full DNA profile, at your request."

"I have had no contact with that uniform since it was cut off me after the explosion. If a match is made, the link between trafficking and the bombing will move from tenuous to solid."

The tribunal all looked at Kelley's monitor, which did not show any indicators of deceit. Their faces remained immobile, but there was some shifting in their seats, as they processed what he was telling them.

"Your sister, a civilian?" asked General Paine, his tone slightly derisive.

"Yes, sir. Dr. Turner is a highly intelligent woman who became somewhat familiar with the police procedures when she lived with me when I was a Blerreon 4 police officer. She has indicated her willingness to testify, if you would like to question her handling of the evidence," Kelley replied.

"But why did she have reason to believe the uniform had any importance, especially after the investigation was closed?" the General pressed. "For that matter, how did evidence leave Fleet possession?"

"Sir, I cannot answer that. I have not discussed the evidence with her since she told me it existed. I recommend asking her directly."

The tribunal elected to take a recess.

After the Battle

During the break, the team asked if things were going well. Franklin told him his presentation was excellent, but she thought he could have answered the General better. Kelley replied that speculating would have been worse.

He assured them that things were going as well as could be expected, though he had a gut feeling that General Paine was not done with him.

Chapter Sixty-Six

The hearing resumed as the Generals walked back into the hearing room and up onto the riser to sit down. Kelley watched their body language closely.

General Paine placed his elbows on the table, leaned forward and just stared down at Kelley. Kelley returned his stare, ready as a runner is when they are in the blocks, waiting for the sound of the starting pistol.

Crane had helped him with that analogy. It was meant to help keep his mind focused to keep his physiological cues from spiking too high.

"*Agent* Kelley," General Paine sneered, "You present an interesting theory, one yet to be substantiated." He paused, giving Kelley a chance to respond.

Kelley kept breathing and didn't say anything, his monitors indicating an uptick in emotions.

"Are you saying we should open an investigation and waste countless resources running down tenuous allegations all over the sector, based on your word, *Agent* Kelley? Because you say that you saw a fellow agent in an elevator for a *second* over three years ago? Is that what you want us to do?"

Kelley's monitors flared as his emotions spiked.

"Permission to speak freely, sir," he asked through gritted teeth, his mouth dry.

"Oh, by all means, Agent Kelley. You go ahead and speak your mind," General Paine said.

"Thank you, sir," he said barely audible. He took a deep breath, opened his mouth, and let it all come out.

"What I want you to do is give me some answers." His tone hard and even. "Yes, this is personal. I want you to find out who tried to kill me and why. I want you to tell me who tried to slander me when I was flat on what was left of my back *and* why they felt the need to slander me at all. And, I really want you to tell me where Fleet was during all this, because it sure as hell wasn't behind me, sir."

"This case has merit. I want Fleet to take a sector-wide trafficking case seriously, regardless of whether it involved murder or even just attempted murder."

"I saw other soldiers reamed for minor infractions because Fleet has a reputation to uphold. What I want you to do is show me Fleet has accountability, across the board, down and up, the chain of command, sir."

"This isn't just a trafficking case. A bomb went off *inside* a Fleet base and the investigation was *shut down*. I don't know the reasons that were given to shut it down, but I want to know if you are going to condone that decision now, in light of new evidence."

"You want to know why I'm not in uniform? You think I am disrespecting Fleet for not wearing my uniform? I'm not wearing it because I can't. I can't put it on without feeling as betrayed and disgusted now as I did then."

"I want you to give me back what I lost three years ago. Respect for the uniform, loyalty to Fleet, and belief in its purpose. I hate the hollowness I feel because of what got ripped out of me *after* I was blown up."

"What do I want you to do? I want you to give me thirteen years of my life back. I want you to tell me they meant something by looking into the allegations presented to you here today."

"The Galactic Investigative Services is here because the evidence we have suggests that somebody deliberately murdered an agent on a Fleet military base. We suspect this was done to cover up their trafficking activities. The events following the explosion suggest that somebody high in the chain of command covered it up."

"So, yes, sir. Yes, I am asking that you open a sector-wide investigation based on the evidence provided to you here today by me and my fellow agents."

His team's monitors were spiking wildly even though the well-trained agents appeared to be statues in their seats. His monitor was leveling out.

General Paine stared at Kelley for a moment, then asked, "Feel better?"

Kelley took a very deep breath and let it out slowly. "Yes, sir. Thank you, sir."

The General glanced at his peers and sat back against his chair, considering Kelley's testimony for a time.

"Were you a part of the trafficking network?" General Paine suddenly asked, hard and fast.

"No, sir."

"Can you tell me why you were there on the day of the explosion?"

"No, sir. I have limited recollection of that day."

General Paine sat back again and gestured to his fellow generals. The other two leaned in close towards General Paine and they spoke quietly amongst themselves for several minutes.

Once their impromptu conference was over, the three sat back in their chairs, faces stern and solemn.

"Based on your testimony Agent Kelley, I am going to have to ask you to leave," General Paine told him.

Kelley's entire body went numb, his jaw slack.

"Yes, as your involvement is not able to be determined at this time, we need to ask you to remove yourself from this hearing room, while we continue to discuss the case with your colleagues."

Agent Franklin came over and stood beside him. "I believe the General is saying that since we don't know if you were a target or just in the wrong place at the wrong time, it is possible that you may have information as a *witness,* not just a victim, that is unknown to you and is, as yet, uncovered. As such, you cannot be part of any further discussions regarding this *investigation.*" She looked to the General for confirmation.

The General nodded, his face still impassive.

Kelley's monitors fluctuated as he tried to process what was happening. He turned to Agent Franklin and said, somewhat dazedly, "I guess I will see you back at the office."

She smiled reassuring, nodded and said, "Yes you will. Thank you for everything you have done." She looked straight at him and said, "It's okay. We've got it from here."

He turned towards the rest of the team who were on their feet, their monitors fluctuating with their emotions. They were each murmuring their own assurances.

Still numb, he gathered his things and turned to leave. He heard chairs being pushed back as the three generals rose to their feet.

He turned back and saw the three generals standing straight and proud with the Fleet colors behind them. His chest got very tight. He saluted them. In unison, they returned the salute.

PART III – BEGINNINGS/ENDINGS

After the Battle

Chapter One

Kelley returned to Visnia alone. To his surprise, Fi, Mel, and little Brian met him at the Port. Mel and Fi took turns giving him big, long hugs before taking him home.

They already seemed to know all he could have told them, that Fleet had accepted the case and opened an investigation. He assumed Franklin must have told them, only finding out much later that it had been Dr. Crane.

Kelley took a couple of days off work and spent the time with Mel and Brian showing them around Visnia. Once he had convinced Mel that he was fine and that he was sleeping better, she confided in him that she was seeing a therapist.

Though she didn't say anything specific about divorcing Hugo, she did talk to him about his experiences with dating, like she was getting used to the idea and maybe would like to try it herself. He talked to her but didn't press her.

Fi loved having Mel around. They spent the afternoons together once Fi got home from school while Uncle G enjoyed his time with Brian. They would all do something together in the evenings after dinner.

When Mel and Brian left for Nibiru, Kelley returned to work, to his team, with renewed energy. He had been gone for less than two weeks, but it felt longer. He felt like he was getting used to his team and his job all over again. It was okay though; it was a good fit, and everything felt right; righter than ever before. He was finally able to say that not only did he like his analyst job, but he also found it rewarding and fulfilling.

He resumed his sessions with Dr. Crane. Over the years, the frequency of their sessions had increased or decreased, depending on what was going on with Kelley at the time. They were back on more frequent check-ins, but Kelley didn't mind. He had a lot to talk about.

He first wanted to talk about Sofia. She had left Visnia after being given another temporary assignment and their last meeting had not gone well.

Kelley hadn't thought she would apologize to him, but he did think she would have been happy at Fleet taking the case; she wasn't. She was still angry at him and everything was his fault, including her latest assignment.

He agreed the new assignment was the equivalent of being told to go clean toilets. There were no official rules, but agents could get a general idea of how their careers were going based on their assignments, and Sofia's current assignment was a clear message of where her career was.

During one of their sessions, Crane discussed with Kelley the possible reasons why Sofia wasn't happy at Fleet taking the case. Kelley also wanted to talk about why she thought everything was his fault. He did understand the part where he went behind her back and over her head but, he had been right to do so. He felt vindicated and he didn't understand why she didn't agree.

In his opinion, her career and her assignments were all her own doing; he wasn't going to take the blame for any of that. It was her choices that got her reprimanded; not his. And he felt that her bad choices had started long before she met him. Crane counseled him that perhaps, as angry as she was, she wasn't quite ready to see things as plainly as he was just yet.

He told Crane that he thought she needed help—Dr. Crane's kind of help. When Crane reminded him that attempts had been made, he asked if it couldn't be mandatory. Crane didn't see how that would be beneficial. If the subject wasn't willing to put in the effort, it would just be a waste of time for both the patient and the therapist.

Kelley also wanted to understand why Deleon had not been kept on Agent Franklin's team, at least part-time, while they completed the hand-off to Fleet. Deleon had been directly involved for years and he assumed they would want her expertise. Crane said he did not know, but he suspected that it could be argued that her evidence was tainted. It was possible they preferred to reconstruct the evidence for themselves.

As the weeks passed, Kelley was eventually ready to talk about what the Fleet investigation meant to him personally. Did it mean that Fleet had listened? Did he feel like they had heard him and had his back after all this time?

They discussed the possible outcomes and what effects they might have on him. Kelley talked about how he would feel if an individual was never identified, as well as the possibility if one *was* identified, and what would he do.

Kelley was grateful for Crane's guidance. Once the investigation was over, whatever the outcome, he knew this was it. After it was over, he had to move on with his life.

Chapter Two

Fi finished her first year at Verbier Polytechnique with high honors. She insisted on taking summer classes, even though Kelley advised against it. He argued she should get a summer job instead. She agreed in that she did both, she took classes and got a job.

She somehow found time to date. Nothing serious, which pleased and concerned Kelley so much that he talked about that with Crane, too. Dr. Crane assured him that Fi's casual dating was entirely normal for someone her age.

As for himself, dating wasn't so bad, a bit boring, but he enjoyed it for the most part. He didn't feel he really *sparked* with anyone, but Crane told him not to worry, just relax and have a good time. Kelley didn't argue, though he felt that it was similar to what he had been doing before, just with more talking over coffee, but whatever.

Towards the end of summer, Kelley took Fi to Nibiru. They celebrated Fi's belated birthday, Brian's early birthday, and unofficially celebrated Mel's divorce and new place.

Mel assured them both that she and Brian were doing great. She had a job and they were comfortable. Brian had regular visits with Hugo and seemed to be adjusting to his new family dynamic.

Unlike her brother, Mel was very happy to be dating. She confided in him that she was still seeing a therapist and that it was helping. Kelley was very happy to see the light starting to come back in her eyes.

In the fall, Fi started her final year at Verbier. He got his courage together and started to ask her about life after school. What did she want to do? Where did she want to be? He assumed she would want to go to university, but she told him she was still thinking about it.

Kelley was getting tired with waiting for results of the investigation. He was tired, but also *ready* for it to be over. He was prepared as he was ever going to be for whatever answers he would get; he wanted to move on.

Chapter Three

Late in the fall, Kelley received a private communication directly from Chief Belletor saying he was to report to the Fleet base on Gaclite. Gaclite was Visnia's outermost moon, where Fleet had a repair station. The message was brief, apart from the time and location, Chief Belletor only said that he expected Kelley to be dressed properly.

Kelley reported as ordered, in his service dress uniform and was immediately shown to a small conference room where a JAG Captain was sitting.

The Captain got to his feet and saluted him. After Kelley returned the salute, the Captain turned and thanked the ensign who had been Kelley's escort, dismissing him. He waited until the door had closed before turning back to Kelley saying, "Captain Royce Moser, JAG Corp."

Kelley offered his hand and replied, "Major Garrett Kelley, retired."

The two shook hands briefly, then the Captain politely indicated to Kelley to take a seat, before sitting opposite him on the other side of the conference room table.

Kelley seated himself and waited. He was not sure what was going on. He hadn't been called to give testimony or questioned in any way during the past year. If they were going to call on him now, it wouldn't be like this.

The Captain regarded him for a moment without saying anything. Then he said, "I have been asked by General Bataar to brief you on the results of my investigation and the outcome of the resulting trial as it relates to GIS Preliminary Investigation 2621-KD/KG-Trafficking-Sector 3 & 4."

Kelley managed to keep his face reasonably impassive, but his eyebrows twitched in surprise at the mention of a trial in the past tense. He politely waited for the Captain to continue.

"I hope you appreciate how irregular this is and how important it is to be delicate and discrete." Moser was stern; it wasn't a question.

"Yes, Captain. I am listening."

The Captain opened his mouth to speak, but before he could, the door on the other side of the room opened and a General walked in, closing the door on his aide before she could follow him in.

Both men quickly stood and saluted him, Kelley only a fraction behind the Captain. Moser crisply said, "General Bataar, sir."

The General paused, giving Kelley a brief once over before returning the salute. They remained standing as the General seated himself at the end of the table. Kelley and Moser exchanged looks across the table. Moser gave him a brief, warning look in answer to his questioning one.

"Be seated, gentlemen." General Bataar said in a quiet, tired voice.

To Kelley, it seemed as if the General was more than tired. He had a hollow, almost dazed look in his eyes.

"I'm retiring soon, but before I go, I wanted to talk with you, Major Kelley." He stopped talking.

Uncertain, Kelley gave a non-committal, 'yes, sir.'

"I read the transcript of the hearing, what you said before the tribunal. I wanted to make sure you got some answers." He stopped again.

"Thank you, sir. I appreciate that very much, sir," Kelley said in earnest.

The General nodded. Silence. "Captain Moser will see to the details."

Moser gave the General a crisp, "Yes, sir."

More silence. Kelley and Moser kept still and silent. The General seemed to collect himself and looked directly at Kelley. "I also wanted to say on behalf of Fleet, on behalf of myself, I am sorry for what my son did to you and that GIS agent."

Kelley's body jerked as he swore loudly in his head. He swallowed, eyes down and tried to pull himself together.

General Bataar went on. "Fleet lost a good solider and a fine officer that day."

He looked up at the General, his throat tight, at a loss for words.

The General gave a slight nod, saying, "Right. I will be going now." He stood up to leave.

Moser and Kelley leapt to their feet. Kelley forced words out and said, "Sir. Please wait." The General stopped.

He inhaled a couple of times to loosen his throat. "Sir. I am sorry, too. As a father myself, I can't imagine...I mean, I know it's not my place to say." Kelley broke off, hesitating, then said, "I am sorry for your loss, sir." The General nodded curtly, accepting his condolences.

Kelley gathered his courage and added, "Don't retire."

Taken aback the General looked at him in surprise. Moser equally surprised, looked between Kelley and Bataar and back to Kelley, but didn't say anything.

"No need to make a bad situation worse, sir."

"I left Fleet because I didn't see any other choice. And every day since, I've wondered if I should have stayed. Should I have stayed and fought? Was I a coward for leaving?"

"I don't know. It may be that leaving was the only way for me to survive long enough to come around for an attack from a better angle."

"Regardless, you say Fleet took a loss when I left. If I may say, sir, I believe Fleet would be worse off if you left." He paused briefly, the General was still listening.

Kelley stated quietly, but firmly, "I think you should stay and ride out the storm."

Bataar looked at him and said, "You haven't even heard the facts of the investigation yet."

"Sir, I know enough. I don't have to know the details to know a good General when I see one."

Bataar turned to Moser. Moser first closed his mouth, then opened it again to say, "Yes, sir. I agree with Major Kelley. You owe it to those who look up to you to stay and lead them through this, sir."

General Bataar thought for a moment and said, "I appreciate the advice, gentlemen. I will consider the matter. Good day."

Kelley and Moser snapped salutes in unison, barking out, "Yes, sir. Good day, sir."

General Bataar returned the salutes. He nodded at Kelley before leaving the room, closing the door with a slight bang. It seemed to Kelley that he left with more energy than when he had entered.

Chapter Four

The door had barely closed before Kelley turned to Moser, his own energy high, and asked him, "What the hell?"

Moser gaped back mockingly, saying, "Hey, I do what I'm told." He sat down hard in a chair and unbuttoned the first several buttons of his uniform around his throat.

Kelley also sat down and leaned back; eyes closed for a long moment. When he opened them again, Moser's head was back, taking a hit from a flask.

He swallowed and offered the flask to Kelley, who accepted it and took a healthy swig, before handing it back.

"Right. You are here, under orders, to give me answers?" he asked Moser.

Moser nodded agreement but clarified, "Within reason."

There was a short silence before Kelley said, "Seriously? You are going to make me ask? Can't you just tell me what you know or are you going to make me say 'please'?"

"Okay. Okay. Yes, we confirmed there was an illegal trafficking ring being run out of Fleet by Fleet officers, no less. They used Fleet personnel and worked through civilian intermediaries to coordinate the buying and selling of goods across two Sectors."

"Most of the personnel we interviewed told us they didn't know anything; they were just following orders. We believe this was true, the trail up from them certainly never led anywhere."

"It wasn't until we confirmed Agent Kendell's connection and started to work the case from that angle that the pieces started to line up."

Kelley interrupted, "So you did test my uniform?"

"Oh, yes. Iaso had preserved the evidence very well. And your sister was able to provide sufficient details to assure us as to the integrity of the sample."

"She also explained how the uniform was given to her by Fleet personnel without telling us the investigating officer's name." Kelley thought he could tell Moser was impressed by Mel's testimony.

"According to Dr. Turner, she believes the team who investigated the bombing didn't take being told to close their investigation too well. And they liked you leaving Fleet even less. Dr. Turner couldn't say for sure what they thought, but in her considered opinion, she believes giving your uniform to her was their way of protesting; it was their way of saying they wanted things made right."

Kelley was silent as he absorbed this new information, then he said quietly, "I appreciate the precautions you took with her, Captain Moser."

Moser briefly nodded in acknowledgment. It had taken a lot of effort to question Mel. Dr. Crane had passed information via Agent Franklin that informed Fleet of Dr. Turner's unusual situation regarding her 'collar,' but not precisely what might trigger it. Fleet had questioned her with a medical team standing by.

"Ultimately it was worth it. GIS provided us with the necessary samples for Agent Kendell, and Iaso ran a blind test. They matched you, of course, as well as blood and cranial matter to Agent Kendell."

"Tracking Kendell on the base that day led us to Lt. Bataar and General Sarro. Once we started with them, it was easy enough to work our way down."

"Were you able to get their intermediary contacts, outside of Fleet?" Kelley asked.

Moser shook his head. "No. We could only get so far down. Agent Deleon burned possible connections when she went after the small fry. We had no leverage to get them to talk and no way of prosecuting them again. The only thing we could establish is that once an underling was tagged, they were cut loose, ostracized to protect the network and those above them."

"Okay, so you had proof of the trafficking and suspicions of who was running it. Your investigation was limited to those within Fleet and most of them weren't guilty of anything chargeable. That took close to a year to figure out?" Kelley asked.

"Hey. It isn't easy investigating a General or his aide, you know. Not without alerting them too soon." Moser was defensive.

"Fair enough," Kelley conceded. "You mentioned General Sarro. How was he involved?"

Moser didn't immediately reply. He took a small sip from the flask, capped it, and set it down on the table. "Officially, he knew nothing and was so distraught at finding out what his aide was doing that he walked out of an airlock."

"And unofficially?" Kelley pressed him.

"We have no proof that he either ran the ring himself or jointly with Lt. Bataar. Somehow the fact that we reopened the investigation into the Tydfil CF48 base explosion leaked out. We are still trying to contain suspicions that he was involved in any sort of cover-up or that he spaced himself to avoid prosecution."

"He did avoid prosecution," Kelley grumbled.

"No," Moser said simply. "There was too much mud on Fleet, too much blood. He was tried on other charges in absentia and convicted. His name is disgraced, and his family has been denied all rights and benefits," Moser said staring straight at Kelley.

"I can feel for his family but I'm not sorry," Kelley said staring straight back at Moser.

After a moment, he asked, "Did you find out which one of them decided to blow up Kendall? And why? I mean, from what I learned, the guy was an idiot, certainly not much of a threat."

Moser snorted. "Yes and no. He was persistent. And a GIS agent who wouldn't take no for an answer. Either Sarro or Bataar decided that eventually someone in Fleet was going to listen to him."

"Kendell was lured on base, gulled into thinking he had found an informant. He thought his 'informant' had given him the keys to his case."

"But why on base? Why go to the trouble of dressing him up in a uniform, which looked real to me by the way, and bringing him to the very place they didn't want him?" Kelley asked.

"Kendell was suspicious of back-alley meetings. And he told them he had full use of GIS resources. We know now that he was lying, but General Sarro and Lt. Bataar believed him."

"A Fleet military base was one of the few places Kendell couldn't bring GIS tech into play."

"They had no idea he would try and open the evidence package while still on base," Moser finished flatly.

Kelley reached out and took the flask, feigning calmness.

After a time, Kelley said roughly, "So, blowing me up was a mistake. It wasn't personal. Okay then. So why slander me? Why question my record?"

"As you said, it wasn't personal. They were desperate, they were trying to deflect attention from Kendell and on to you. Remember, they had a body that couldn't be identified as being anyone from Fleet, wearing one of Bataar's uniforms. They did anything they could to raise suspicions anywhere they could, as well as influencing what investigation there was."

Kelley snarled out his opinion of their tactics.

When he finished, Moser calmly continued. "You know, you leaving Fleet did more for this case than you realize. You were no longer there to be their stooge. They couldn't shift suspicion or accuse someone who wasn't there, though they initially tried."

"You left after the results of the preliminary investigation were released. Those we interviewed told us that the accusations made after your discharge only inflamed the situation and brought the attention they were trying to avoid. It forced the General to step in and quash the investigation and the slander campaign that had so very badly misfired."

"That saved them until we could prove who the victim had been. We were able to get the bombing investigation unsealed and reopened. That gave us irrefutable evidence that the General both lied and was directly connected to Bataar's activities."

Kelley put the cap back on the flask and set it gently on the table.

Chapter Five

After Moser's revelation, Kelley sat quietly for a time, processing the information. Moser was patient.

Finally, he said, "And Lieutenant Bataar?"

"Within Fleet, his trial was more public. It was necessary to show that Fleet holds all its personnel accountable for their actions."

"He was given a fair trial and convicted on all charges. He recently declined to appeal and is scheduled for execution within the next seventy-two hours," Moser related quietly, but somewhat tensely.

Kelley looked at him a moment, then said, "I don't want to see him. I mean, I don't have a need to talk with him or anything like that."

Moser relaxed. "Good to know. Thank you."

"Could I get the details of the trials that were released to Fleet personnel?"

"I don't see why not," Moser replied. He tapped on his tablet for a minute. He then pushed his tablet towards Kelley's. Kelley accepted the connection and the file Moser had pushed his way.

"Anything else, Major?" Moser asked.

Kelley thought for a minute and shook his head. "No, thank you, Captain. I appreciate everything you've done regarding the case and coming here today."

After the Battle

"All part of my job," Moser said standing and buttoning his uniform.

Kelley did the same, then offered his hand. Moser shook it strongly. "Thank you," Kelley said again.

Moser nodded. "Thank you for what you said to General Bataar. None of us wanted to see him go."

Moser took a step back and snapped him a salute. Kelley returned it promptly. Moser turned on his heel and left the room, closing the door quietly behind him.

Kelley inhaled deeply and let it out quickly. He didn't want to process his feelings here. As he picked up and put on his cap, he noticed the Captain had left his flask.

He had no idea if it was intentional or merely an oversight. It didn't matter to him; he pocketed the flask without a qualm. If Moser wanted it back, he knew where to find him.

Chapter Six

Kelley left the base and returned to Visnia. When he got back, he was surprised to see Fi already home from school.

She was equally surprised to see him, especially in full uniform.

"Wow," was all she said, looking him up and down.

"Yeah. I had a meeting on the base on Gaclite. What are you doing home so early?"

"We had a half-day because of a teacher's conference. Can I get a picture?"

"You've seen me in uniform before," he said, a little embarrassed.

"No, I haven't," Fi protested and started getting out her device.

He grumbled but posed as requested until she was satisfied. Then he went to his room and changed out of his uniform. When he came back, he asked her to join him on the couch. She flopped down next to him asking him what was up.

"I don't think I ever gave you my pictures, did I? I mean, the ones after I left Blerreon 4?"

"No," she confirmed, starting to get excited. "I have the ones you gave me from Aunt Mel, but nothing after that."

They sat together as he shared pictures of his life during his Fleet career as well as many of the stories around them. The daughter-safe versions anyway. Fi was thrilled and loved listening to his adventures.

She commented that he had a beard back then. He paused briefly before answering honestly and telling her that he had preferred a beard to being clean-shaven, but that things change. He shrugged. You adapt, you move on. She nodded and moved close to give him a hug. He hugged her back as he kissed the top of her head.

PART III – AFTERWARDS

After the Battle

Chapter One

After the unofficial briefing on Gaclite, Kelley was able to get on with his life, his battles on and off the field over and done. Dr. Crane would say he had 'closure.' For Kelley, that meant tying up a couple of loose ends.

He gave Agent Franklin and the team the official version of events, including Lieutenant Bataar's execution. There was general appreciation all-around; Kelley thanking them, the team thanking him, capped by Agent Nandi personally congratulating the entire team on a job well done.

Franklin and Kelley had a brief disagreement as to which of them should update Deleon. Franklin challenged Kelley to a game of mini missiles, which Kelley won; Franklin had to update Deleon.

The following spring Fi graduated from Verbier Polytechnique summa cum laude. There was a lot of speculation between Mel and Kelley as to which university Fi would apply to and what she would study. Kelley repeatedly told Fi that the cost of tuition should not to be a factor in her decision.

Therefore, it came as a complete shock when she announced she wanted to enlist and join Fleet. To compound Kelley's shock, Mel accepted Fi's choice and was surprisingly supportive.

After the Battle

It was Mel who seemed to understand Fi's decision. Fleet could match Fi's drive and ambition, as well as her general thirst for excellence. Kelley was proud and as supportive as he could be.

Maybe Fi's choice influenced him or maybe he was just ready, but he started to reach out to old friends from his Fleet days; the results varied.

A couple of good friends responded, though he had to deal with the fact that several of his old buddies had been killed or were otherwise unable to reach back. He kept in touch with their families where he could.

He was also shocked to learn some of his friends, who he had thought were career soldiers, had left Fleet for various reasons of their own. He liked that he wasn't the only one who was on the outside, but at the same time, it was disconcerting. It made him realize that he had had a very narrow viewpoint while in service.

On the positive side, he especially liked reconnecting with a former buddy, a machinist who was also one hell of a shot. They had been on a number of missions together and had hung out a lot in between. Specialist Amelia Strom had been a good friend of his. Just friends; he had liked her too much to chase after her as he did with a lot of other women.

Fi made it through basic training and started her training as a pilot before Kelley and Strom met up again, face-to-face. When they finally did, they immediately clicked. And when she kissed him, he felt a spark.

Chapter Two

Kelley settled into life with Fi gone and off on her own adventures. He missed her but he was doing good where he was. And he still had family close by; when Brian grew old enough, Mel sent him to school at Verbier Polytechnique. She and Brian both moved to Visnia, where they got their own place near Kelley's.

Amelia transferred to Gaclite where she and Kelley could see each other regularly. The best part was that it was a promotion for her. Mel's partner made the move to Visnia with her, and they all got along great.

Fi loved the challenges and opportunities offered by Fleet. She met them with the same passion and fervor she did with anything in her life. In due course, she earned her wings, as well as a law degree. Law would take a back seat while she was actively flying missions. She didn't make it home often, but she did keep in frequent communication with her family.

She was promoted to First Lieutenant about the same time Senior Agent Ibbota retired and Kelley took his place. Kelley was now in-charge of an entire Sector with multiple teams reporting to him. With Brian graduating Verbier, things couldn't be better; however, they could get worse.

Chapter Three

Kelley received a communication from Fleet saying that Lieutenant Kelley's fighter had been brought down and was currently missing.

He told Amelia but not Mel, until two days later, when he got a very brief message from Fi saying she was okay and not to worry. He believed the message was from Fi, but not that she was okay.

Several days later, she contacted him again in real-time. She said she couldn't talk about the mission, but she didn't tell him about her injuries either.

From what he could see, the left side of her body got the worst of the crash. He couldn't get a close look at the impact injuries, but he could see that she had burns on the left side of her face, shoulder, and arm, and probably down from there. She flipped the screen around to show her right leg under the hospital bed blanket; her left leg was mostly gone. She quickly flipped it back again.

Kelley took the hint and didn't mention it specifically, but he stayed on the call and talked to her as long as the nurse would let him.

When she was released from Fleet hospital, Mel and Kelley insisted she come home. Fi initially protested but agreed when faced with the united front.

The day Fi arrived at the Visnia Port, she was surprised but glad that her Dad and Aunt Mel weren't waiting to ambush her. They apparently respected the fact, that even now, she could take care of herself.

It did take a bit of coordination for her to get her luggage into the transport. She was on crutches because she hadn't wanted a wheelchair. Once home, she asked the driver to take her luggage to the elevator, but only because her right leg and hip were hurting, and there was no one in the lobby for her to ask for help.

When she got out of the elevator, the apartment door opened, and Aunt Mel pounced on her there in the foyer, hugging her tightly.

Her Dad let her get into the apartment before he gave her a big hug. By the time he let go, Brian had already taken her luggage to her old room.

They had a pleasant, quiet evening. Everyone was there, including Amelia and Mel's partner, Cass. They enjoyed a delicious dinner with good wine and easy conversation. Brian talked about his new job, Aunt Mel talked about her latest paper, and no one talked about Fi's last mission.

As the evening went on, people gradually went home until it was only Kelley and Fi sitting on the couch. This time, they both had a beer in hand with a bag of cookies between them.

"So, how are you holding up, kid?" Kelley asked her.

"Fine," she answered, stuffing a cookie into her mouth.

He gave her a droll look and said, "Really? Now you start lying to me?"

"What is there to say?" she grumped, her mouth half-full.

"You tell me."

She glared at him while she finished chewing. She reached for another cookie, but Kelley moved the bag to his other side, away from her.

"Come on. Give them back. It's been ages since I have had anything this good," she protested.

"Tell me about the crash."

She shrugged, "I don't call it a crash. I got hit, couldn't eject, and had to put it down. It was a good landing, all things considered."

"You are okay with how everything turned out?" he asked her.

"NO."

He waited. After a short staring contest, she went on.

"What do you want me to say? No, I'm not okay. I'm freakin' angry. I am so flippin' mad, I can barely see straight. And I don't know why. I mean, I got shot down, but I survived. There was a fire, but the suppression system worked like it was supposed to. I got rescued. They came and found me. I got taken to a hospital where I got good care. So, why do I feel like I could put my fist through a wall?"

"Are you a fighter pilot anymore?" he asked.

"No. Fleet requires that a pilot have at least two working legs," she answered mechanically.

"Was this your choice?"

"No, I didn't choose any of it. And I still can't believe I'm never going to get back into my rig," she said vehemently.

He maintained eye contact but didn't say anything.

She stared back at him, then asked, "Is that what you expected to hear?"

"Doesn't matter what I expected to hear. I just know it's better to talk about it than not."

"But what difference does it make? It doesn't matter if I wanted it or not. It doesn't matter if I'm angry or sad. It won't change anything if I talk about it or not. I'm no longer a pilot."

"You've forgotten how to fly a plane?" he asked her.

For the first time ever, Fi looked like she wanted to hit him. She didn't say anything; she just ground her teeth.

He went on, "I'm just saying you are still a pilot. Downgraded at the moment, yes, but not out on your six. Remember, what happened is still fresh. You are in a lot of pain, and as much as you think you can, you shouldn't be making too many decisions until you have had a chance to think things through, and yes, talking things through with someone, *will* help."

"What is there to discuss?" she snarled. "I *know* I have my degree to fall back on. I have no experience but they'll send me over to JAG. I just have to ask."

Her tone was full of emotion; he could tell she was upset with him and didn't like him poking at her and messing up the equilibrium she thought she had achieved.

"Fi. I know you know it's not that easy. You didn't choose to stop being a fighter pilot. You got something you loved taken away and you have no recourse to get it back. That's tough. It's tough for people like us to deal with a dead end. We are used to being able to fight or to find a way to get what we want."

"If I say I agree, would you give me the damn cookies back, please?" she asked. He knew that she didn't agree, but at least she wasn't as angry at him as she had been. She just wanted him to stop talking about it.

He gave her the cookies and said, "You know I know what I am talking about, don't you?"

She stared at him for a short time and then shook her head slowly, saying "Do I?"

"You'll get there," he assured her. He saw her tense up and she looked at him with pleading eyes. He thought he knew why. She didn't want him of all the people to parrot what everyone else had already been telling her.

"Oh hell no. I'm not going to say it," he told her.

She said warily, half skeptical. "Say what?"

"I am NOT going to tell you anything about how it 'just takes time' or to 'give it time'. No, ma'am. *I* won't feed you that space slag."

A short burst of involuntary laughter broke out her. "Well, thank you for that! So, tell me what you do understand?"

"I understand what it's like to go from making real decisions, hardcore, life and death decisions on the fly, under fire to being told 'it just takes time.' Time as in days of tedious, monotonous, excruciatingly boring chunks of doing nothing but *waiting*. Waiting to heal, waiting for something to happen, hell, even waiting for the pain to just be less. I preferred getting shot at."

She nodded in agreement. "Yes!" Then her eyes dropped as she looked down at her leg. "Everything hurts."

"You know you will heal." She nodded but didn't say anything. "When I got blown up, it wasn't just that I literally lost a part of me, it was that I wasn't going to get it back. Even when I healed, I wasn't going to be the same man as before. I liked me, and it felt that by looking like a different man, I was going to be a different man. Someone other than me."

Fi pulled her leg up under her, like she used to, and squirmed until she got comfortable facing him. He waited without saying anything.

"Yes. I can see what you are saying. I think. It's that, in a way. I mean, you're right, I'm not ready to be a lawyer right now, but I thought I would be one, someday. So, it's not that far a stretch for me to get to that person," she told him.

He just nodded and let her talk.

"It's that, in a way," she repeated. "It also is that I'm not pretty anymore." She started talking fast, as if he was going to interrupt. "I know I was so petty. I mean, I'm here, mostly. I'm alive, what do I have to complain about? A lot of others didn't make it out. I feel like such a jerk for being so self-centered."

He shrugged. "It's normal. It's completely normal. You were confident in who you were and now that person has dramatically changed. Something like that can shake a person to their core. It's no surprise you are unsure as to who you are now. You *are* a different woman." He paused before asking, "Have you been talking with Fleet therapist?"

She made a face. "Yes. I don't feel like I need to though."

"Therapy is a tedious, slow, pedantic, and sometimes painful process, that I highly recommend," he said earnestly. "Be open and honest and keep with it," he advised. "It can and does help."

She was honest enough with him to let him see that she was doubtful. He stayed quiet and gave her time to consider his advice. After a while she said, "I'll give it a shot."

He reached over and took her hand and just held it. They sat without talking until she suddenly squeezed his hand tightly as she inhaled quickly, like something had hit her.

"It's big and it hurts, and it's going to take a long time to go away, isn't it?" she asked him, tears starting to slide down her face.

"Yes. I promise you, you will get through this," he assured her gently but firmly, as he moved over to hold her.

When she stopped crying, Kelley got up and brought her a blanket and some tissues. He also made them both a cup of tea.

He handed her the tea as he sat down, saying, "You have a long road ahead of you, but I can tell you now that people aren't going to notice the scars as much as you think."

"Really? Because I am just *so* bright and beautiful on the inside? My energy is just so wonderful?" she asked. She was facetious but trying not to be openly sarcastic.

"I mean it. Want me to prove it?"

"Hit me," she said, as if she was game and not dubious.

"Over the years, you've seen me, I mean my body. In shorts, swimming, stuff like that. And the only thing you've even commented on is my lack of beard. Was that just because you were being polite?"

She looked completely surprised. "Well, no. I mean, it's not like you ever walked around naked or anything like that, but no, I never noticed anything. What was there to see?"

He tapped on his tablet for a minute, then handed it to her. She gasped, and her jaw dropped as she looked at the pictures.

"Those were taken when I arrived at the rehab facility. They like to take 'before' pictures," he said without emotion.

She looked from the pictures to him and back again. "These are you? What happened?"

"Explosion in close quarters, right next to me. I was lucky to have lived. They tried the guy who did it the year before you graduated from Verbier."

"Ohhh," was all she said at first. "Can I see?" she asked, looking at his torso.

"I'll show you mine if you show me yours."

She nodded and pulled her shirt half off, so he could see her left side. He then took off his shirt and let her look.

"Wow. I never saw them before," she said referring to the faint scars.

"That's right. And you only saw them now because you were looking for them," he said putting his shirt back on. "And Fi, I have to say, your wounds aren't *that* bad. I hope you understand what I mean. I just mean, they *will* heal."

"I understand, and I believe you." She looked at the pictures a minute or two longer before handing the tablet back.

"Last thing to consider. I know the medical care Fleet is giving you is good. I know they take care of their own. It's just their focus is on bringing you back to full functionality and not much past that."

"Just keep in mind that you don't have to stop there. I don't look this good because I just happen to heal really well. I elected to have some cosmetic surgery done because I wanted to. It was something I wanted to do for *me*. I want you to know as you go through your healing process, that you have options in addition to the ones Fleet is giving you."

"It's early days yet, but have you looked into what they would pay for? It may not be covered outright, but they might kick in a percentage. And if they don't, and if you want, I can always help out. I'm sure your Aunt would, too."

She reached over and gave him a big hug, saying, "I love you."

"I love you, too, kid," he told her softly, hugging her back.

Chapter Four

It did take time and a lot of hard work, but Fi was able to adjust; her family with her every step of the way. She agreed to therapy, at first only because she had promised her Dad, but later she admitted that it did help.

Fi also took her Dad's advice and really thought things through. She went back to her flight crew and talked with them. They understood it was goodbye and they appreciated the chance to say it, too. They let her get back into a fighter, just to be in one, until she was ready to get out for good.

It helped. It helped her decide to maintain her pilot certification. Being a fighter pilot was out, but there were other options that she could explore.

Fi also took Kelley's advice and opted for a civilian leg replacement. She was much happier with the one she got; she said it made the transition easier. She was too proud to take credits from him or Mel.

Kelley stopped worrying as he watched Fi find her stride. She threw herself into her new career at JAG with a passion, the same passion she always had. He was never prouder of her than the day she was promoted to the rank of Lieutenant Colonel.

When asked how she did it, how she made the transition from the cockpit to the courtroom, Fi gave credit to her family. She learned tenacity, faith, and courage from both her Aunt and her Dad.

She said her Dad especially taught her that finding a different objective was better than fighting for ground that was no longer there. Moving on wasn't saying you didn't love and miss what was gone, but it was okay to find something else to be passionate about.

When accused of being lucky or favored, she replied that being aware and being prepared were certainly Kelley traits, but not exclusively theirs.

No one has it easy, despite what it looks like from the outside. Everyone has a battle they are fighting and are in the trenches one way or another. Just get on with it and remember to look after each other. Soldiers take care of each other on and off the battlefield; together they find a way through.

Fi made it a point to say that she hadn't found it easy to transition, and that admitting she needed help outside of her family, from professionally trained therapists, had been difficult. She was grateful for her Dad who had shown her the way by example.

When Kelley heard Fi talking, at first, he was embarrassed. He didn't feel like he was so wise, like some great sage. He remembered just trying to get through each day, every day. He remembered Mel had told him a long time ago that it would all work out. He hadn't believed her, just like Fi hadn't believed him; but it had, it most certainly had all worked out.

Life is good. Go live it.

ABOUT THE AUTHOR

Stephanie Stieglitz was born and raised in Dover, New Jersey. She graduated Rutgers University with a degree in Comparative Literature. *After the Battle: Kelley's Story* is her first novel, which finally puts her degree to some use. Kelley is a reminder that the best part of life is what is yet to come.

www.ingramcontent.com/pod-product-compliance
Lightning Source LLC
Chambersburg PA
CBHW022206010726
47493CB00002B/435